COOPER

A NEW YORK PLAYERS NOVEL

LULU MOORE

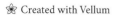

To all the second albums everywhere; the hard to write follow up
I'm in good company

Nirvana - Nevermind
Oasis - What's The Story
Blondie - Parallel Lines
Amy Winehouse - Back to Black
Madonna - Like a Virgin
Adele - 21
Kanye - Late Registration

SOUNDTRACK

FIND COOPER'S PLAYLIST ON MY SPOTIFY
@LULUMOOREBOOKS

NINA SIMONE - Feeling Good
LIZZO - Truth Hurts
THE KILLERS - Mr Brightside
BLEACHERS - Don't Take the Money
MAGGIE ROGERS - Light On
OASIS - Wonderwall
SAM SMITH - Promises
MASSIVE ATTACK - Angel
JAMIE XX ft ROMY - Loud Places
LAMB - Gorecki
PRINCE - Paisley Park
EARTH, WIND & FIRE - Fantasy
YOUNG MC - Bust a Move
THE DOORS - Light my Fire
FLEETWOOD MAC - Everywhere

PROLOGUE

COOPER

Have you ever fucked up so bad you don't know how to get out of it?

Like really and truly monumentally fucked up?

Because I have.

Have you ever had something so perfect, so incredible, so complete and then thrown it away?

Because I have.

Which is how I ended up here. At 2.36am. Nursing a broken nose.

Where I've been for the past five hours. In the dark. Staring at the bottom of a bottle.

Because my nose isn't the only thing broken.

My heart is too. Into a million pieces. A heart that has only ever been owned by her.

I'm in mess of my own creation and now I'm doing everything I can to fix it.

Starting with a love letter.

Except it isn't a letter. It's a mixed-tape. A love playlist.

Me, a professional athlete and grown-ass man, making a playlist like a fucking teenager.

How can I find the words to convey how I feel?

That I'm not just missing her, but that a piece of me is missing because she's not here.

Hindsight is a powerful thing.

To quote Janet Jackson, 'You don't know what you got 'til it's gone'.

I definitely know.

And I'm getting it back.

1

FREDDIE

I could hear my phone ringing in the depths of my bag as I pulled up in front of my house. I reversed as quickly as possible into the available space but it stopped before I could turn the engine off and reach for it.

Oh well.

Jumping out, I opened the trunk and stared down at the contents. It was currently filled with a dozen rolls of wallpaper. Pulling out as many as I could fit under one arm, I walked toward the front door and dumped them on the step before going back for the rest.

I don't know why I agreed to this.

My assistant, Carrie, was supposed to pick these up and take them over to the client to go through. But instead of ordering swatches, like normal, she'd ordered entire rolls at four hundred pounds each. Twelve rolls, all different. So, they needed to be sent back. Today.

Not sure why this was my problem, but Carrie begged me to take care of it so she could get ready for a big date. So I agreed and added it to my mountain of other jobs I had to do.

I rummaged around for my keys before I realised they

were already in my hand and opened the door, bringing everything inside. And by bringing I meant picking up what I could carry and kicking the rest to roll along the floor before stopping where I'd deposited the rest on the hall floor. I was so tired I could barely make it through to the kitchen and immediately fell onto the big corner sofa, face first, closing my eyes.

What. A. Day.

I owned an interior design business for high net worth individuals. I was lucky enough that I didn't have to take on any client I didn't want to, which meant I could spend my time working on projects I loved, believed in and that challenged me. I'd thankfully moved on from the days which had been taken up with running errands and sourcing the impossible.

Life size, gold plated elephant? No, because that's disgusting.

But right now, apart from having to sort out an order gone wrong, I was organising my sister's wedding reception and bachelorette.

Not a small task. And being the control freak I was, there's no way I'd have let anyone else do it.

My sister, Wolfie, had moved to New York for a few months last year and met her now fiancé, Jasper. The wedding was in two weeks', in the English village where our parents lived, a forty-minute drive outside of London. The reception was being held in the barn on my parents' property and I'd been tasked with making it look presentable.

Wolfie wanted a 'fairytale glen' theme and so that's what Jasper was giving her via me.

One room in my house was currently dedicated to massive boxes of fairy lights all ready to be strung up. I'd spent the day with the florists organising miniature blossom trees to be delivered, along with what seemed to be miles of ivy and thousands of tea lights.

4

A shrill ring burst through the silence, startling me out of my daze. I let out a loud groan as I blindly reached around me, trying to find my phone. Which was still at the bottom of my bag.

Incoming call: Stuart

Nope. Didn't want to deal with that. I pressed decline and my home screen popped up.

MISSED CALL: STUART x 3

MISSED CALL: COOPER x 2

My heart skipped an involuntary beat.

Cooper.

Cooper Marks.

Hottest man on earth.

Current bane of my life.

He was Jasper's best friend and we'd met last year when I'd been visiting Wolfie. I'd seen him for the first time where he and Jasper worked together. And by work, I meant played ice hockey. At the New York Rangers.

And ice hockey players were a whole other level of sexy man, a level I didn't even know existed but had definitely become a massive fan of. I remember that first match, it was like watching foreplay – raw, sexy and fully charged with testosterone and adrenaline.

Cooper Marks absolutely had all of that.

Over the months I'd spent in New York with Wolfie, we'd all started hanging out with Jasper's friends more. And as I'd got to know Cooper better, we'd become friends too. With things in common. Such as our love for design and architecture.

And naturally, I'd offered my help with any advice he needed for designing the house he was building. His dream house.

That was my first mistake.

It had started off simple enough, pointing him in the right direction of the finest kitchen designers or where he would source the best shower heads. All well within my remit of an experienced and well-respected interior designer.

But the request had slowly changed to daily messages on the best tea pots or curtain rails. Or trying to make me decide the better shade of blue between two identical pictures.

At which point it became clear he was deliberately trying to wind me up.

Which it did.

And as I was Maid of Honor to his Best Man, our need to be in contact had increased, so I couldn't ignore him quite as easily.

At least that's how it felt.

He'd become the hottest, most irritating person I knew. Sitting in prime position right under my skin.

I got up and walked to the fridge, pulling out a bottle of rosé and poured a glass. Better get this over with.

I dialed through on FaceTime, propping the phone up on the counter.

A ripped torso and broad, muscular chest came into view before he tipped the screen up. His warm, amber eyes flashed with amusement, as a grin spread across his face. Days' worth of stubble only highlighted his perfect bone structure and strong jaw. He'd definitely won the handsome lottery the day they were handing out tickets.

A hot flush ran through me, tingles shooting down my spine. My body and my head were not aligned in thinking when it came to Cooper Marks.

"Hello Tiny. Nice of you to call me back."

Tiny. Grrrr. He wasn't wrong, but everyone was short compared to him. What did Shakespeare say? 'Though she be but little, she is fierce'.

"Marks. What's up?" I raised an eyebrow at him, taking a sip of my wine.

6

He was clearly outside in his garden. I could hear splashes in the pool, so he wasn't alone.

"I have an emergency entertainment question. I'm entertaining and I wanted to ask what are the best straws for cocktails." He deadpanned.

"What?"

"Cocktail straws. Drew wanted those curly ones for the party today. Do you know where I can get them? Can you order them for me?"

This is what I was talking about.

"Cooper, you have an assistant. And if you don't, please let me find you one so you stop annoying me."

"Oh, come on Tiny. You know you're the best at this."

"Best at what? Finding straws?" My annoyance flared. "What is the matter with you?"

He started laughing at me, his mouth open wide, his pink tongue peeking out.

"Calm down. I was calling to ask if you can send me Murray's number. He and Jamie arrive later today and I need to give them some details for getting here."

"Coop, hurry up, we want drinks." Called a whiny, saccharine voice.

"Who's that?"

"No one." He moved away from where he'd been standing.

"Cooper, come on."

That was definitely not a voice I recognised.

"Have you got a bunny there?" I frowned.

"No, Felix and Drew are here." He mentioned two of the more promiscuous members of the team.

"With bunnies?" I pressed.

"There are a few girls here."

Gross.

My temper started to flare. "Why are you calling me when you're entertaining?"

Not that you did entertain a bunny.

The corner of his mouth tilted up a fraction.

I'd called him.

Bollocks.

I rolled my eyes. "Well, I'm not going to keep you. Don't do anything stupid with Jasper this weekend. I'll send you Murray's number now."

"Thank you, Tiny." He smirked.

"Yeah, yeah." I hung up and sent my brother's number to him.

A message came back immediately.

Cooper: *Thank you, Tiny. I promise to be on my best behaviour, just for you X*

I took a deep sigh, then downed the rest of my wine and poured another glass hoping to push away the visions of his rippled torso currently flooding my brain.

2

FREDDIE

Nina Simone was feeling good and I had to agree with her.

A decent night's sleep had worked wonders in ridding me of my irritability at Cooper, as well as the sadness which had been creeping up on me lately. Sadness at Wolfie leaving and moving permanently to New York.

As well as my sister, she was my best friend. I was going to miss her terribly, but at least it gave me an excuse to visit New York more often.

The bachelorette party was taking place this weekend and, while small and super low key at Wolfie's request, I'd still been working hard to make sure this weekend would be a brilliant send off for her.

"What are you making me for breakfast?" Wolfie stretched her arms out with a yawn as she walked into the kitchen.

"Hey, I said I'd bring it to you in bed." I poured fresh squeezed orange juice into a large jug, soon to be mimosas.

"Yeah but I was awake and excited. And hungry. So, what are you making me?" She walked over to the kitchen island and pulled out a stool, sitting on it.

I grabbed a bottle of Bollinger from the fridge and popped the cork, topping up the orange juice. Although with my generous hand it wasn't so much topping up, more like even split. I filled a glass and handed it to her.

"Happy Bridal Shower Day." I kissed her cheek.

She grinned. "Thank you."

"Oh, I forgot," I ran to the drawer and pulled out a crown, placing it on her head. "You're the Queen today." I kissed her on the cheek again before curtseying.

"Why, thank you." She laughed. "But seriously, what are you making me for breakfast."

"Pancakes."

"Cooper's pancakes?" Her eyes opened wide.

"Of course." I grabbed the coveted recipe from the kitchen pinboard. Cooper Marks' pancakes were almost as delicious as the man himself.

I pulled out the mixing bowl from the cupboard as the doorbell rang.

"I'll get it, you make my pancakes." Wolfie ran to the door.

I walked into the pantry to grab the flour, as well as buttermilk and eggs from the fridge. As I opened the drawer looking for a whisk, I heard a screech.

"Freddie! Fred, help me." I threw it down on the counter and sprinted towards the door, before skidding to a halt.

She wasn't being attacked, unless it was by pollen. She was standing in the doorway holding a display of flowers almost as big as her.

"Why are you shouting? You can carry this."

"I know I can, but I can't carry all that too." She nodded into the road where three men were emptying a van of giant balloons all filled with glitter, streamers and little balls.

"Alright love," One of the men shouted at me. "There's some more in here if you want to grab 'em."

I jogged over to the van, where I was handed an enormous bunch of tied balloons.

"Won't give you too many, you'll float away." He winked. "Having a party then?"

"No, this is a regular Saturday round here." I replied dryly, turning around before he had a chance to respond.

We walked into the house, passing by the last delivery guy who'd already deposited his balloons in the kitchen. I let them drift to the ceiling before showing him out and shutting the door. There were easily fifty balloon floating between the kitchen and the hall.

"Wolf, I'm curious, at any point have you expressed to Jasper a love of balloons?" I looked around at them all.

I went back to making the batter, before spooning it out into the griddle. Soon I had a giant stack of the fluffiest pancakes.

"Wolf…" I glanced at her. She was miles away, buried in the note which arrived with the flowers, a wistful smile across her face. "Wolf?" I called again and she lifted her head to me. "Order's up. We have to eat up here because of this egregious display of Jasper's love. Bring the drinks over."

She walked over to the breakfast bar, through a sea of ribbons and streamers hanging from the balloons and pulled out a stool.

"I have the best fiancé." She said sliding my glass over to me, her giant engagement ring catching the light. It was so pretty and sparkled constantly from every angle.

"You certainly do." I straightened her crown which had slid down the side of her head and held my glass up in toast. "Now let's eat the best pancakes in the world."

I took the maple syrup from her, after she'd poured an excessive amount onto her plate and forked in a mouthful.

"You know, I think you might make these as good as Cooper. They're better than Jasper's…" Her eyes narrowed at me in a glare. "But tell him I said that and I'll hurt you."

I motioned a zipping of my lips. "What did the card say?"

"Just that he loved me and can't wait to marry me." Her

face lit up. It was like she had cartoon hearts and cupids spinning above her head.

"Who wouldn't be excited to marry you."

"I know, right?" She raised her glass and took a sip. "Hey, do you know what they're doing this weekend?"

"You don't know?"

"I know the gist, I just didn't want to ask Jasper the details." She swirled a forkful of pancakes around her plate, soaking up more syrup before putting it in her mouth.

"Oh babe, it's going to be so lame." I cackled. "Jasper literally doesn't want to do anything without you. Jamie and Murray got there last night, Jamie said they went to a strip club and Cooper went home with Jasper ten minute after they arrived, they didn't even see a stripper."

She started laughing. "I told him he'd be in a world of pain if he touched a stripper."

"You know, you're getting really comfortable making threats in your old age." I raised an eyebrow at her.

"Whatever, not like you're unhappy that Cooper didn't enjoy the naked spoils either." She smirked. "You can't even deny it."

She wasn't wrong.

Jealousy irrationally fired up. I had no claim on Cooper but my brain and my heart were constantly warring over this fact.

His was a life of casual sex and bunnies. And while I had no issue with the casual part, I was certainly no bunny.

"Cooper can do whatever and whomever he wants. We're just friends. Nothing more."

She rolled her eyes at me.

"You talk every day, several times a day in fact." She picked up her mimosa, looking at me as she sipped.

I reached for more pancakes off the stack, forking one onto her plate before mine. "Your point is?"

She shrugged. "No point, just sounds like you're trying to convince yourself, that's all. I know you think he's hot."

"He is hot. Insanely hot. Even blind people can tell he's hot. It practically permeates the air around him. Doesn't mean we're more than friends though."

"Does he know that?"

"Does he know what? That we're not more than friends? Yes, I'm pretty sure he's aware since we don't have sex." I took another bite of my pancakes. I'd made too many but they were too good not to eat.

"You definitely could though."

"No thanks, he's got bunnies lining up around the street corner for that." I remembered that saccharine whine.

The first time I'd met Cooper and the hockey boys, Wolfie and I had gone to the bathroom and overheard a conversation between three young women who'd barely had a brain cell to rub together. They were deciding between them which hockey player they were going home with that night. They were so confident it would happen and they didn't care with whom, for them it was a brag on social media. Even then, when Cooper's name had come up in their prospect list I'd been raged.

And disgusted.

But that's what they were used to.

"I'm never going to be someone he can take home at the end of the night for a quick shag, I have a bit more self-respect than that."

"Word on the street is that he's not been with a bunny in a while."

"First, stop gossiping about me and Cooper with Jasper. Second..." I paused, thinking for a moment and came up blank. "Well, I don't have a second."

"Okay." She said in that tone that people use when they don't believe a word you're saying.

"I like him as a friend, but that's it. Also, you've met him, he's way too annoying and bossy."

She smirked into her mimosa. "You're literally describing yourself."

"I'm not annoying." I protested. "And I'd prefer you to use the word assertive, thanks." Her grin got wider as I continued. "You know how annoying he was when I was trying to help him with his house. He still sends me daily texts about one inane thing after another as though I'm his assistant. Not even sure why he asked me, he just did everything he wanted to regardless of my advice. He's so fucking stubborn."

Her eyes opened wide as she pursed her lips.

"I'm not stubborn!"

"Oh please." She poured some more maple syrup on her pancakes, wiping the drip off the top of the bottle with her finger before sticking it in her mouth. "All I'm saying is that you and Cooper are very similar."

"And all I'm saying is that we're friends." I ran my finger around the last of the syrup on my plate. It was the most acceptable step before licking it clean.

"What do you talk about then?"

"I don't know." I threw my hands in the air. "How about the wedding?"

She grinned. "And?"

I shrugged. "Sometimes music. Mostly about how annoying he is though."

"Have you ever sent him music?" She tapped her index finger on her lips, like she was trying to make a point.

"I send him the playlists I make everyone." I leaned back in the stool, tucking my feet under me. I was so full.

"A-ha! Case closed."

"What the actual fuck are you talking about? What case?" I glared at her.

"You always say music is an expression of feeling and you only send it to people you like."

14

"Yes. To my friends, you loon."

She jumped off her stool and kissed me on the cheek. "If you say so." She took the bottle of champagne from the fridge and grabbed two fresh glasses, filling them and finishing it off. "So, tell me about the plans for today."

I stood up taking the empty bottle from her. Rounding the counter I placed it in the recycling bin and started pulling the empty plates towards me.

"We're meeting everyone at the Corinthia for massages and then we have dinner and party time."

Her eyes opened wide. "We're going to the Corinthia? Oh my god, I'm so excited."

I looked at the clock, we had an hour before we needed to leave.

"The car will be here at eleven and I have some things for you upstairs." I opened the dishwasher and loaded it before taking her hand and dragging her out of the kitchen. "Come on."

Wolfie flopped onto my bed as I turned on some music and walked through to my closet. "Wolf, come in here."

I held out two dresses for her. "This is for you to wear now." I shook the hanger which was holding a delicate, white and blue silk sundress. "And this." I shook the other one, a silvery, shimmery evening dress. "Is for you to wear tonight."

"Oh Fred, they're beautiful." She ran her hands over the silk as I picked up a weekend bag and placed it on the low ottoman.

"Here's your weekend bag, everything you need is there, just add your toothbrush."

She wrapped her arms around me, holding me in a tight hug. "Oh Fred, thank you so much, I can't wait. This week has been exactly what I wanted."

She let go of me and walked over to a shelf, picking up a frame containing an old photo of my birth parents from when they were younger. They'd been best friends with

Wolfie's parents and had died in a car accident when I was little. So, Jack and Diane, Wolfie's parents, had adopted me right away and become my new family.

I'd been so young that it could have turned out very differently. And because they'd been close since their own childhood they were able to tell me stories of their times together, we celebrated them and talked about them constantly. They'd ensured my parents were a huge part of our family, not just for me, but Wolf, Murray and Jamie too.

"Hello Danvers, you have the best daughter in the world." She pressed a quick kiss to the photo before putting it back on the shelf.

I grinned at her. "Go and get your arse in the shower, but don't bother washing your hair, it'll get greasy from the massage. And you'll have it done properly later."

"Okay." She ran off, shouting. "Woo hoo, I'm getting married."

3

FREDDIE

The driver carried our bags through the hotel lobby and over to the private lift. We took our things from him and got in. Taking it to the only floor it stopped at, our suite.

"Oh wow." Whispered Wolfie in reverence as the doors opened where we were greeted by a butler.

"Jesus." I followed, taking in the room, and burst out laughing. There must have been another dozen balloons floating around. "They're everywhere." I turned to the butler. "Hello, there."

"Hello, Ms Danvers, I'm Gerard, I'll be here for anything you need during your stay. Everything is set up as you requested."

I smiled.

"I do believe a couple of your guests have already checked in and are in their rooms. Would you like me to call them up, or would you prefer to settle in first?" He raised his eyebrows in question.

"Please call them, that would be great." I smiled.

"You're booked in for two pm at the spa. And then you have stylists arriving at six for your dinner on the terrace at eight."

"Super, thank you." I replied.

He gave a brisk nod, before leaving through another door and closing it behind him.

I walked into the suite to find Wolfie roaming around before she headed off to the next room. There were huge vases of flowers on every surface, their fragrance fighting against the scented candles flickering throughout the rooms.

"Hey, come up here." She hollered from upstairs and I ran to find her.

She was out on the terrace.

The view stretched across London, up and down the River Thames, the turrets of London striking a balance against the Eye and the Shard. It was my city and I loved it.

Wolfie wrapped her arms around me from behind. "It's incredible. Thank you. I was right earlier, you are the best."

"You're welcome. You deserve it." A lump appeared in my throat and I hugged her arms into me. "I'm going to miss you, Wolf."

"I'm going to miss you too, but you already have your own room ready for whenever you visit. And you can fly over as often as you want. Come on, let's get a quick pic for the boys before everyone else arrives." She held her phone up, taking a snap with the skyline in the background.

"Wolf, Fred?" Voices called from inside the suite.

"We're up here."

Molly and Amy bounded out of the doors. They'd flown in together from New York, arriving last night. Amy was Jasper's sister and a fellow bridesmaid, Molly was Cooper's sister and she'd become a really good friend.

"Oh wow." Molly walked slowly over to the balustrades edging the rooftop, taking in the view before we all fell into a group hug.

"We've missed you guys." We cried in unison.

"The balloons are cool." Said Molly.

"Jasper." I replied. "There must have been fifty delivered to our house this morning too."

"My brother does nothing by halves, that's for sure." Amy took a seat on one of the squashy looking outdoor beds.

A butler suddenly appeared with a bottle of chilled champagne and glasses. He was so silent he could have been a ninja. He began pouring it out into the glasses, before handing it around.

"We're gonna be wasted before we even get to the massages." Molly took one from him, smiling at him in thanks. "What's the plan for the rest of today? Who else is coming?"

As if on cue Alex, our sister-in-law walked out. "Hi there, ladies."

Wolfie and I got up to hug her.

"Everyone this is Jamie's wife, Alex." The girls got up to introduce themselves as the last of our friends, Sophie and Olivia, strolled onto the terrace.

Introductions were made throughout our little group of eight women as more champagne was poured and we got comfortable on the sofas, the combination of sun and alcohol allowing us all to relax. Wolfie's phone started ringing, she grinned as she looked at the screen before standing up to answer it.

"Hi baby." She made her way over to the other side of the terrace.

Sophie sat down in her empty spot, pulling me into a hug. "Fred, this is incredible, you've done a banging job. Have you been here before?"

"No, but I thought it would be fun. You know she didn't want to go big, so I wanted to find something nice enough where we could have our own party, be totally spoiled, waited on hand and foot, and not have to go out. Best of both worlds." I tapped my glass to hers before we both took a sip.

Molly was right, we were going to be wasted before massages.

"This is where Beyonce stays, you know." She looked around as though imagining her here.

"Well, what's good enough for Queen B, is definitely good enough for us."

"Cheers to that." She flicked her bouncy curls facetiously off her shoulder. She tilted her head. "Seriously, Freddie, you've done a great job. And how are you feeling about all this?"

"You mean Wolfie leaving?" I looked over to where Wolfie stood, still grinning like an idiot into her phone.

She nodded.

"I'm okay, I've tried not to think about it too much. Obviously I'm going to miss seeing her so often, but it's not like we won't speak. When she was over in the States last year we still talked all the time. It's just the little things, like not being able to go and see her for dinner and drinks, you know." I sucked in the side of my cheek, a habit of mine whenever I started to get uncomfortable.

"Yeah, it must be hard." She rubbed my arm empathetically. "And you know we're always around for dinner and drinks too, just call us whenever."

I smiled. "Thanks Soph."

After being massaged to within an inch of our lives, we'd all spent the rest of the afternoon on the terrace laughing and catching up before being primped and preened by a team of experts. Something I could definitely get used to.

I was so relaxed I may as well be walking on a cloud.

I zipped up the side of my dress as Wolfie walked into our room, her blonde hair had been blown out into Hollywood waves which fell softly down her shoulders. Her silvery dress shimmered in the sunlight, making her appear almost mermaid like.

"Well, aren't you a vision. Jasper is one lucky boy."

"He sure is." She twirled in her dress. "Hey, let's call them." She placed the phone on the dresser where we could both see the screen.

Jasper's face peered out as he answered. "Well, look at you two beautiful ladies."

"Why thank you." I replied. "We were just saying how lucky you are."

"And don't I know it." He chuckled. "Are you having fun, Cub?"

"So much, are you?" She asked him.

He shrugged.

"Oi." Called a voice. "I've worked fucking hard planning the best Bachelor party ever. At least have the courtesy of pretending you're having a good time, you moody shit."

Jasper grinned as Cooper's face came into view. "Wolf, Tiny, both looking lovely I see."

I watched, mesmerised, as his tongue peaked out and ran along his plump bottom lip.

Fuck, he was sexy.

I had no doubt that tongue could do wicked things.

I shook my head, trying to clear my thoughts. It had been too long since I'd had sex. Or since I'd had decent sex anyway.

"Thanks Coop." Wolfie answered. "How are Murray and Jamie?"

"Drew and Clevs have taken them under their wing. I'm not sure they'll survive, if I'm honest."

"Yeah, we're not worried, you should watch out for them. They're deceptive and if you're not careful they'll drink you under the table."

Cooper smirked. I was certain he'd already become well aware of what our brothers were capable of.

"Wolf Cub, I'll let you go and enjoy your evening but call me before you go to bed, okay. I love you. Can't wait to marry you." Said Jasper and I could see Cooper in the background rolling his eyes.

"Okay baby, have a fun afternoon. I'll speak to you later. I love you."

She hung up and we headed out to find the rest of the girls on the terrace. Even though we weren't going out I'd still wanted to make the evening formal, so the dress code had been set at 'Black Tie'. The girls were in a brilliant array of dresses, each one more stunning than the last.

"Holy fuck, we look absolutely incredible. It's a good job we're not going out tonight, we'd be hounded." I laughed.

Cocktails were being poured as everyone relaxed, the sun still warm in the sky, hours away from setting. The terrace had been filled with candles of all sizes, one of Jasper's balloons tied to each chair at the table. I'd made a playlist for tonight and the music pumped gently out of the speakers.

"It really does look awesome up here." Alex walked over to me, her pink dress flaring out like a flamenco dancer. "You have done a good job."

"I just booked it, Al. I really haven't done anything. Save the praise for when you see the barn." I pulled a face.

She laughed at me. "Does it look good?"

"Not yet, but it will." I winked. I was quietly confident it would be some of my best work. "Have you heard from Jamie?"

We walked to join the rest of the girls. Canapes were being handed out and I took one, popping it in my mouth.

"Yes, earlier. He said he's so hungover he thinks he's crying tequila. So, fuck knows what went on. I'm not sure I want to know either."

I laughed, shaking my head. "Ha, that sounds about right.

Week away from you and the kids, it's a rookie mistake to go out hard on the first night. When are they flying to Vegas?"

"Tomorrow. Then back here on Thursday, land Friday morning." She perched on the back of a chair, crossing her ankles out in front of her.

"It's going to be carnage. They'll be so fucked up when they land." I laughed.

"I know, stupid dickheads." She nudged my shoulder. "So, come on then, what are these hockey boys like? Any hot and single ones?"

Alex had been trying to set me up for a long time, and right now, Cooper's naked torso flashed before my eyes.

"None that I want to get involved with."

Which might not have been entirely true.

One of the butlers waiting on us passed by with a tray of cocktails and I switched out my empty glass for a full one.

"That's not an answer." She smirked as she took a fresh one too.

"Well, it's all you're going to get."

The less I thought about Cooper before he arrived in London, the better.

Unlike the rest of the boys, he was staying at my house with Jasper, which filled me with dread and excitement in equal measure. We'd be spending a lot of time together in the week before the wedding and things would be easier if I could keep him at arm's length. But with Alex and Wolfie trying to pry information out of me at every opportunity, it was going to be harder than anticipated.

Wolfie came over and joined us, kissing Alex on the cheek. "Al, you look so pretty, I love your dress."

"Thank you." She stood up and slowly spun, the bottom of her dress floating around her. "I was just asking Fred about the hot, single hockey boys."

"Oh yeah, did she tell you about Cooper?"

I narrowed my eyes at her.

She was such a shit stirrer and between her and Alex I was right in the middle of their pot of trouble.

"No, she didn't." She looked at me, then waved her hand out gesturing at Wolfie to continue. "But feel free to."

"There's a lot of chemistry between them. And they talk every day. He's hot too, not as hot as Jasper obviously, but hot."

I glared at her again, trying and failing to silence her with my eyes.

"Is something going on with the two of you?" Alex raised her eyebrow.

"No, there is not." I frowned. "We're just friends." I saw Alex look at Wolf, something silent passing between them. "Oh, fuck off, the pair of you. Stop stirring shit."

They cracked up laughing.

"Ladies, dinner is served." Interrupted Gerard.

Saved in the nick of time, thank fuck. I pushed Cooper out of my head once more and walked off before those two clowns could make it worse.

We all moved to the long table, which had been rearranged so we looked towards the river. The light was slowly dying but only moved to make the candles all the brighter. They glowed in oversized hurricane jars, positioned down the table.

"This is so beautiful." Sighed Wolfie, before taking a seat at the head of the table. "The perfect Saturday night date. Surrounded by all my girls."

Laughter levels increased as twilight hit on the horizon. The drinks and conversation flowing steadily as dinner was served Italian style. Giant sharing platters piled high with food were placed on the table and we all dived in.

"Freddie?" Molly spooned a helping of meatballs on her plate. "What happened with that guy you were seeing?"

"Which one?" I passed a bowl of big, leafy greens across the table to Alex.

"Fred has the best dating stories! She's found some absolute horrors." Wolfie turned to me. "You should tell a few."

"Christ, I don't know where to start. There's been too many. Which probably isn't something I should admit to." I sat back in my chair, thinking.

I definitely didn't have the best record when it came to dating. Wolfie would tell you that I just didn't pick the right guys, which wasn't wrong, but I'd yet to meet someone that I knew would add to my life in the best way. Until then I was living on a diet of fun dates and mediocre sex.

"What about Crazy Louis?" Wolfie sipped her cocktail.

I smirked, remembering the story. "Well, we'd been on a date and he'd come back to my house. He'd seemed relatively normal, bit quirky, but he was funny. Anyway, we were having sex and half way through he stopped to tell me he didn't like the dress I'd been wearing that night."

"Nooooo." Molly's hand flew over her mouth as her eyes opened wide.

"True story. He was still inside me. I didn't know what to say." I grinned at their expressions.

The laughter levels went up another notch and my sides were beginning to hurt.

"Oh god, I once matched with a guy on Tinder and we were chatting, then out of nowhere he sends me a dick pic with the caption 'Do you like big clocks?'" Sniggered Sophie. "So I wrote back 'yes they're really helpful for when I need to tell the time in a hurry'."

We all burst out laughing.

"He never replied." She finished.

"That's genius, boys are such fuckwits." Amy's face was creased up with laughter and she was using her napkin to dry up the tears flowing down her cheeks.

"Cheers to that." I raised my glass in the air.

The war stories continued on full throttle each one funnier than the one before, and we must have sounded like a pack of hyenas to the waiters who were clearing the empty plates, bringing another course.

Before we knew it the sun had set, its orange glow gone for another day.

"What about the guy that moved next door to you? Jamie said he works in trading or something." Alex picked up again, my love life clearly a topic of interest to everyone bar me.

A shudder ran through me at the thought. Simon, my neighbour, was the epitome of a sleaze. In fact, look up the definition and you'd see his repulsive face leering back at you. He never missed the opportunity to make an innuendo.

Or just blatantly proposition me.

Or touch me.

"Oh god no." Wolfie ticked her finger back and forth in a no gesture before I had a chance to. "He's so gross, I've never met anyone so arrogant and he's such a sleaze. He pops over all the time uninvited, but only ever looks at our boobs, so I've stopped answering the door. He thinks he's god's gift to women. And he really isn't."

"Yeah, he's bad. I just can't be fucked to start a turf war with my neighbour." I pushed my chair back and stood up to find the bathroom.

"I bet he's got a micro penis." Laughed Olivia, which set everyone else off again.

Molly held her hand up. "As a doctor and speaking from a strictly medical standpoint, you know who don't have micro-penises?"

She looked around, mischief sparkling in her eyes.

"Hockey players."

Oh fuck.

Do not think about Cooper's cock.

This conversation needed a swift derailing.

"Oh I can't wait for this week." Sniggered Sophie. "Bridesmaids get first dibs, right? Come on Fredster, we've got some fun times ahead."

"No thanks." I shook my head and I walked off before Wolfie and Alex could add their penny's worth.

I wasn't getting involved with anyone this week.

Definitely.

No question.

4

COOPER

My phone buzzed as the cars drove through the gates and pulled up on the concourse beside the plane hanger.

We were done with Vegas.

"Well, you look less like shit than I thought you would." Freddie announced over FaceTime, more loudly than she needed to.

"Don't hold back, will you?" I raised my eyebrow.

A sly grin spread across her face, making her ice blue eyes sparkle. I'd never seen a colour like it, as though a water droplet had been caught in the sunlight. The shade of the palest sapphire.

"What time are you getting in?" She asked.

I looked at my watch. "Ten hours from now. Whatever time that is in London."

My brain wasn't working, although it definitely wasn't the worst I'd ever felt leaving this city.

I watched as she pursed her lips. They were full and pouty, the type of lips I'd seen on plenty of bunnies, but these were one hundred percent natural. "Are you going to tell me what happened?"

"That's a negative, Ghostrider."

She scrunched her nose up. "Come on, I won't tell anyone."

I laughed at her because we both knew that wasn't true. Anything she knew, Wolfie would know within a matter of minutes. Seconds even.

"No, it's a universal rule. What happens in Vegas stays in Vegas."

Which was fine, because there wasn't actually anything to tell. Nothing happened. It would go down in the record books as the most boring Vegas trip ever.

And I mean EVER.

"Yeah, yeah, I'll get it out of you eventually." She threatened. "Okay we'll see you in ten hours. And get some sleep, you and I have work to do!"

I groaned at the never ending list of Best Man jobs I'd been lumped with. Freddie had clearly been channelling Napoleon as the world smallest tyrant. She was so fucking bossy, but for whatever reason I never seemed to put up an argument.

"Noted, see you at the airport, Tiny."

I hung up and looked around at the pitiful group in my car. Each and every single one of them were hungover to the eyeballs. But honestly, drinking was the extent of our trip to Vegas and there was really nothing interesting to tell Freddie or anyone else for that matter because nothing had happened, or as far as I was concerned it hadn't. Unless you counted Jasper nursing a bottle of whiskey and whining about how he wasn't good enough for Wolfie.

No strippers, no gambling, no sex.

At least not for me and definitely not for Jasper.

As Best Man, it had been my responsibility to stay by him all night and as he'd had zero interest in doing anything except talk about Wolfie, that's what I'd ended up doing too. I'd missed out on all the fun.

The rest of them, well, that was a different story.

In the car ahead I could see our teammates Felix Cleverly, Drew Crawley, Brogan Bartlett and Carter Rice as well as Wolfie's two brothers crawl out of the passenger doors and make their way slowly up the stairs of the plane. None of them had removed their sunglasses from the moment they'd woken up, although I'm not sure they'd even been to bed.

Fuckers.

"Sir, we'll load your luggage, feel free to go ahead." Said the driver, turning around to us.

"Thanks man." I handed him a wad of cash as a tip.

"Coop, can you move? I need to get out of this car." Grumbled Tate, Jasper's brother.

I opened the door. Tate pushed passed, taking in a deep breath of air.

"If you're going to be sick, don't do it near me. And do it before you get on the plane." I said as Jasper climbed out, followed by two more guys from our team. Apart from Jasper and me they were all in a sorry, sorry state.

"Everyone get on the plane." I called out as another car pulled up and I walked over to greet it.

"Are you the hangover guys?" I asked as the driver's window lowered.

"We are, Mr Marks." Said the driver.

"Perfect. They're all on the plane, can you come up?"

"No problem, Sir. We'll unload and be up shortly. Just need everyone in their seats. There's eleven of you? Correct?"

"Yes, eleven. Thanks, Man, see you up there."

I entered the large cabin and could see the boys already in various states of incapacitation, some already asleep, some drinking and Felix had a barely dressed woman on his knee. Where the fuck had she come from?

"Clevs, what the fuck?" I shouted and glared at him, until he knew exactly what I was shouting for.

"Chill out. She's leaving soon."

"She needs to leave now." I waited until he tipped her off his knee and stood up, walking her to the entrance of the plane before giving her a long kiss goodbye.

I shook my head at him until he sat back down. It was a mystery how he managed to get women following him around like some type of god. He was a moron at the best of times.

"Guys, heads up." They all groaned at me. "We've got a long flight ahead, and I have something for you. So I need you all to sit the fuck down and listen."

"Mr Marks?" A voice called from the stairs.

"Yes, please come in." I motioned them in, before turning back to the messes in front of me. "This is my present for all of you."

"Is it girls?" Yelled a voice from the back.

"No dickhead, it's a medical present, so roll up your sleeves. Before we take off you're all getting an IV drip so we don't land in London looking like hungover pieces of shit."

"I fucking love you, Coop." Called Drew as one of the nurses got to work on him.

"I'll remember that." I took a seat next to Jasper and rolled up my sleeve. "You okay?"

"Yeah, just want to get to Wolfie." He held out his arm for an IV.

"We'll be there in ten hours and you'll be asleep for most of it." I reassured him.

A year ago my mouth would have dropped open at such a statement, but since Wolfie literally crashed into his life he'd become a different man. Jasper had been the quintessential bachelor playboy with almost a different woman every week, just like I still mostly did, until he'd fallen head over heels in love. And, as much as I hated to admit it, it was for the better.

She 100% owned his balls and he loved it.

He now couldn't bear to be parted from her, even for the

night, and although he was my best friend and our relationship had changed, I loved seeing him so happy.

He'd got lucky.

Wolfie had fitted into our lives so easily, even bringing along her own friends.

Speaking of which, I pulled out my phone and found the latest playlist Freddie had sent me, titled 'Vegas Hangover.'

"There you go, Mr Marks. This will take up to forty-five minutes then you're all good to go." The nurse examined the IV before walking round to check on the rest.

"Thank you." I pulled on my headphones and pressed go, closing my eyes.

Freddie had introduced me to so many new bands, The XX playing out now had quickly become one of my favourites, the electro-melodic beats relaxing me.

Our best friends were getting married and we'd become close by default. She was actually the first girl friend I'd had.

The last girl I'd been really close to had left me with a broken heart. Our relationship had been the true definition of a whirlwind romance. I'd been going through the draft, she was training to be a physio and we had fallen in love. Then we were married within a month and soon after reality hit. Our relationship lasted a total of eighty-six days.

Everything I'd believed to be true, every feeling I had for her, turned out to be a big fat lie. I buried myself in hockey and swore I'd never put myself in that position again.

Never allow my emotions to carry me away.

Never to be owned by a woman.

Bunnies had been the life for me ever since.

Although recently the appeal had become less and less.

Freddie had come along as part of a package deal with Wolfie and I'd soon found myself really looking forward to hearing from her. It had been ages since I'd met someone who made me laugh as much as she did and I loved winding her up. Loved seeing how far I could push her.

She was just so fucking funny.

Fiery too.

When she was helping me with my house, I realised how amusing she was when I didn't listen to her advice. I'd enjoyed winding her up, letting her think I'd paid no attention to anything she said, when in reality most of my house had been designed from her suggestions.

And the closer the wedding got the more frequent our messages had become, until they were several times a day.

I was speaking to her more than my teammates. More than my family.

I'd grown used to seeing her face over FaceTime. Usually in a scowl at her annoyance at me, mostly deserved from one stupid request after another, but I couldn't help it. I'd even caught myself thinking about the next inane thing I could ask.

And when I wasn't winding her up our conversations veered away from wedding chat and mostly involved music. I thought I had a love of music, but Freddie was at a whole other level.

My eyes started to droop as I took a deep breath and absorbed the lyrics.

"This was a fucking genius idea." Bellowed Brogan from the back of the plane, half an hour later. "Coop, I feel absolutely banging."

The nurses were walking around, removing the IVs which had been done with. The boys were definitely starting to look less like the walking dead, although a few still hadn't taken off their sunglasses.

The pilot walked over to Jasper and me. "Sir, wheels up in ten if you're ready."

"As soon as possible." Grumbled Jasper, not looking up from his phone, no doubt texting Wolfie.

"Ten is great, thank you." I nodded to him as he walked back to the cockpit.

I turned around. "Hey, we'll be leaving in ten. Sort your shit out and sit down."

The stewards prepared for take-off, sealing the doors as the pilot came over the intercom.

"Gentlemen, we'll be wheels up in two minutes. The air looks clear for the journey and we should be arriving in London ahead of schedule in nine hours and seventeen minutes."

The plane moved smoothly off into a fast taxi before a steep climb into the clouds until it levelled out.

As the stewards unbuckled and started moving around the cabin, handing out drinks, two bodies plopped themselves into the seats opposite Jasper and me - Jamie and Murray, looking less worse for wear than they did a few hours ago. They weren't small guys either, they could definitely hold their own in the bar with the rest of the boys.

"Alright guys?" Said Jamie. "How are you doing?"

"Better now we've taken off." Jasper seemed to have cheered up significantly.

"How are you two doing?" I raised an eyebrow.

"Yeah good. Fucking awesome weekend." Murray grinned. "I feel like I could go another night after that drip."

They looked at the pair of us, before their eyes settled on Jasper.

"Look Jasper, mate." Jamie cleared his throat. "Before we land, Muz and I need to have the talk with you."

I watched Jasper frown in confusion as I clocked what they meant. Ohhhh this was going to be awesome.

"What talk with me?" He frowned.

"Well, you know the one about making sure you look after Wolfie."

I snorted, this was fucking hilarious. Mainly because Jasper was so obsessed with Wolfie that he'd almost rather die than let her be hurt from even a paper cut, so this talk was one hundred percent pointless.

"Right, okay. Guys…"

"Let's not pretend we're any threat." Interrupted Murray. "You beat people up for a living, but if our dad asks, we had the talk. Deal."

Jasper laughed at them, "Deal. But I do think you'd be able to give me a run for my money, although you have nothing to worry about. I would never hurt her. And to clarify, I don't beat up people for a living, I just knock them out of the way. Coop is the one who beats people up."

I glanced up as the steward approached us.

"May I offer you gentlemen any refreshments?" She handed us the flight menu.

"I'll just take some water thanks." I replied, as the others ordered beers.

They all looked at me as I stood up. "Freddie said I need to sleep as I've got a full day of work when we land. So, if you're going to stay here yapping I'm leaving to sleep elsewhere. Someone wake me up an hour before we get there, please."

Murray took his beer from the steward. "Glad we're not the only ones she bosses about."

I walked to the bedroom at the back of the plane, passing several of the guys already back on the booze, stuffing burgers into their faces as they played a game of poker. Tate and Drew, oblivious to the noise, had passed out cold, lying flat on the reclining chairs.

I entered the bedroom and fell onto the bed, sleep taking over almost immediately.

5

COOPER

I woke up to heavy breathing and turned to find Jasper next to me. A knock at the door followed.

"Mr Marks, we'll be landing in an hour. You asked us to wake you." Came a voice through the panels.

"Thanks." I called. "Jas, wake up." I shoved him as I looked at my watch. I'd managed to get a solid eight hours.

"What?" He grunted in confusion.

"We're landing in an hour. Then you'll see Wolf."

It was alarming how quickly that made him sit up.

"Do you want to get in the shower first? Otherwise I'm going." I stood up.

"Yeah you go." He fell back on the pillow.

Ten minutes later, I wrapped a towel around my waist and walked out. He was fast asleep again. No big surprise, Jasper slept like the dead and as we roomed together whenever we played away games I was more than used to his sleeping habits.

"Jas! Wake up." I shouted, throwing a clean towel at his head. "We're going to be landing soon. Get your ass in the shower."

"Okay. Calm down." He flung back the duvet, standing up.

He turned just before he walked into the bathroom. "Hey Coop, I love you man, thanks for this weekend. It was brilliant. I'm glad you and I got to spend time together without the clowns out there too."

I pulled on some clean boxers, followed by my jeans. "Yeah me too buddy, but we've got a big week ahead of us now. And Wolfie's put me in charge of you this week, so please get in the shower."

He grinned and shut the door behind him.

I yanked a shirt on as I walked into the main cabin, expecting absolute carnage, and found myself pleasantly surprised by mostly sleeping bodies on recliners. It was like being at camp, except if the campsite was a fifty million dollar plane.

"Fellas." I was greeted by silence. I clapped my hands loudly. "Hey dipshits, wake up! We're going to be landing soon." I heard a few more grunts. "You've got ten minutes to get your shit together before I need you to pay attention so we can get off the plane."

"You got it, bossman." Mumbled someone who sounded like Drew.

The stewards were handing coffee out as Jasper emerged from the cabin. He grabbed one and we took seats together near the front.

As the plane landed I could feel Jasper's leg tapping against the floor and he was out of his seat almost before the plane fully stopped.

"Jas, sit down." I pulled on his sleeve. "We can't get off until the plane has been checked, then you can go."

He groaned and sat back down.

I stood up.

"Gang, listen up." Nine bleary faces turned to me. "When we get off the plane Wolf and Freddie will be outside along with a couple of cars to drive you to the hotel. Freddie has itineraries for you, but have today to do what you want, then we have the concert tomorrow night, then we're heading to the country on Tuesday for the wedding. Pace yourselves and fucking behave, to be very clear I'm not coming to bail any of you out of jail."

Jesus, I sounded like a fucking camp councillor.

The doors to the plane opened and Jasper was first off, down the steps like a shot, running as quickly as he could. I picked up the bag he'd left, along with mine, and felt a slap on my back as I headed towards the door.

"Nice job, Coop. If you ever decide to quit hockey you'll be snapped up by the Boy Scouts in no time." Huck Sands, of one our defensemen, put his arm around me.

"Fuck off." I smirked.

"Awesome, awesome trip though buddy, thanks so much."

As we walked into the arrivals hall Jasper was already wrapped around Wolfie. Freddie was leaning against the railings looking bored as she tapped her phone screen. One foot flat against the wall only served to jut a hip out and emphasise her mouthwatering curves. Curves I don't think I'd ever properly appreciated before now.

She was wearing tight yoga pants which hugged her lithe thighs, making them seem much longer than her miniature stature, miniature compared to my six foot three frame anyway. A faded black vintage t-shirt stretched across her chest and as I got closer I noticed the artwork. It was the album cover for Bon Jovi's Slippery When Wet. My dick twitched and my mind fell into the gutter before I could stop it.

I gave myself a second to compose myself, suddenly feeling so fucking excited that I was going to spend the next ten days with her.

I was in front of her before she noticed me and bent down to nearer her eye level.

"Hi Tiny."

She looked up from her phone, boredom replaced by a slow smile spreading across her face.

"Marks." She pushed off the wall.

I pulled her into a hug, lifting her off the ground inhaling the scent of citrus and cedarwood.

"You took your time. These two haven't taken a breath since he stormed through the doors five minutes ago." She grumbled, making me laugh.

I suddenly felt a sharp pull, like my heart was beating double time, and put her down.

"It's good to see you too, Tiny." I rubbed at the weird feeling in my chest.

The rest of the boys made their way through the doors.

"Wow guys, you really look like shit."

Drew picked her up into a hug, followed by Felix.

"I'm feeling so much better now I've seen you, you're like a miracle cure, Fredster." Winked Felix.

I growled under my breath. Smooth fuckers.

"Yeah, yeah." She made her way around the rest of the guys, greeting them all with hugs.

I walked over to Wolfie, where she'd managed to unglue herself from Jasper's mouth, although he was still holding her as tightly as he could.

"Hey Wolf, how're you doing?" I leaned in to kiss her on the cheek.

"Coop! You look good!" She gave me a one handed hug. "Thanks for bringing Jas back to me in one piece."

"It was the most boring Vegas trip on record." I whispered to her. "Jasper and I were in bed by ten."

She rolled her eyes. "I'm going to choose to believe it, whether it's true or not."

"I wish it wasn't true." I winked.

A shrill whistle pierced the air and several of the guys flinched.

"Right guys." Shouted Freddie. "Cars are outside. Can you shift your arses please?"

We made our way out of the terminal where the cars were waiting, Freddie handing out instructions to the boys as they climbed in.

"You and Fred are driving together? Just the two of you?" Jasper lowered his voice as I put my bags in the trunk of his car to take back to the house for me. Unlike the rest, we were staying at Freddie's.

"Yeah we've got some work to do."

"And she's driving?"

Jamie and Murray got in the back of the car and they all started laughing, shaking their heads.

"Yeah?" It came out as a question.

"Good luck!" He grinned and slapped me on the back.

"What?" I frowned.

He winked at me and got into his ride, next to Wolfie.

I opened the passenger door of Freddie's SUV and climbed in, wondering what Jasper was talking about. A faint smell of leather with citrus and cedarwood, the one I'd smelled on her earlier, was lingering in the air and I felt a calmness wash over me.

She opened the door, hoisting herself in and I let out a chuckle.

"What are you laughing at?" She looked at me.

"Why do you have this car, you can barely see over the steering wheel? Let alone get in." I grinned.

"Well, Jasper struggled to fit in my car. And we can't fit everything we need in the trunk of a Porsche. So I've got Pops' car for the week."

"Fair point. Let's go then, Tiny."

She started the engine, accelerating off.

"Want to play DJ?" She handed me her phone, opening up Spotify.

I flicked through some of her playlists before settling on

the track I'd been listening to on repeat since she'd shared it earlier. The XX Dare You.

"I knew you'd like this album."

"I do. A lot. I've been enjoying my musical education." I turned to her, taking in her side profile as she was driving.

I don't think I'd ever really noticed how striking she was, almost ethereal. I'd always thought she was beautiful no question, but I'd never had the chance to properly study her without her noticing or a phone between us.

Thick lashes framed her eyes and the pale blue of her iris appeared almost translucent from this angle. She had a little button nose and high cheek bones. Her jet black hair, poker straight and so glossy I could almost see my reflection in it, rested just below her collarbone.

I felt weird and I couldn't put my finger on why. I must be jet lagged.

"Has your hair grown?"

"Yes. I need to tie it back for the wedding, so I've been growing it, but it didn't get far." She laughed.

A loose strand had fallen forward and I fought a sudden urge to tuck it behind her ear. An ear that was scattered with tiny diamond studs, except for a little arrow half way up and a miniature gold heart inside the shell.

As we hit the main roads heading into London I understood what Jasper meant about wishing me luck. It was almost as though she was competing in the Indy 500 with every other car on the road, and the Range Rover's engine was powerful enough to let her as she swerved in and out of the traffic. I grabbed hold of the ceiling handle as she squeezed between two cars moving across the lane.

"Fucking hell, slow down. I have a dangerous activities clause in my contract."

"What does that mean?" She glanced at me with a side eye.

"It means I'm not allowed to partake in them, so I'd

appreciate it if you slowed down. Maybe stick to one lane." I gritted my teeth.

She grinned at me in a way which would have made my crotch tight if I hadn't been scared for my life. Minutes later we pulled up on Saville Row, outside a red brick store front and rang the buzzer.

"Hello?"

"Hi, it's Francesca Danvers. I'm here to collect the suits for the Jacobs' party."

The door buzzed again and we pushed in.

"Good morning, Ms. Danvers. We have the suits here ready for you." We were greeted by a sharply dressed man with measuring tape hanging around his neck. He pointed to a hanger filled with suit carriers, each one had our individual names on. We'd had our suits custom made for the wedding.

"Oh great, thank you. These will be good to lay flat in the car, right?" She asked.

"Yes they should be fine, just hang them back up as soon as you can."

She turned to me. "Do you think we should drop the suits off to the boys? The hotel is just by here."

"Fuck no, don't give them anything to have responsibility over. We need to take these back with us."

"Yeah, okay." She nodded in agreement, before turning back to the tailor. "Can we wheel this hanger out?"

"Yes of course, I'll help with that. And can I offer you both something to drink? Sparkling water perhaps?" He held out a couple of chilled cans.

"Yes please." Freddie took them, handing one to me. I took a sip, it was a fucking weird tasting water, I looked at the can – fizzy cucumber.

Bloody English.

We grabbed the hanger and wheeled it out of the shop. Unlocking the trunk, it was full of large boxes.

"Freddie, what's all this shit?"

"Oh fuck, the fairy lights. I forgot I hadn't moved them."

I opened the back doors and pulled the seats down, making the trunk space bigger before pulling all the boxes back through, creating room for the suits.

"Thanks Coop." Freddie grinned at me. "Thanks for coming with me."

"Didn't realise I had a choice." I raised my eyebrow as she passed me the last suit and I laid it down.

"Yeah, you didn't really."

"Ms Danvers, is there anything else you need?" The tailor walked out of the shop.

"No, we're good, thank you for helping us."

"You're very welcome. Enjoy the wedding." He wheeled the hanger back into the shop.

I looked down at Freddie. "Where to next, Boss?"

"Oh shit." She mumbled looking past me. I was about to turn around when she grabbed the front of my shirt dragging me down, my lips crashing onto hers. Soft and pillowy, they were the most delectable lips I'd ever had the pleasure of having against mine.

But what the fuck?

I pulled her head back. My hands spanning the width of her face, I looked into her eyes searching for an answer.

Her tongue brushed across my lower lips and from that moment on I had no control over myself and covered her mouth with mine. She tasted like mint and cucumbers from the sparkling water she'd been drinking and as I opened up for her, allowing her access to me, our tongues collided in motion sweeping together.

I'd never felt anything so perfect.

She was a human defibrillator shocking my body back into life.

She let out a soft moan, which shot straight to my groin. I didn't know what was happening and I didn't care, this was the best kiss I'd ever had.

She was standing on the tips of her toes and as I reached down to cup her ass, she lifted up wrapping her legs around me, rubbing right up against my dick which was getting harder by the second.

"Fuuucck Freddie." I groaned into her mouth before our tongues continued their journey, tangling together stroke after stroke.

Her hands were scraping through my hair, trying to pull me in closer. Pushing herself further into my mouth, devouring me. This girl was a demon. I'd never felt so much passion and I couldn't remember the last time I'd wanted someone so intensely.

And then she started rocking against me.

Screw shopping, I wanted to go straight to bed. Bury myself so deeply inside her she'd feel me for days, weeks, months. She was lucky I wasn't taking her in the back of the car. She groaned into my mouth again as my grip on her ass tightened. One slip of my finger and I knew it would be drenched in her.

"Fred?"

"Freddie?"

Where was that voice coming from?

"Fred, is that you?"

Who the fuck was calling her name?

She pulled away from my lips and turned her head slightly. Her grip loosened and she slid down my body, turning in my arms so her back was to me, thankfully hiding my erection pushing painfully against my zipper.

There was a man standing in front of us, looking at us with a horrified expression. Not that I blamed him, I'd have probably had the same if I was passing two people dry humping on the street.

"Oh, hi Stuart, how are you?" Freddie asked, trying to sound as casual as possible and failing.

"Is this why you're not calling me back?" He pointed to

me, anger written all over his face. Anger directed at me. Not that he was remotely intimidating, he looked like he would crumble under the weight of my hockey pads.

She shuffled uncomfortably, moving out of my arms. "Look Stuart, we had a few fun dates, but I think we both know that it wasn't going anywhere."

What in the actual fuck was happening?

"I thought it was going to go somewhere."

Oh Jesus.

"I'm sorry Stuart, but it wasn't, we don't have any chemistry. You're a nice guy, but just not the guy for me."

Stuart's face dropped, no one wanted to be nice guyed. And suddenly I felt awkward as fuck. I'd had that face once before and it was fucking horrible.

"I'm going to leave you two to talk." I slammed the trunk door shut.

I walked around to the driver's door to get in, although the seat was so far forward I couldn't even fit. Fuck's sake. I tried to block out their conversation until I could finally squeeze in, closing the door behind me.

I sat there processing what had just happened. I was sporting a semi and I could still feel my heart beating as hard as it did when I'd just finished drills. Freddie had kissed me, possibly the hottest, most sexually charged kiss I'd ever experienced and she'd done it to send a message to another fucking dude.

She'd seen him coming and grabbed me.

A revenge kiss?

Whatever it was, she'd used me and I didn't fucking like it. I could feel my blood start to boil.

Why did I care?

Because there was no way she hadn't felt that too. That passion and need hadn't been just one way. She'd nearly set me on fire.

The driver's door opened and I turned to see Freddie staring at me.

Fuck me she was beautiful. More beautiful than she'd been ten minutes ago, her lips pink and swollen from our kiss.

"Thanks Coop, you can get out now. He's gone."

Fuck that.

"I'm driving now."

She frowned. "What? No, it's my car."

"That's irrelevant. I'm driving."

She was a second away from stamping her foot, which would have made me laugh if I wasn't so fucking angry.

"Cooper, stop messing around, I'm not in the mood. Please just get out." She sighed.

"Yeah, I'm not in the mood either, Francesca. So, get in the passenger seat or I'll drive off and leave you here."

Her jaw clenched at my use of her full name.

"Why do you have to be so fucking infuriating?" She held onto the door frame her eyes shooting daggers at me.

"I'd like to see this wedding through and the likelihood of that happening is significantly decreased if you continue driving, so get in. Or I'll send you an Uber."

She narrowed her eyes at me as she slammed the door, stormed around to the passenger seat and climbed in with a huff.

"Just because you were a bitch to him doesn't mean I'm going to let you be one to me. So, tone down the grump."

"I'm not grumpy."

I smirked at the blatant lie.

"Oh really? Daily occurrence that is it? Just leaving broken hearts all over London, are you?"

"Hardly." She huffed again but staring out of the window this time.

I watched as she picked an invisible thread off her yoga pants, pants I wanted to rip off her and continue where we'd

46

left off, burying my face in her dripping pussy. Our relationship had shifted gears in the last five minutes and I needed to take control of this situation.

I took a deep breath. "You've done him a favor, he wouldn't haven't been able to handle you anyway."

"What's that supposed to mean." Her head whipped round and she glared at me.

"It means what I said. You'd have been too much for him and his little puppy heart."

"You're making me sound like Cruella de Vil."

"Not at all." I said as softly as I could. "You have a big heart and it has a lot of power. You need someone who can take that. And he wouldn't have been able to. In fact, if the all the guys you go for are anything like him they're never going to work out. If he was man enough to be with you then he'd be with you. No one worthy would let you go."

Christ. First a camp counsellor and now I was Dr. Phil.

She grumbled out of the window. I could hear her muttering to herself.

"And Tiny?" I waited for her to turn back and look at me. "Let's get one thing straight. Don't ever fucking kiss me to get out of breaking up with someone else. Got it?"

She nodded silently.

"Next time you kiss me, it's because you can't not."

And you can bet your fucking ass there's going to be a next time.

I watched her eyes open wide and I started the engine.

"Now, I need you to give me directions."

6

FREDDIE

Cooper pulled up in front of my house and I jumped out before he could turn off the engine, storming in past Jasper who'd opened the door.

I could barely contain my anger.

"Yeah, I'll bring these in don't worry." I heard him shout.

I ran up the stairs and slammed my bedroom door shut.

How could I have been so stupid?

What had come over me?

I was one hundred percent placing the blame for this on Alex and Wolf. They'd been winding me up so much about Cooper this week and it had clearly sunk into my very small brain.

He was my friend.

My friend who was a wall of unyielding muscle, of bulging biceps and rock hard pecs. So hard. As though he was carved from granite.

But this morning.

This morning I had them pressed against me and felt him in all his solid glory. Felt his power. Felt what he was capable of.

After five minutes of pacing up and down, I laid on the

floor. Programming Fleetwood Mac onto the speakers I closed my eyes, trying to calm myself with the dulcet tones of Stevie Nicks.

I thought back to the journey home, to Cooper words. *"Next time you kiss me, it's because you can't not."*

He was fucking dreaming if he thought I was going to kiss him again. Presumptuous arsehole.

How fucking dare he.

I wasn't a bunny at his beck and call.

But holy shit, he could kiss. Those lips were now imprinted onto mine. I don't think I'd ever been kissed like that. Like he couldn't get enough, like he'd die if he couldn't taste me. And when he lifted me up and rocked against me, oh god his dick.

It was like what dick dreams are made on.

I pressed my eyelids down trying and failing to erase the memory.

And fucking Stuart. Cooper was right, he was like a puppy and I'd kicked him. I was a horrible, horrible person.

I banged my head against the floor, trying to rid myself of my spinning thoughts.

"If he was man enough to be with you then he'd be with you. No one worthy would let you go."

And what was that supposed to mean?

Oh god, I'd kissed him. And he'd been so angry at me.

But the way he looked at me, like he could ignite me from the inside out. I felt a heavy throb between my legs.

That could fuck off for a start.

I heard my door open and turned to see Wolfie walk in.

"Fred, what are you doing? We're going to the pub." She stood over me, looking down. "Are you okay?"

"Yeah." I groaned.

"Then why are you listening to Fleetwood Mac?"

It was a valid question, she knew I only listened to Fleetwood Mac at times of existential crisis. They had been my

49

parents' favourite band, having met at a Fleetwood Mac concert and I listened to them when I needed help solving a problem. She lay down on the floor next to me.

I turned to her. I couldn't tell her yet, because I wasn't even really sure what to tell her. There wasn't anything to tell. It definitely wasn't a big deal. But she would make it one, without a doubt. Her and Alex.

Not to mention Molly.

"I'm fine, I'm just a fucking idiot sometimes."

"Okay, well I could have told you that." She nudged me in the ribs. "Come on, come for lunch with us."

"No, I can't, I need to drive out to Mum and Pops and check up on how the barn is coming along."

"Okay." She turned and kissed me, then stood back up. "I love you Francesco, thanks for working so hard to make my wedding so beautiful."

"You know I'm too much of a control freak to let anyone else do it." I grinned.

"Yeah, I know, I still love you though."

I heard her walk down the stairs and the muffled voices of the three of them before the front door shut. I stayed on the floor for another five minutes, then got up.

I pulled up in front of my parents' house and ran inside. Rookie and William, our family Labradors, ran to the door to greet me and I bent down to give them a cuddle. We'd always had dogs growing up and these two were the most recent additions, although Rookie was getting pretty old.

"Anyone home?" I walked through to the kitchen, where I found Murray against the Aga cooking some bacon. The dogs immediately sat underneath him. "What are you doing here?"

"Jamie dropped me off." He replied.

"Why didn't you go back to your house?" I frowned.

"I realised I didn't have anything clean and needed to do some washing." He flipped the bacon before taking some bread from the breadbin.

I pulled my hair back into a messy bun and walked over to the window, staring out at the lawn. "What's wrong with your place?"

"The washing machine's broken and I haven't had time to get it fixed." He answered. "Do you want a bacon sandwich?"

He opened the fridge, taking out the ketchup and squeezing it onto the bread.

"Yes please and a cup of tea."

"You make the tea. Anyway, what are you doing here?"

"I needed to drop some stuff at the barn." I filled the kettle and switched it on, moving past him to take the mugs from the cupboard.

"Is Cooper with you?" He piled the slices of bread with crispy bacon and cut them in half.

I spun around to him. "No, why would you ask that? Why would he be with me?"

"Because you were supposed to be doing jobs together today? He went to sleep on the way back specifically because you had a full day of jobs."

He walked over to the long, scrubbed wood table, putting the sandwiches down.

My shoulders dropped and I let out a sigh. "Oh."

I put two mugs of tea in front of us and sat down.

"Franks, what's with you?" He eyed me as he passed me a bacon sandwich.

I'd never admit it out loud but Murray was my favourite brother. He'd come along a few years after Jack and Diane had adopted me and I'd taken to him as though he was my own personal baby doll. Even though he was six years younger than me we'd always been close as we'd grown up and I shared everything with him. He was also the only person, apart from Jack occasionally, who called me Franks, never Fred, like it was something only we shared. With Wolfie in the States more than London we'd been spending a lot of time together.

"I did something stupid." I shrugged as I bit into my sandwich. "Oh, this is good."

"I'm going to need you to elaborate." He stared at me before stuffing his own into his mouth. A dollop of ketchup fell out and hit the table.

I pulled my hair out of the tie again and then put it back up. "You remember that guy I went on a few dates with? Stuart?"

"What that the weirdo you were with when I bumped into you the other week?" He scrunched his face up as he chewed.

"He wasn't weird." I protested and he raised his eyebrow at me. "Yeah alright, well anyway, I wasn't really feeling it and we'd never made plans for another date and I've been busy with the wedding so I haven't called him back."

"And?" He leaned back in his chair, taking a huge gulp of tea.

"I bumped into him this morning when Cooper and I were loading the suits into the car." I took another bite of my sandwich. There really was nothing like a bacon sandwich and a cup of tea to make you feel better.

"Oooh awkward. I hate the ghost and bump." He grimaced.

"Yeah, hang on, that's not the worst bit." I sipped on my tea.

He looked at me, his eyes open wide and mocking like he was hanging on tenterhooks.

"So, I saw him walking down the street..." I squeezed my eyes shut. "And kissed Cooper to get out of him seeing me."

I heard Murray cough into his cup. At the same time,

Rookie let out a loud groan from his basket. I scowled at the pair of them.

"You kissed Cooper?" He leaned forward across the table, as if needing to get closer to believe it.

"Yeah, I know, I'm a fucking idiot." My face fell in my hands.

"What happened?"

"By the time Stuart got to us I was practically dry humping him. It was so awkward, and Stuart was so upset at me. I don't even get it, it was three dates and he barely even kissed me! Then when I got back in the car, Cooper was really pissed off and he wouldn't let me drive."

Murray smirked.

"It's not funny, he's living at the house for the next few days and I just want to avoid him."

"Oh Franks grow up. He probably just thought it was funny. You don't have to avoid him."

I wished that were true.

"Murray, he said to me 'Don't ever fucking kiss me to get out of breaking up with someone. And next time you kiss me it'll be because you can't not'." The words were tattooed on my brain.

"Oh, he is a fucking lad." He was openly laughing at me now.

I scrunched my face up. "Murray…" I whined.

"How was it?"

I stared at him. I could lie, but I'm not sure I could hide it very well. Not from Murray at least, and I needed to rid myself of this burden.

"The best kiss of my life." My face fell back into my hands.

"Franks, you're so dramatic. Have you told Wolf?" He asked.

I shook my head. "I didn't want to make a big deal out of it."

"It's not a big deal unless you want it to be one. But

honestly don't stress about it, he doesn't seem like the sort of guy who'd care if you kissed him."

"Yeah because he gets women throwing themselves at him all the time." I grumbled.

"Exactly so he probably won't even remember you among the masses." He stood up, picking the plates off the table and putting them in the sink.

The thought that he might not remember it sank heavy in my stomach.

"Murray!" He was trying to wind me up and it was working.

He leaned back against the counter, his arms crossed over his chest and narrowed his eyes at me. I could see the corner of his mouth twitch.

"Franks, do you want him to remember you..?"

"Well, I don't want to be lumped with the masses and he clearly thinks I'm going to kiss him again. Which I'm not."

I wasn't. Definitely.

He shook his head at me. "You're a dickhead aren't you. How do you get yourself into these messes?"

"I don't know." I stood up, done with the conversation. "Do you want to come and see the barn with me? Can you help me unload the fairy lights?"

He thought for a minute. "Yeah, if you drive me back?"

"Deal. But we're not going back until later so I can be sure Cooper is asleep."

Yes, I was absolutely a dickhead.

But needs must.

I drove the car around to the large barn on the far side of my parents' property, the dogs following us running along the outside. Wolfie had always wanted to get married here and Jasper had spared no expense. We had one more week to get it looking like the fairyland glen she'd requested.

The place was a bustle of activity, currently filled with workers erecting platforms, rolling in tables, hanging ivy, sectioning the space up for the dinner. The blossom trees were on the way and the marquee would arrive over the weekend to extend the space for the dancing and the after party to be set up.

The dogs started sniffing around in case a spare biscuit could be found somewhere.

I saw Carrie, my assistant, ordering some guys about in the corner before she clocked me and ran over.

"Hey guys." She gave us both a hug. "We're getting there, do you want a tour."

"Definitely." Answered Murray, although I think that had more to do with the fact that he'd always fancied Carrie than actually wanting to see the place.

"We brought the fairy lights, do you want to ask some guys to get them from the car?" I pressed the fob to make sure it was unlocked.

"Oh yes, good idea." She radioed over to the foreman who quickly arrived with two burly men.

Murray's eyes widened at the entourage. "Franks, exactly how many fairy lights are in the car?"

"One hundred thousand." I grinned.

"Well let's hope you don't have to go through them all to find the inevitable faulty one in the middle." He raised an eyebrow at me.

"Idiot. Come on, let's see the place."

We started walking around the site, with Carrie pointing each designated space out to us.

"Are you going to have a fire pit?" Murray asked.

We'd exited the barn at the point the marquee would be attached and walked outside.

"Yes, over there." Carrie pointed to an area that currently looked like a box in a field.

Murray turned to me, his hands on my shoulders looking at me in earnest. "Franks, do you know what would be really cool? You need to have loads of little secret places where people can hook up. Make sure you have that okay, Wolfie's got loads of hot friends."

"Calm down Romeo, I'm pretty sure you getting laid isn't the top of Wolf's agenda." I patted his chest.

"Who says she has to know?" He waggled his eyebrows at me.

"I'll see what I can do." I laughed at him.

"That's all I'm asking for…"

I shoved him away as he grinned at me. "Come on, let's see the rest."

7

FREDDIE

Fucking birds.

I pulled the pillow over my head trying to block out the chirping noise from the dawn chorus which took place hours earlier than I ever wanted to open my eyes on a Saturday morning. I'd had a shit night, tossing and turning through broken dreams of Cooper.

I willed myself to go back to sleep, which didn't work so instead I pulled on my running gear, stuck in my ear pods and headed out into the early morning park life.

When I returned an hour later the house was still quiet. I doubted Wolfie and Jasper would emerge for a while seeing as they'd been apart for two weeks, and Cooper, well he was probably exhausted from Vegas.

Fucking Vegas.

I grabbed my favourite mug from the cupboard and switched the coffee machine on, then opened up the fridge pulling out yoghurt, berries and milk. I turned around, nearly dropping everything in the process. There, leaning against the door frame, was Cooper in all his solid, muscular glory, with a giant smirk on his face.

How long had he been standing there watching me and why had I suddenly lost the power of speech?

"Good morning Tiny." He grinned with that impossible grin, his delicious caramel eyes glinting in amusement.

"Good morning. Would you like a coffee?" I focused on being cheery and mature, something I'd had to dig very deep to find. Especially as my heart rate was beating double time and I don't think it had anything to do with the run I'd just returned from.

Beads of sweat started rolling down me.

"I would, thank you. And I'm glad to see your filthy mood has disappeared." He walked towards me, the corner of his mouth twitching.

I gritted my teeth and smiled. "It has."

"I missed you yesterday, I'd been looking forward to spending some time together."

"Well I had some things to do and ended up spending the day with Murray." I put the mugs under the coffee machine.

When I turned back around he was standing right behind me, pining me in and it suddenly felt like I couldn't breathe.

"Cooper wh.. what are you d..doing?" I stuttered.

"Did you think about me yesterday?" His voice like gravel as his eyes trailed across my body, before they stopped at my rib cage, a slight frown creasing his brow.

I startled as he touched me, his hands moving slowly up my sides before his thumb grazed back and forth across the four dates I had tattooed under my heart. My heart which he would definitely be able to feel banging hard against my chest.

So hard that I could feel it between my legs.

"No I didn't." I snapped and his eyes shot up, blazing into me.

He knew I was lying.

"No? You didn't think about our kiss? About how perfect

our mouths were together? Because it's all I could think about." His eyes locked onto mine.

Fuck I need to get out of here.

"Fred are you making coffee?" Wolfie's voice called through from the stairs, causing me to jump again.

I turned to the mugs under the machine.

"Yes." I shouted back as she walked into the kitchen.

Cooper had already taken a seat at the table, his eyes boring into me, as he ran his thumb along his lower lip. I couldn't look at him, I could feel my entire body heating up from his gaze, damp seeping through my knickers.

Wolfie gave me a once over. "God have you been for a run already? You're so keen."

"I couldn't sleep." I passed her one of the coffees, putting the other on the table.

Cooper took it from me before I had a chance to let go, brushing his fingers with mine. Electricity shot through me and it felt like I'd been burned.

"Coop are you making pancakes?" Jasper ran down the stairs and joined us in the kitchen.

"I can." He answered, his eyes still trained on me. "Tiny, would you like pancakes?"

"No thanks. But everything you need is in the fridge so help yourself. I'm getting in the shower." I turned to walk out as quickly as I could.

"Fred, what's the plan for today?" Wolfie pulled out a chair and sat down.

My phone pinged and I looked at it.

Murray: *How's Loverboy?*

I choked on my saliva and ended up having a coughing fit.

"Francesco, are you okay? You're acting like a weirdo."

"I'm fine. It's all fine. Everyone's meeting for lunch then we have The Killers in Hyde Park later." I forced a smile on my face.

"Are you coming with us?" Jasper took Wolfie's coffee and sipped it.

"Yes I'll be at lunch but I said I'd pick Murray up so we'll meet you there."

I could see Jasper's eyes narrowing at me.

Shit.

I wonder if Cooper had said anything to him.

Fuck I need a cold shower.

"Okay guys, see you at lunch." I ran up the stairs as fast as I could.

Freddie: *Change of plans. I'm picking you up before we go to lunch*

Murray: *Oh I can't wait to hear why*

"So why did you need to pick me up again?"

Murray and I were in the back of a cab on the way to the restaurant I'd booked for lunch. The whole wedding gang of Jasper and Wolfie's friends was meeting before we headed to Hyde Park to watch The Killers. It had the potential of an epic day as long as I managed to avoid being around Cooper at all costs.

"I need your protection. Promise me you won't leave my side all day." I looked at him with pleading eyes.

"Fuck no. I'm not promising that. You have got to be joking." He was rummaging through the box I'd been carrying and pulled out a t-shirt. "Franks, today is where I pick which one of Wolfie's hot friends I hook up with at the wedding, it's almost like an audition for them without them knowing."

"God you're disgusting." I groaned. "Muz, I really need you today."

"Sorry, no can do. If you really don't want to be around him then stick with the other guys. Maybe Tate, he seems a safe bet. Huck, Carter, Felix and Drew will definitely be on the prowl. And probably Brogan, come to think of it. Oh, and Dante."

Useless.

"What am I looking at?" He held a t-shirt up.

"I've had t-shirts made for everyone. The front is a picture of Jasper and Wolfie, the back is names of us all, like a tour shirt. I thought it was funny."

He pulled a face at me. "Do I have to wear this?"

"Yes, we all are. Look, I have mine on." I held it out to show him.

"Okay fine." He whipped off the shirt he was wearing, replacing it with one from the box.

We pulled up outside the restaurant, Murray jumped out with the box and headed inside while I paid the driver. I followed him in and could see them all sitting at a long table by the window, where he was already handing around t-shirts to everyone.

Big platters of food were spread out down the middle, along with several empty glasses.

"Hey, Freddie's here." I heard Felix call and spied a spare seat between him and Huck, so made a beeline.

"Hi gang, how are you all doing?" I waved to everyone without looking at anyone particular, not wanting to see where Cooper was sitting.

Felix got out of his chair and picked me up, giving me a big kiss. "Freddie you look good enough to eat. I've saved you a seat next to me and Huck."

I laughed at him, I felt the tightness ease in my chest. This is what I needed, some light-hearted fun.

"Hey guys, how are you, what've you been up to since you got here?" I asked as Huck gave me a kiss.

"Oh man, we went out last night. You English ladies are wild." Felix smirked.

Jesus Christ. They'd been in the country twenty-four hours.

This is exactly why I needed to avoid Cooper at all costs.

Revolting.

"Seriously? You already got laid?" I reached out and took some fries from his plate.

"Yeah, why do you think Carter and Dante aren't with us yet?" Brogan sniggered from across the table.

I looked around and realised there were still some people missing.

"You're a horror show." I shook my head. "Okay I'd like to get very drunk, who can help me with that?"

"Fuck yes." Huck barely had time to put his hand in the air before the waitresses were flocking.

In fact, as I looked around, there seemed to be plenty of young waitresses hovering around our table, something I wasn't going to complain about seeing as several bottles of champagne arrived within minutes.

"She was hot." Felix's leaned around Huck as he watched the waitress walk away.

I raised my eyebrow at him.

"Fred, unless you take me home with you then I'm going home with someone else. But you have first dibs." He batted his long boy lashes at me.

Maybe I needed to go and sit with the girls.

"I'll pass, but thanks."

Felix laughed at me, "I'm joking, I've already committed my night to finding girls with Muz and Tate."

My nose wrinkled. "Ewww gross."

Drew put his arm around me. "Don't worry Fred, you can stick with me tonight. I'll look after you."

"Thanks Drew." I rested my head against his shoulder.

My phone buzzed with a message.

Murray: *Fucking hell, Cooper looks like he's about to murder someone*

I looked up, straight into a deep glare and my breath caught in my throat. Cooper was staring at me, unblinking and I could see a muscle twitch underneath his right eye. It reminded me of the first time I'd watched him play hockey where he'd been so angry he'd smashed his hockey stick into pieces and shattered the glass door of the penalty box.

The throb started hammering between my thighs.

Oh my fucking god, what's the matter with me?

I quickly looked away, then back up seconds later. He was still staring and my entire body flushed hot.

Jesus why was this turning me on so much.

The tension was broken as a cheer went up, Carter and Dante had finally made an appearance. They walked over to the table, their arms in the air, still wearing sunglasses.

"It's okay guys and dolls, we've arrived." They high fived Jasper and kissed Wolfie, before they sat down in the remaining empty chairs at the other end of the table.

Drinks continued to flow, the waitresses never far away, it was a wonder the place hadn't run out of glasses. Most of them seemed to be on our table.

"Huck, switch seats with me." Molly came over and shook the back of Huck's chair.

"Huh, what?" He looked at her, confused.

"Go and sit over where I was, I want to sit with Fred for a bit." She gave me a hug.

"Nah, sit on my lap." He pushed his chair back so she could fit.

She shrugged and took a seat. "How are you? I missed you yesterday at lunch."

"You went to lunch with Wolf and Jas?"

"Yeah plus Cooper and Amy. It was fun, although Cooper was in a foul mood." She moved forward in Huck's lap so that he could turn his head to speak to Felix, blocking him from our chat.

"He was?"

"Yeah, just his usual grumpy self but more so. Where were you anyway?"

"Oh, I had to drop some things at my parents." I tried not to think about why Cooper was in a mood and I didn't dare look over to where he was sitting.

"How's it looking?"

"It's coming together, but it's going to be amazing. I think I've actually created the fairyland glen of Wolf's dreams." I grinned at her.

"Cheers to that then." She raised her glass to me and we downed them in one as more food was placed in front of us.

The boys were like vultures on a bowl of chicken wings, I managed to snatch one up before they all went.

"Fred, Muz said you're putting in hook up areas." Huck turned back to us, throwing the empty bones onto his plate and sucking the sauce off his fingers. "And I want to thank you for that."

"Oh god, don't let Wolfie hear you say that." I could see her down the other end of the table, laughing at Jasper as he played with her hair.

"What's a hook up area?" Felix took a long sip of a fresh pint which had been put down in front of him before wiping his mouth with the back of his hand.

"A designated area where we can hook up with girls." Huck replied.

"Oh nice! I'm down with that." Felix tried to high five me which I ignored, Huck taking it instead.

"Jesus, there are no hook up areas. And don't fucking go around saying that there are." I hissed.

"Alright, calm down we'll keep it on the DL. You know you're the only girl I'd want to take there anyway." Felix winked at me.

"God Felix, you're so cheesy, how you ever manage to get girls is beyond me. The stuff that comes out of your mouth." Molly rolled her eyes at him.

"Not everything that comes out of my mouth is bad, Mol." He flicked his tongue in and out at her.

"I'm going to be sick." She scowled.

"I've told you before, don't hate the player." He ruffled her head.

Drew, Brogan and Huck cracked up laughing as Wolfie walked over. She stood behind the back of Brogan's chair.

"Hey Francesco. What time do we need to head off?"

I looked at my watch. "We can go anytime, bands are on from four pm. Killers on at nine. You want to go now?"

"Yeah, let's get the bill and head over, everyone's getting too pissed here. We need some fresh air."

I glanced around the table, volume levels at an all time high, food and drink decimated. Jasper was standing at the end with his arm around Cooper, along with Tate they were laughing at something Jamie was saying. Cooper suddenly looked up at me and his expression instantly changed, his eyes filled with so much heat that butterflies started to flood my stomach.

I watched as a slow, sexy smile curled on the edge of his lips.

It was definitely time to leave.

8

FREDDIE

"Guys we have twenty minutes to get drinks and head to the stage. What does everyone want?" I called to the group although it was just girls left.

The boys had disappeared well over an hour ago, Cooper included, which meant I'd been able to breathe easier.

I was not faring well under his constant glare.

With the boys gone we'd been able to sit around and gossip, enjoying the balmy London evening we'd been blessed with.

"Gin and tonic." Came the unanimous cry.

I made my way back to them ten minutes later with a tray of drinks and they each leaned in to grab one.

"Jas said they're near the front and twenty metres in to the left of the speaker." Said Wolfie.

"Come on then, let's go." Molly stood then fell back down giggling.

Amy pulled her up, also giggling before linking arms with her and Sophie. I took Wolfie's hand and we walked towards the boys with the rest of the girls in tow.

"There they are." Screeched Wolfie as she pointed to the crowd of thousands.

It took me a second before I spotted the boys. Even in the throng they weren't that hard to find, the majority of them taller than most men. An imposing wall of muscle. We squeezed through the people until we reached them, Wolfie automatically falling into Jasper's embrace.

"For fucks sake, I can't see anything." I grumbled.

"I got you Fredster." And I was suddenly thrust into the air underneath a pair of strong shoulders.

"Thanks, this is much better." I patted Felix on the head as Wolfie joined me sitting on Jasper's.

"Oh my god, this is brilliant. We can see everything." She cried. "We need to always bring the boys to festivals."

Molly appeared next, on Huck's shoulders.

"Molly!" We called in unison.

"Don't fucking drop her." A deep growl ordered.

I looked down to find Cooper glaring at Felix, not at Huck who had his sister, before looking up at me. The twitch under his eye was back.

"Oh fuck off. I'm not going to drop her. Stop being such a grumpy bastard." Felix shot back.

Suddenly the spotlights on the stage started to change colour, dry ice billowing out as base notes pounded from the speakers.

"Oh my god it's starting." Screamed Wolfie bouncing up and down. The Killers was one of her favourite bands.

"Cub, stay still, you can't bounce like that otherwise you'll fall."

"Sorry Baby." She bent down to kiss him.

I grinned at her.

"I love you Francesco. Thank you, this is so epic." She grabbed my hand as the music properly started up and the band arrived on stage. Mr Brightside suddenly blasted out and the crowd went wild.

"Anything for you." I leaned over and kissed her.

I could see Sophie and Olivia jumping around with Amy,

Murray had his arm around someone I couldn't make out. Brogan was trying to get Carter on his shoulders. Dante, Tate and Drew had their arms in the air and were yelling the lyrics as loudly as they possibly could.

I could feel the vibrations from the giant speakers running through my body.

Cooper turned and approached us as another song kicked in, "I'm going to the bar. Tiny come with me."

"No, I'm good here." I didn't dare look at him.

"I'm not asking, come with me. Felix put her down." He ordered.

Felix lowered me to the ground.

"Thanks a lot." I grumbled.

"I'll have a beer if you're getting them." He winked.

Before I had time to answer, Cooper had grabbed hold of my hand and was dragging me through the masses to the bar.

"Ouch, you're hurting me. Cooper, what the fuck?" My arm was practically being removed from its socket.

He ignored me as we cleared the crowd, pulling me along until there was hardly anyone around. He stopped when we reached some hoardings, pushing me against them.

"Cooper what the fuck are you doing? The bar is over there."

"We're not going to the bar." He growled.

"What? Then what the fuck are you doing? I'm going back." I tried to leave and he blocked my path.

"You're staying right here and you're going to answer some fucking questions." His hands were either side of my head.

"What the fuck is your problem?" I shouted.

"I could ask you the same." He spat back.

"What?" I looked at him, confusion written all over my face.

He pinched the bridge of his nose and closed his eyes, taking a deep breath. When he opened them again, they burned into me with what felt like the heat of a thousand fires, hitting me straight between my thighs turning my insides to liquid.

"Why the fuck have you been ignoring me all day?" He snarled.

Oh shit.

"Cooper…" I pushed back on his chest, but there's no way I could move him.

"No really, please tell me why the fuck you've not said one word to me and instead been throwing yourself at Felix." His voice was low and steady as if he was having trouble controlling his anger.

Woah.

"What the actual fuck are you going on about? I haven't been throwing myself at anyone."

"Then why did I have to pull you off his shoulders just now and why was I watching him all over you at lunch." His eyes narrowed at me.

"Are you serious?" I crossed my arms across my chest.

"Do I not appear serious?"

"You appear unhinged." I smirked.

He pinned me into the wall, his musky, earthy scent overwhelming me. He would definitely be able to feel my heart pounding in my chest if he got any closer.

"I swear to God, Francesca. Do not push me right now."

I watched his tongue run along his lower lip, mesmerising me again, causing my breath to quicken. The way he said my name, like I was in trouble and about to be punished only added to the fire coursing through me.

"Do you remember what I asked you this morning?" His voice was barely above a whisper.

"Yes." I breathed out.

"And do you wish to change your answer? Have you been thinking about our kiss yesterday?"

The beat between my legs was growing heavier, he was

turning me on so much I could scarcely catch a breath. I thought about his words and looked up at him.

"Maybe you should remind me."

His eyes locked into mine and I watched the corners turn up slightly as he smirked, before crashing his lips down to meet me.

Holy fuck, this man.

His tongue plunged into my mouth, aggressively sweeping round, staking claim, before softening against me. He sucked in my bottom lip as his hands roamed across my ass, lifting me up and wrapping my legs around his waist.

It was indisputable. His mouth was made for mine.

I tightened my arms around his neck, pulling him into me but I couldn't get close enough. My fingers moved up into his hair as he rolled his hips to the rhythm of his tongue and, somehow, the beat of the music. My body melted against him, like hot wax dripping down a candle.

His tongue continued its assault, my lips completely consumed by his.

"Fuck." He murmured into my mouth as he pulled away, nearly taking me with him. I wasn't ready to let go yet.

I didn't want it to stop.

He gave a low chuckle. "Come on, we need to go back with beers before they notice us missing. But you're going up on my shoulders this time and don't let fucking Felix touch you again. Understand?"

I nodded, so affected by him I wasn't able to speak.

"Good, because this is far from finished tonight." He growled against my lips, pulling me to him one last time, grinding against me, making sure I could feel how solid his cock was, how much he wanted me.

He put me down on the ground, then took my hand, silently leading me to the bar.

"Drinks." He called when we got back to the group, all of them still bouncing around. "But you'll have to share as we couldn't carry one for everyone." He handed them around before turning to me.

"Ready, Tiny?" He crouched down so I could climb onto his shoulders.

My legs hooked behind him, his big hands resting on my knees. I could feel his thumb sweeping back and forth over my skin.

Murray looked up at me, catching my eye and raised his eyebrow, a grin spreading across his face. He was so drunk.

"Fuck off." I mouthed back, shaking my head, because there wasn't anything else to say.

"Francesco! You're back." Shouted Wolfie excitedly over the music, grabbing my hand, nearly toppling her and Jasper over.

"Cub!" He definitely had his hands full.

I started laughing, I could even feel Cooper laughing at her, his bad mood gone. She was so drunk and happy, and suddenly so was I, the music taking me again, helping me to ignore the pounding of my heart.

Music, the magic elixir. The solver of problems.

The concert wrapped up and we slowly made our way out of the park, towards a taxi rank.

"I need to get Wolfie home." Jasper was holding onto a swaying Wolf, who was still singing Mr Brightside.

"Wolf you're getting the lyrics wrong." Yelled Murray.

"Who's coming to the club we went to last night?" Shouted Felix. "I want to keep partying. Freddie you're coming."

"No, she fucking isn't." Shouted back Cooper.

I saw Felix smirk at Drew and Murray, I had the distinct feeling he was baiting him.

"Can everyone stop shouting? I can do what I fucking

want." I wanted to go home, I just didn't want to be told I was going home. For some reason all my decisions seemed to have been taken away from me.

"We are going home with Jas and Wolf." Cooper growled in my ear, goosebumps instantly breaking out across my body.

"Okay, well you lightweights can go home, the rest of us are going clubbing." Murray high fived Felix.

"Fred are you sure you don't want to come out?" Molly hugged me.

I looked over at Cooper who was talking to Tate. I'd never met anyone so intense, I don't know how I'd not been aware of it before. I thought about our kiss and felt my body heat up, he had stayed close by all night and every time he touched me it reignited the fire that burned between my legs.

"No, I'm pretty tired. I'm going to head home with Wolfie. Have fun though and I'll speak to you tomorrow."

"See you bitches later." Called Huck as he got into his taxi with most of the boys. The door shut and he stuck his head hung out of the window. "I'm telling you, I'm not mad. I'm just disappointed."

I heard them all giggling as I climbed into the cab behind Wolfie. Jasper got in, followed by Cooper who sat down opposite me, his smile almost sinister, his eyes never leaving mine. As we arrived back at the house Jasper carried Wolfie inside and Cooper held onto me as he paid the driver.

Gripping my chin, he pulled my lower lip down with his thumb.

"Go up, I'll come and find you in five minutes." He leant into me, touching his lips to mine.

I swallowed the lump in my throat and ran inside, Jasper and Wolf had already disappeared.

Shutting my bedroom door, I walked straight into the bathroom to run the shower. I needed to calm down.

I had no idea what was about to happen, the anxiety was

swirling around my stomach and I could hear my heartbeat pounding in my ears. I stepped in allowing the hot water to wash over me, rinsing away the day, soothing my nerves until I could breathe normally again.

Wrapping a towel around me, I walked back into my bedroom, stopping as I reached the entrance, where my jaw dropped.

Holy fuck.

Cooper was sitting back on my bed wearing only a pair of shorts, his deeply tanned skin warm in the glow of the bedside light. The shadows emphasised his smooth, broad shoulders and chest atop rows and rows of incredible abs.

His massive biceps, covered in slices of delicate tattoo work and such a contrast to his hard body, were accentuated by his arms lightly crossed in front of him. He was so masculine, sex literally oozing out of his every pore and he looked so cool and calm, whereas I was nothing but a puddle of arousal, my insides liquid.

I don't think I'd ever seen anyone so sexually confident in my entire life.

His abs rippled and contracted as he moved to the edge of the bed, placing his feet on the floor. His eyes trailed the length of my body and my breath caught in my lungs.

"Come here." He whispered, hooking his finger at me.

My resistance vanished. This man seemed to have absolute control over me in a way no one else ever had. I don't know how it had happened but I knew I liked it. I walked over to him, the adrenaline coursing through my body.

I'd never felt like this before.

Never felt like my heart was about to burst out of my chest.

Never been so turned on from a single look.

He pulled me to stand between his legs. He was so tall that our eyelines matched. He took my face in his hands and rubbed his thumb across my cheek. His hands were so big that I could feel his fingers wrapping around my neck while my cheek fitted neatly into his palm. I leant into his caress.

"You are so fucking beautiful." He brought his mouth to mine, kissing me on and on with absolute tenderness, until I could barely stand.

His tongue was so soft and gentle sweeping around my mouth that I melted against him for the second time that night. Pushing his fingers into my hair, raking through it, they removed the tie so it flowed freely.

He pulled back as a moan escaped my lips, his eyes burning through me with a force I'd never experienced before. His hands trailed down my neck until they reached the edges of the towel. I took a deep breath as he released it from the knot, dropping it to the floor.

I'd never felt so naked.

I heard the air suck through his teeth as his eyes trailed across my body, his pupils dilating as he watched my nipples tighten even more than they already were. A flood of wetness poured out of me, down the inside of my legs, my body trembling with more desire than it had ever known.

"Christ, Tiny, you are perfect." His hands wrapped around my waist, running over my stomach and underneath my breasts, marking me. Claiming me.

He leaned forward, licking along the tattoo over my heart before taking one of my nipples between his teeth, twisting and biting. A loud groan escaped my lips. I could hear him murmuring French to me as his tongue continued its journey while his hands travelled across my body, stroking my ass, his fingers brushing between my legs before they moved down the back of my thighs causing them to buckle.

"Open your legs and sit on the edge of my knees." He commanded.

I held onto his shoulders as I straddled him, his legs moving mine wide apart exposing me to him. I could see his massive cock, hard and heavy in his shorts. I was so close to the edge of the abyss, I was sure I'd combust as soon as he touched me.

His eyes flared and as he studied every inch of me, his tongue tracing back and forth along his lower lip. And in that moment I knew I'd found his tell, the one thing he did when he was aroused, like he was contemplating his first taste.

My breath was coming in bursts, everything building inside me.

"Cooper, please…" I moaned.

His head tipped up, a dark smile curved the corner of his lip. "Tell me what you need."

"I need you to touch me."

He brushed his lips against mine. "Je n'ai jamais rien voulu autant que je te veux. Tu me rende dingue."

His hands moved to my hips and he parted me with his thumbs, I shot back as they danced over my clit.

"Shhhhh, Tiny." He breathed against my chest. "Look at yourself, you are exquisite. So pink and perfect. Look." He repeated and I looked down, watching his fingers disappear inside me, his warm, tanned skin contrasting with my pale tones.

Jesus Christ.

He groaned loudly as his finger curled inside me. "Fuck, you're so wet for me. And so tight. I'm gonna make it feel so good for you."

He bent down, biting on a nipple, causing me to cry out, the pleasure and pain fighting against each other. My back arched to give him more as his fingers hit my G spot again and again. I started riding his hand as he added another finger and this time it was my turn to groan, the pressure so intense I was going to explode any second.

"Freddie, kiss me." Before I had a chance to move, his lips crashed onto mine as his fingers pumped into me.

The air was sucked from my lungs as the most intense orgasm I'd ever experienced ripped through me, I could only manage a silent scream as his lips surrounded mine. His tongue swept round my mouth, caressing me, bringing me back to life. His fingers continued stroking, calming me down until I was so sensitive I needed to pull his hand away.

A smug grin spread across his face as he put his fingers into his mouth, groaning as he sucked off my juices.

I nearly came again from the sight.

He pulled my face back down to his, cupping my jaw, nipping at my lips before running his nose along the column of my neck, breathing me in. I could feel his tongue gently trailing around my ear, sending shockwaves down my body, before peppering me with kisses. His arms wrapped tightly around me, bringing my sweaty drenched body against his rock hard chest, strength radiating through him.

"You are incredible." He kissed my nose as he closed his legs, bringing mine with him and swivelled around placing me on the mattress, before curling us up together.

"Time to sleep now, baby." He kissed my head and covered us with the duvet.

"What?" I pushed up on my elbow and looked at him, searching his face for a reason. "No, Coop…"

He brushed my lips with his.

"You're not ready for me yet. But soon." He pulled me against his chest and stroked my hair as we fell into a deep sleep.

9

COOPER

I looked down at her, her breathing deep and even. She looked so peaceful and calm, not her usual mouthy self.

I smirked into the dawn light.

A lock of hair had fallen over her eyes and I gently brushed it away. I don't know what the fuck had happened to me in the last forty eight hours, but the last time I'd spent a whole night in bed with a woman was thirteen years ago.

I felt my dick get hard as my mind drifted to last night.

How open she'd been.

How responsive her body was.

How powerfully she clenched around my fingers.

How sweet she'd tasted.

And she was so tight my dick would need CPR after she'd squeezed the life out of it with her perfect pussy. Even on my fingers, that velvety warmth pulsing around me had nearly sent me over the edge. She had absolutely no idea how sensual she was. I wanted to bury myself inside her so badly and didn't ever want to leave.

Fuck.

I rubbed away the tension in my chest that kept popping up, I should probably stop drinking so much.

I needed to get out of here before anyone else woke up. I didn't want to have to explain what I was doing creeping out of her room at the crack of dawn before Freddie and I had a chance to talk about it. I kissed her head and eased out from underneath her, heading back to my bed.

"Oh mate, I am absolutely hanging." Murray strolled into the kitchen, followed by Tate, Drew, Carter, Huck, Brogan, Dante and Felix.

I watched him go straight to the cupboard and get out eight glasses, while the others took a seat at the table next to me, Carter and Tate resting their heads on their arms.

"You guys fucking stink. Have you even been to bed? What are you doing here?" I looked at the clock, it wasn't even eight am.

Murray sat down with the glasses and filled each one with the contents of some sachets he'd also grabbed from the cupboard, diluting it with water.

He handed them out.

"Here, you absolute legends, drink these." They each took a glass, downing it in one.

"That is rancid." Carter looked like he was about to vomit.

"Yeah but it'll make you feel better."

I stared at the group, Dante looked like he was having trouble swallowing. Tate and Carter had their heads back down on the table.

"Guys, what the fuck are you doing here?" I asked again.

"More's the question, what are you doing here? I thought you'd be up guarding Freddie's door." Giggled Felix, who was clearly still drunk.

Did I hear that right?

"What?" I narrowed my eyes.

"Oh dude you were absolutely raging last night." Huck

stretched his arms above his head. "You looked like you wanted to rip someone's head off."

"What?" I repeated.

"That reminds me." Drew reached into his pocket, removing a wad of cash and started peeling off fifty pound notes before handing them to Felix.

Felix giggled again. "Nice doing business with you."

"I'm sorry. Can someone please explain to me what the fuck is going on?" I could barely keep the anger out of my voice.

Murray, Huck, Drew and Felix all started pissing themselves laughing.

I gritted my teeth. "I'm not going to ask again."

"Calm down. You're always so fucking territorial about Freddie so we thought we'd have a bit of fun. To be honest I didn't think it would happen so soon, but you snapped pretty early on. Felix had a bet on it happening yesterday, Huck had today. Brogan and Tate thought you'd last until the wedding." Drew was crying with laughter.

Fuck, did they know what happened?

"Are you serious?" I narrowed my eyes at each and every one of them.

They looked back at me with grins so wide I wanted to punch their lights out.

"Oh man, you're just so easy to wind up."

"You're a bunch of dicks." I was so fucking angry.

"Dude, chill out. It's not like anything happened." Huck put his head in his hands. I hoped it was pounding.

"But you bet on me hooking up with Freddie?" I scowled.

"No, just losing your shit over her. You're always so fucking weird about her, never letting anyone get near her but you don't have the balls to make a move." He lifted his head and looked up at me.

I had the fucking balls last night, dipshit.

I tried to keep a poker face but could sense Murray staring at me. I had a feeling he knew what was going on.

"Freddie better not find out about this or I will take each and every one of you out the back and beat the living shit out of you." I growled.

"Freddie find out about what?"

We all turned to look at her standing in the doorway in an oversized t-shirt and shorts.

My heart stopped.

She looked so fucking beautiful.

I had a flashback of her sitting on my lap riding my hand. Her face when she came was one of the most perfect things I'd ever seen.

I felt my dick get hard again and moved my shorts before they got too tight.

Stop it.

"Fredster!" Cried Felix. "You're a sight for sore eyes, come and sit on my lap and make me feel better." He winked at me.

I'm going to murder him.

She looked at me, her ice blue eyes piercing through me before she turned to Felix. "I'll pass, but thanks. Are you guys still drunk?"

"We might well be." Hiccupped Huck.

She looked around the group, shaking her head. Tate and Carter had definitely fallen asleep at the table.

Murray got up and pulled her into a hug. "Franks, please make us all better, we're begging you. Can you make us tea and bacon sandwiches?"

She scowled. "Christ, you could be having room service at the hotel right now."

"But then we wouldn't get to see your beautiful face." Drew batted his eyelashes at her.

And I'm going to murder him too.

She rolled her eyes, walked over the fridge and started

pulling out bacon and eggs, fixing breakfast. The aroma of food and coffee soon filled the air.

"Hey Fred, what's that?" She turned to find Huck pointing to a huge, framed sign on the kitchen wall titled 'Freddie's Rules'. Which listed as follows:

1. Saturday Mornings Are For Emergencies Only
2. Say I Love You Every Day
3. Don't Be A Dick
4. Chocolate
5. When In Times of Crisis – Fleetwood Mac

"They're my rules." She grinned. "I invented them when I was a teenager and then Wolf had that made for my birthday one year."

"Do you stick to them?" He asked.

She paused before answering. "I do actually, for the most part."

"When was the last time you listened to Fleetwood Mac?" A sly grin crossed Murray's face.

She narrowed her eyes at him and I watched her swallow. "Friday morning."

Yeah he definitely knew.

"Oh Fred, what was the crisis?" Drew jumped up and hugged her.

"Having to deal with you fucking imbeciles." She grumbled, pushing him away and turned back to finish breakfast.

I couldn't hold back the smile from spreading across my face. She was so snarky and prickly, taking zero shit and I loved it, especially as she'd been putty in my hands last night. I'd seen a side of her that I was willing to bet the pile of cash on the table not many people had seen. In fact, the thought of anyone else seeing it the way I had made my blood boil.

She put a pile of bacon sandwiches in front of us, along with some fresh orange juice and two big pots of coffee.

Everyone tucked in.

"Oh god this is good." Said Brogan with his mouth full. "I like English breakfasts."

Everyone murmured in agreement as the pile was swiftly depleted.

"Anyway, Coop, what are you doing up so early? You look liked you'd been here for a while." Dante placed a cup of coffee in front of me.

I ran my hands through my hair. "I'm trying to finish my speech."

"Oh yeah, how's it coming along?"

I pulled a face.

I'd been working on it for the past month, struggling with a bad case of writer's block. Best Man's speeches were hard. All the really funny stories were definitely not wedding appropriate and likely to land Jasper in the dog house.

"Hey, have you got props?" Piped up Felix as he slurped down his juice.

"No I haven't got any props, dickhead." I took a sip of my coffee.

"Everyone loves speech props."

"Yeah but I'm trying to make sure Jas and Wolf don't get divorced within a week."

"Thoughtful of you."

I raised my eyebrow at him. His face was really starting to become punchable.

"Just make sure you've got the bit in about how much he was crying when he first met her and she rejected him. And our James Bond trip to downtown." Smirked Drew.

I looked up as I heard Freddie laugh.

"You think that's funny?" I asked her.

"Yeah it's a funny story. You guys were such morons."

"Hey, it got him the girl didn't it?" Felix shrugged.

She scoffed.

"Come on then Fredster. If that doesn't work for you, then what would work for you?"

I sat up. *Okay now I was listening.*

"Oh god, the guys Franks dates are sooo lame." Murray smacked his fist on the table.

Something I could agree with.

"Hey!" She protested. "My love life is not up for discussion."

She was looking at anyone but me.

"No seriously. Tell them about Stuart." He laughed.

I smirked into my coffee. Fucking Stuart. It made me rage he even had the audacity to think he was in the same league as her.

"Murray, what the fuck." She tried to kick him but he grabbed her foot and pulled her over to him until she was sitting on his knee.

"Franks, he didn't even kiss you. I don't really like thinking of guys dating you." He looked at me. "But even I can admit that's fucking lame."

"He was a gentleman. And he was nice to me." She grumbled, wriggling free from his grasp.

"Then why aren't you with him?" I raised my eyebrow at her and she scowled at me.

"Freddie, we're gentlemen." Whined Drew waving his fingers around, pointing at us.

"None of you is a gentleman." She shouted. "You've been here three days and you've already had sex with someone. You're too used to bunnies doing whatever you want them to do, you treat everyone you meet like a bunny. But more fool them for acting like one." She glared at me.

I'm sorry, what? She thinks I think she's a bunny?

Everyone was staring at her.

"Franks…" Murray reached for her but she jumped away.

"And you're the worst." She turned on him, her anger really boiling up. "You can forget about these hook up spots."

"Woah woah woah. Let's not be too rash with this." Huck grinned.

"You're all disgusting."

And with that she stormed off, leaving us in silence as we stared after her. I didn't like how I felt about that. She thought last night was something I did with just anyone?

With a fucking bunny? Fuck that.

I didn't chase women.

"What's a hook up spot?" Dante pulled me from my thoughts.

"I'd convinced Franks to add these secret areas outside at the wedding. Places we can take Wolfie's hot friends and have a little privacy." Murray grinned as Dante high fived him.

I wasn't listening.

Fucking bunny.

I'd slept in her bed all night and we didn't even have sex.

I took a deep breath and stood up.

"Where are you going?" Smirked Felix.

"The bathroom."

I stormed up the stairs and into her bedroom where music was blaring out, shutting the door behind me.

"Knock much?" She grumbled, turning the music down.

"You wouldn't have even heard it over this racket."

"Don't you call Lizzo a racket. She's a Queen." Her anger was still very near the surface.

"Whatever. What the fuck was that just now?" I crossed the room to where she was standing, invading her space.

"What?" She avoided my glare.

"Don't play dumb, it's beneath you. That little speech back there about bunnies, felt like it was aimed at me."

She rolled her eyes. "Not everything is about you, Cooper."

"I'm aware of that." I said through gritted teeth. "But it felt like this was. Is that what you think last night was?"

She shuffled her feet and looked at the floor.

"Francesca, answer me."

"Urgh! You're so used to people doing what you want to try to please you." She moved away and stomped through her closet into the bathroom, me following like a needy puppy.

"You never do one fucking thing I want. Or try to please me." This fucking woman. I'd never met anyone who riled me up so much.

"You seemed to get me to do what you wanted last night." She shot out.

I watched her chest rise and fall.

Did she really have no clue?

"So this is about last night?" I said slowly.

"Look Coop, I get it. I kissed you to avoid Stuart, you returned the favour. It was fun, but let's just leave it now." She picked up the toothpaste, squeezing it onto her brush.

"Ex-fucking-scuse me?" I seethed.

"I know I kissed you. And it was hot. But I shouldn't have done it. I wasn't coming onto you, you've misunderstood the situation. I'm not a bunny to hook up with." She turned her back on me.

"Don't you dare lump yourself in with the bunny brigade. Do you even know what a bunny is?"

She rolled her eyes again and started brushing her teeth.

What the fuck was happening right now?

I walked over and stood behind her, pushing her up against the counter top. Her breath hitched and I knew she could feel my cock turning hard, because I seemed to have zero self-control around her.

"All I wanted was to make you feel good. You think what we did last night I do with just anyone? You think I treated you like a bunny?" I hissed at her.

"Well you weren't here when I woke up." Her mouth full of toothpaste as she looked at me in the mirror.

So that's what this was about?

"I was here until seven am. I left while you were still snoring away because I didn't think you'd want me explaining what I was doing creeping out of your room if Wolfie saw us." I threw my hands in the air.

She paused as if thinking about what I'd said to her before taking in a deep breath.

"Cooper just forget it. We were drunk."

"What the fuck is going on with you? I'm not going to forget it." I spun her around. "And if you think I'm that forgettable, you've got another thing coming. There's no fucking way you've ever come like that with another man."

And now I wanted to rearrange the face of any man who'd even been lucky enough to touch her. Why the fuck was she under my skin so much?

She shrugged.

A fucking shrug.

I felt my teeth grind together. "You know you're breaking one of your rules."

"What?" She frowned.

"You're being a dick." I stared her down.

"Whatever. Go back to your bunnies. This conversation is over."

"No, this isn't over until I say it's over." I turned and stormed out.

10

FREDDIE

The door slammed so hard the walls shook and I sat down on the loo seat letting out the breath I'd been holding in.

Last night was... well, I didn't really have any words to describe it.

Hot as fuck was probably the official term.

But when I woke up and he wasn't there, then went downstairs to see them sitting around the kitchen table all cocky and testosterone filled, I did what seemed like the perfectly normal thing to do and lost my shit.

Stupid dickhead boys and their hook ups.

But he'd been right, I'd never come that hard with anyone before and we hadn't even had sex. The way he'd made me feel, the heightened level of arousal I'd been in all day and the control he'd had over me, was off the charts hot.

Like, volcanic hot.

The hottest.

As though he'd voodoo magicked me and I'd fallen under his spell.

How had it moved so quickly from him being my friend, a hot as fuck friend but a friend no less, to this sex god who could make my body do and feel things I'd never thought possible?

A rush of nausea ran through me at the idea of him doing that to anyone else.

Fucking bunnies.

I turned the shower on, stepping under the water and tried to wash it away.

"Fred?" I heard Wolfie call.

"I'm in the shower." I called back as she walked in and sat on the rim of the bath.

"Why are all the boys downstairs and what's with the slamming doors?"

"Cooper is still in a mood, the boys are still drunk and haven't been to bed." I rinsed the shampoo out of my hair and ran conditioner through the ends.

"Oh." She said. "Why's Cooper still in a mood?"

I shrugged while I rinsed all the soap off, closing my eyes under the water so I didn't have to meet hers. She'd know I was lying.

"Can you pass me my towel please"

She picked it up off the towel rail and handed it to me.

"Thank you. Anyway, did you have fun last night?"

"One hundred percent, it was brilliant fun. Thank you, really. Can't believe Jas let me stay on his shoulders the whole time, he said I kept nearly falling off." She followed me into my closet and laid back on the ottoman.

"You did." I dried myself off and pulled some knickers from my drawer, nearly falling over as I put them on. Maybe I wasn't sober either.

"Are there any plans today?"

"No, we figured that everyone would be pretty hungover so didn't make any plans. I think it needs to be a chilled one today. Are the boys still in the kitchen?" I opened my wardrobe, trying to find something to wear.

She nodded.

"We could have a barbecue I guess? We'd need to get some more food though. There's definitely not enough to feed that monstrous pack downstairs."

She jumped up. "That's a great shout. Hurry up and get dressed."

After brushing my wet hair and roughly drying it with the towel, I threw on my favourite white maxi dress and headed down. Someone had opened the French doors and a warm breeze was in the air, I could see a couple of the boys asleep on the sun loungers in the garden.

"Where's Jas?" Wolfie asked.

"He and Coop went for a run. He said to tell you he won't be long." Replied Drew without opening his eyes.

"Oh okay. Hey guys, do you want a barbecue? Fred and I thought we'd do one seeing as you're all hungover to the eyeballs."

"That's the best idea, I'm going to make Bloody Marys. Franks what have you got?" Murray stood up walked over, pulling me into a hug. "Also, I love you."

"I'll remember that next time I ask you to do something for me and you say no." I grumbled.

"Oh come on. Looks like it's working out." He nudged me.

I glared at him. It absolutely wasn't working out.

"Anyway, Bloody Marys." He rubbed his hands together.

"I have everything but I think we need supplies, I don't mind driving if you want to come with me."

"Okay but obviously I'll be the one driving." He turned to the group. "Freddie and I are going to do a supplies shop so we don't run out of anything. Put your requests in, we're leaving in five."

As we walked out of the house to the car, Jasper and Cooper were sprinting down the street with their shirts off, muscles upon muscles rippling in all their glory. It was like some kind of athletic porn and I had to actively work to keep my mouth shut at the sight and remind myself to blink.

They stopped when they reached us.

I looked at Cooper, sweat pouring down his massive body, droplets navigating through the crevices of his abs. I felt a well of saliva build up in my mouth, one that I had a lot of difficulty swallowing. It should be illegal to look that hot.

His eyes scanned me from bottom to top. Holy blazing balls of fire, I could feel my insides burning.

"Guys we're having a barbecue and Bloody Marys, we're heading to the store to stock up. Do you want anything?" Murray called from the driver's seat.

"No we're good, thanks Man." Jasper rubbed his face.

"There's only one thing I want." Cooper said so quietly only I could hear it as he pinned me with his glare.

Jesus.

I climbed into the car and Murray drove off. I stared out of the window, my mind still well and truly back where we'd left Cooper and his dripping, sweaty muscles.

"What did he just say to you?" Murray glanced at me with a side eye.

"Who?"

"The Man on the Moon, who do you think?"

"Oh nothing." I tightened the straps on my sundress as I thought about the look in Cooper's eyes.

"Well that nothing just made your face go bright red, so spill it. What happened yesterday?"

He lit me up like a firework and I rode his fingers until I collapsed against his hard, sweaty body. We fell asleep, then I woke up and he was gone.

"Nothing."

"Franks, you can't bring me into this and then not keep me updated." He pulled into a space in front of the store. Switching off the engine, he unbuckled his seatbelt and turned to me, waiting until I gave in.

I'd be terrible under interrogation. Caving immediately.

I sighed. "Fine, but don't fucking tell anyone. I've still not told Wolfie. He was so mad at me yesterday Muz, like actually raging that I'd been ignoring him."

"Yeah I know, I saw. I tell you, I would not want to be opposite him on the ice."

"Tell me about it. Anyway, you know how he made me go to the bar during The Killers?"

He nodded.

"Well, he then shouted at me for ten minutes for ignoring him all day and something about not letting Felix touch me. Then he kissed me."

"Brilliant. I told you he was a fucking lad." He clapped his hands together.

"Murray can you not use this macho bullshit language please? I'm your sister. You should be on my side. Not the one of a 'lad'." I grumbled with air quotes.

"Calm down Franks. I'm one hundred percent in your corner but I get the impression this has been a long time coming. He likes you and he hasn't known what to do about it. I don't think he's told anyone about what's happened between you, but I'm pretty sure he knows I know."

My heart started beating double time.

"What? What does that mean?" I looked up and he grinned at me.

"You know this morning when you came in and asked about what you didn't know?"

"Yeah." I narrowed my eyes.

"Well, the boys had been busting his balls about liking you and being territorial, but not having the balls to do anything about it. But we know that's not true don't we." He nudged me.

I looked down at my dress, running my fingers along the edging of the embroidery.

"And why does he think you know?"

"Because while he was threatening to murder Felix and

Drew, he was looking at me with the worst poker face I've ever seen."

My head shot up. "Are you telling me he likes me, likes me?"

He nodded. "I think so."

Holy shit. Butterflies filled my chest.

"Why's he such a grumpy fuck then? I'm sure he never used to be like this."

"He definitely has, but I think that's just him. Plus maybe he doesn't realise he likes you and just gets totally raged at the thought of anyone else being near you. You probably don't know the half of it but he's always been territorial, even I remember last New Year when we were in the bar and he nearly took out that guy who was trying to dance with you."

I tapped my finger against my chin as some memories started flooding back. "Oh yeah, I'd totally forgotten about that. So you don't think he thinks I'm a bunny?"

"No, I don't. And I'm telling you Franks, if he did, and treated you like that I don't care who he is but I would kick his fucking arse."

I smiled at him, while he was no hockey player he was definitely pretty stacked and I'm not sure who I'd want to bet on for that fight.

"But Franks, question is, do you like him, like him?"

I nodded.

"Good." He leaned over and rubbed my arm. "Because I think that you need to move away from those cretins you've been dating and on to someone who's more at your level. Someone who isn't scared of you."

"What does that mean?"

"The guys you go out with, you always try to mould to them when you're first dating. It never works out because after a few weeks," He paused, searching for the words needed to be uncharacteristically diplomatic, "Let's say your strong-willed personality makes an appearance. Then it goes tits up because they can't deal. You don't need to be anyone else but yourself, Franks. And the right guy is someone who takes you as you are. And I think Cooper can definitely handle you, you're very similar."

This sounded familiar.

I narrowed my eyes at him. "Have you been talking to Wolfie about this?"

He shook his head. "No, why would I?"

I shrugged.

"Look, all I'm saying is there's more to Cooper than you think. Don't write him off too soon."

"Okay, thanks Muzzler." I sighed deeply and gave him a hug. "Right the sooner we get this shopping done the sooner we can get back."

We jumped out and headed into the store.

When we walked back into the kitchen Wolfie was making Bloody Marys.

"Oh thank god, you've arrived back in time. We've run out of vodka."

"There's no way, there's a case in the bar downstairs. Did you look?" I puzzled.

"Oh no. I just took what was off the shelf."

I rolled my eyes. "Hang on, I'll go and look."

I ran down the stairs to the basement, where I had a laundry, spare bathroom, cinema room and a bar. I loved my house so much, my fifteen years as an interior designer meant I'd been exposed to some of the coolest ideas for creative spaces. Over time I'd learnt what worked and what didn't, as well as what I'd have in my own house.

So when I'd bought it a few years ago I'd spent a long time gutting it and fitting it with the most fun things I could think of, one of which was a full size bar and party room, complete with a giant disco ball.

I walked into the party room rounding the bar, looking for the vodka.

"Freddie, your house is fucking ace." Drew walked through the glass doors which led up to the garden.

"Thanks." I smiled, opening up the cupboards under the bar, pulling out a case of vodka.

"Did you do the whole house?"

I nodded. "Yeah."

"Woah, I can't believe you've got a disco ball in here." He switched it on so it spun around, making the room sparkle. "We are definitely coming in here later. I really like it, can you come and do my house?"

I laughed. "Sure, if you want me to."

"I'm serious, will you come and do my house? I just bought one. Here let me carry these." He took the case from me and we walked outside in the sunshine.

"Hey Freddie's got a proper disco ball down there. We're having a party later." Drew called out to everyone.

"We're having a party now. Bloody Marys are ready." Wolfie put a tray down on the garden table.

Gross.

"We can have it for the after party then." Drew reached for a drink.

"Fred, you're not having one?" Felix asked as Wolfie handed me a glass of rosé.

"Tomato juice freaks her out." She replied for me.

I walked into the kitchen where Murray was prepping everything for the barbecue. "Franks go and turn on the grills will you?"

"Yeah okay." I looked around, it seemed quieter than it was before. "Where is everyone?"

He rolled his lips, hiding a grin. "Everyone or Cooper?"

I was just about to answer when I caught a movement by

the door. Cooper was standing there fresh from the shower, hair wet, t-shirt straining across his huge chest. His shorts were slung so low on his hips that I could almost make out the wedge of a perfect V. He looked so fucking edible I could barely stand it and the smirk on his face told me he'd heard exactly what Murray had said.

Bollocks.

"Everyone." I scowled and spun on my heel, marching towards the barbecue.

I was trying to turn the knob on the gas canister, but it was stuck. Fucking Murray must have been here last, twisting it too tightly. God, boys were so annoying.

I got down on my knees, trying to get leverage.

"So, you were wondering where I was, were you?" Cooper leaned over me and turned it with ease.

Stupid gorgeous bastard.

"No, I was not." I looked up at him.

He bent down so we were eye to eye and ran his thumb along my jaw. My stomach clenched.

"You're a terrible liar, Tiny."

I swiped his hand away, before he could feel the heat in my cheeks.

"You didn't seem to mind me touching you last night." He smirked, standing back up.

"What are you two doing?" Called Huck as he and Murray approached the barbecue with a tray of meat.

"Just revisiting a conversation we were having earlier." He stared down at me, jamming his hands into his pocket.

"Yeah, well, step aside Fred. Men need to cook with fire."

I rolled my eyes, doucheness had officially hit insanity levels.

"Christ there is way too much testosterone here today, I'm going to find Wolf." I pushed off my knees and walked off.

I plopped down next to her on the sun lounger. "Hey,

have you spoken to any of the girls today? We should get them here, there are too many boys."

"Yeah that's a great idea, we should have done it earlier." She grabbed Jasper's hand as she walked past. "Babe, where's my phone?"

"I don't know, but here's mine." He pulled his phone from his pocket. "Why?"

"Just want to get the girls over."

"Okay baby." He leant down to kiss her before walking over to join the boys.

They were sickeningly cute sometimes. Wolf was already on the phone to Molly as I looked over to where the boys were. Cooper had his head thrown back laughing at something Murray had said.

He was so beautiful, but that intense, smoulderingly sexy thing that he had going on last night, that was another level hot. I felt the familiar thump between my legs.

I mulled over Murray's words as they came back to me.

I'd never known a guy to get jealous over me before and I was definitely into it. And if last night was Cooper being jealous, then I think that was a notion I could work with.

11

COOPER

"You need to put the chicken on first, they take longer than sausages, otherwise you're going to cremate them." Ordered Dante.

"Dude, stop telling me how to barbecue. I'm the god damn barbecue king." Drew shoved him out of the way.

Morons.

I sipped on my beer and glanced down to the patio where Freddie was sitting with Wolfie. She looked so fucking beautiful in that white dress and the tiny hint of side-boob I'd caught earlier had left me with a semi for the past few hours. I wanted to run my tongue along it, before sucking one of her rosy nipples between my teeth, biting down on it, twisting it, making her scream in ecstasy.

Just like I had last night.

Which, I'm sure, was why my blood was currently on a medium simmer. Because she was down there where I wanted to be, but instead I was up here listening to these bozos arguing about the barbecue.

A growl escaped as Felix sat down with them.

Why? Why did it wind me up so much when I saw other men touching her? Or when she was touching other men.

Right this moment, Felix. Her arm slung around his shoulders as he made her laugh loudly about something undoubtedly stupid.

Those laughs should be reserved for me.

Those touches reserved for me.

I took a sip of my beer to stop my jaw from clenching further.

"...Mate, don't you think?" Murray smacked me in the arm.

I turned to him. "Think what?"

"What were you looking at?" He smirked.

Your sister.

"Nothing."

His eyes narrowed, scrutinising me. I didn't know what he knew and until then, I was playing dumb.

I waited for the puck to drop.

He dropped his voice, turning his back to the guys so they couldn't hear us. "She's winding you up, you know."

I scratched my beard, unsure I heard him correctly. "What are you on about?"

"Felix. She's winding you up, so you can cool your jets."

I subtly pointed over to them. "She's doing this on purpose?"

He nodded with a smirk.

Well, this was an interesting turn of events. The little minx. Although I'm not sure why I was surprised, but I was surprised Murray seemed to be invested in this. I knew Molly dated, but I'd yet to meet any of them and I definitely didn't encourage it.

And I'd be damned if she dated a hockey player.

Not that Freddie and I were dating.

Or that I wanted to date.

"Why are you telling me this?" I tipped my beer back, finishing it.

"Because you like her and I'm sick of the twats she's been dating."

I could certainly agree on those two points.

"Fucking Stuart." I muttered under my breath.

"Exactly."

"I still don't know why you're telling me this."

He crossed his arms and leaned forward, just like Freddie did when she was trying to make a point. Even though they didn't share DNA they were so similar. Same mannerism, same cheeky glint, same open and forthright way of speaking.

"Because I like you and I think you'd be good for her, so I'm gonna help you out. She needs someone who'll put up with her shit and tell her no once in a while. She's headstrong and the guys she's dated thinks the sun shines out of her arse. But not in the way that commands respect, so she gets bored."

I raised my eyebrow at him, waiting for him to continue.

"She's never asked me for dating advice before."

"What. And now she has?"

"She has." His grin got wider.

Jesus Christ. Talk about dragging it out. I was a breath away from grabbing him by the scruff of his neck and shaking it out of him.

"And are you going to share with me what you told her?"

His eyes flickered with amusement, before a shit eating grin took residence on his face. He was as bad as Felix when it came to causing trouble.

"I didn't really say much, but I did remind her of the incident at New Year when you lost your shit over that guy asking her to dance. And may have filled her in on the bet Felix had running."

I coughed, my inhale sticking in my throat. "What? Why the fuck would you do that?"

That night was still etched on my brain.

We were celebrating Jasper and Wolfie's engagement and she looked smoking hot, I'd barely been able to tear my eyes off her all night. And some fucking douche thought he had the right to touch her. I'd simply made it very clear to him that he didn't.

I'd been looking out for her that's all.

"Well, first because she now thinks she has to make you jealous to get your attention." He winked. "But mostly to provide myself with some entertainment."

The pieces started to fall into place.

"And that's what this spectacle is about?"

She was still laughing and Felix was definitely not that funny.

"Yep."

"And what about yesterday?"

"Oh no, that was straight up her ignoring you. She told me she kissed you by accident then she was worried you'd lump her with the bunnies who do that."

"She's the furthest you could get from a bunny." I struggled to curb the anger I felt at hearing that. I looked at Murray. "She's definitely a dickhead though."

He burst out laughing and slapped me on the shoulder.

"That she is, my man. That she is." He shook his head at me. "Coop, just one thing. I like you mate, but dick her around and my fist will be in your face."

I nodded in understanding, rolling my lips together, the cogs in my brain turning.

I wanted to throttle her for trying to make me jealous, but instead a fresh energy filled my chest and I failed to keep a stupid grin off my face.

She liked me.

"Felix. Get over here. And bring more beers." Yelled Murray.

Felix trundled over and I grabbed one of the bottles he'd brought.

"Stop winding up Cooper."

"Dude, I'm not anymore, I swear."

"You better fucking not be." I pulled him into a headlock and rubbed his hair.

"Get off, you fuckwit." He pinched my arm, making me jump back. "I'm not. Also Wolfie said the girls will be here in an hour. Apparently last night was carnage so they're only just emerging."

"They left before midnight." Scoffed Drew as he walked over. "Lightweights."

"What time do you call this?" Felix shouted down the length of the garden, pointing at his watch.

The girls had finally arrived, Molly and Amy walked out into the garden both carrying cases of booze, followed by a couple of others I didn't recognise. We were in for a long night, which meant I needed to get Freddie before she got too wasted, although based on the way she was currently draped around Carter it looked like she was already half way there.

We left the barbecue and walked over to the swarm of hugging.

"I'm going to make more drinks." Freddie got up and walked down the steps to her bar.

Shit.

"Hi Mol, I'll take this." I kissed her quickly on the cheek, grabbed the case of beer she was holding and ran down the steps after Freddie.

She turned around when she heard me walk in. I put the case down on the counter, taking hold of her hand before she could speak.

"Come with me please." I needed to get her somewhere we weren't going to be interrupted and walked her out of the bar into the cinema room where I found Tate and Brogan asleep.

Lazy fucks.

Next was the laundry room.

Yes, this would have to do.

I pulled her in, gently shutting the door behind us.

Stepping towards her I lifted her onto the counter top, positioning myself between her legs, pinning her in.

She was so beautiful and my cock started to stir as I watched her dress rise up.

She pushed it back down.

"Cooper, do you think you could explain to me why I'm currently sitting on the washing machine?"

The sun had warmed her skin, flushing her cheeks, and as she parted her lips waiting for me to answer my cock began punching against my shorts in its eagerness to get to her.

"Yes." I repositioned the strap of her sundress, which had fallen loose. "I'm calling time, I'm done with playing your game."

"What game?" She asked innocently.

Little minx.

"Your game, Francesca." I ran my hands up the front of her shins, trailing along her soft skin. Her breath hitched and her nipples tightened.

"You only ever called me Francesca when you're really mad."

I slowly slid my hand under the hem of her dress. The rise and fall of her chest increased its pace, fighting against her growing arousal.

Baby, you're going to be begging me to make you come.

"Hmmm, well I am kind of mad."

"Why?"

"You see, even though I know what you're doing I still really don't fucking like anyone's hands on you and I can only take so much. So, I'm calling time." I held her stare, daring her to challenge me.

"Oh you are, are you?" Her voice contained a slight tremble as her concentration waned. She was having a hard time holding on to her anger at me.

"I told you yesterday that I didn't like it. And last night I thought we'd put it past us, especially after I made you come so hard you nearly blacked out." I grinned at her as my hands pushed up past her knees, slowly sliding them apart.

She sucked in her bottom lip and my cock punch harder, desperate to be let out.

"But then today you went back to your usual snarky self and now I see you're actually trying to make me jealous and mad. So I have to wonder, why is that?"

"Coop…"

"No, no baby. My turn to talk." I put my fingers to her lips. "And by my powers of deduction I've surmised that you like me mad because it turns you on, because until last night you'd never had someone touch you that actually knew what they were doing with your delicious, perfect body. That you'd never had true passion. And because I was so mad you thought the only way you'd get it back was by winding me up."

My hands were at the top of her thighs, my thumbs within reach of her clit.

Her pupils dilated.

She was so wet and I had no fucking idea how I was managing to hold my cool right now when all I wanted to do was put my face right in her pussy.

I ran my thumbs underneath the elastic of her panties, hooking them over and began peeling them down.

"Cooper," She half-heartedly tried to push me away. "You're so fucking cocky."

"It's not cocky if it's true." I pulled them over her feet and put them in my pocket. I looked up at her. "I know what you need."

Her jaw clenched. "Why? Because you're such a fucking professional. Bunnies must be lining up."

The snark was back.

"No baby," I brushed her lips with mine before running my nose along her jaw line, breathing her in, breathing in her intoxicating citrussy scent. "Because after last night, I know you. Those Stuarts you've been with before were amateurs. And yes, it fucking winds me up that anyone has been able to touch you, but I don't need to be mad to make you feel like that. I will always make you feel like that, this body of yours is mine now. And I intend to pleasure it at any and all given opportunity."

I ran my fingers down her collar bone, along to where that flawless stretch of side-boob peaked out. Dipping under the fabric I grazed her nipple and her jaw went slack.

I pulled her forward until she was on the edge of the counter, spreading her legs further.

Her breath was shallowing.

Her perfect pussy was glistening with need and I could smell her arousal.

She was so close to coming and I hadn't even touched her.

It was making my dick fucking painful.

"You are so beautiful. And you're about to come so fucking hard in my mouth."

Getting as close as I could, I pulled her legs over my arms. Her entire body was shaking in anticipation.

"Fuck Cooper. Please, I need it now." She whimpered.

"I've got you." Her head shot back with a loud groan as I took a long, hard lap to her.

"Shhh, Francesca, you need to keep quiet." I lightly flicked her clit before flattening my tongue again. She tasted like vanilla and honey as I drank her down.

She was so fucking delicious I wanted to eat all my meals here.

I gripped onto her thighs, stretching her out more so I could sink my mouth further inside, my tongue stabbing at her entrance. I was rewarded with another groan, so animalistic and raw it nearly made me blow my load.

Her legs started to quiver and she gripped onto the back of my head, pushing me further in.

"Cooper, fuck. Fuck I'm..." She exploded on my tongue with such violence her convulsions nearly took hold of me.

I licked her up, sucking in all her nectar until there was nothing left.

"Coop..."

My mouth crashed onto hers and I swept round her so she could taste herself, taste how badly she'd needed that release.

How badly I needed her.

"Baby I need you on your knees right now. I need your lips around my cock so badly, I need to empty myself down your throat." My voice was dark, raspy and unrecognisable.

I lifted her off the counter top, making sure she was steady on her legs before I let go of her. I scuffed my lips against hers one more time.

"Get on your knees, Francesca."

She sunk down on to the floor and looked up with her big, blue eyes, filled with so much fire she nearly incinerated me then and there.

Fuck me, I was so fucking hard.

I unzipped my shorts and watched her eyes widen as I took hold of my dick, stroking myself from root to tip in long, slow tugs.

I was going to last approximately six seconds.

"Cooper, you're too big. I'm not going to be able to take that."

"You are. Just relax, open your mouth." I held onto her jaw

and rubbed all my pre-cum along her lips. Her tongue peaked out, licking them as she looked up, before she wrapped her mouth around me, taking me in, sucking hard.

Holy fuck.

"Oh my fucking god, this is incredible." I hissed, hitting the back of her throat.

I pushed her hair back from her face for a better view, watching her perfect, pillowy lips slide up and down my dick.

This is what heaven must be like.

Pressure shot through my spine the second she cupped my balls, gently squeezing them. Pulling off my dick with a loud pop, she flicked her tongue over the tip before taking me back again.

I was a goner.

I fell forward onto the counter, my legs unable to carry my weight.

"Motherfucker." My orgasm suckerpunched me in the nuts, stealing the air from my lungs, and I exploded down her throat.

She swallowed everything.

My dick was still pumping while she licked me clean as the throbbing subsided, causing aftershocks to run through me.

That was, without a doubt, the best head I'd ever experienced.

I pulled her up, taking her face in my hands, enveloping her mouth with mine. I couldn't get enough and kissed her on and on and on, our tongues crashing together.

"Bébé tu es tellement parfait." I whispered against her lips.

"I have to say, the French is sexy. I do like that." When she grinned at me my heart nearly split in two, as though it was the first smile there ever was.

"You'll get more of that later." I wrapped my arms around

her waist. "Now we need to get back out there before anyone notices us missing."

"Okay. I need my knickers back."

I kissed her nose. "No, they're staying in my pocket."

She pulled back, a frown crossing her face. "I'm not going to go out there with no underwear on."

"Oh yes you are." I kissed her again. "And you're going to enjoy it, because you'll be remembering why you have no underwear on. Every time you look at me you'll know they're in my pocket, then tonight when you're so dripping wet with desire for me I'm going to come and fuck you like you've never been fucked."

I watched her pupils flare and suddenly wasn't sure how long I could play this game. I straightened her dress and turned her around, smacking her on the ass.

"Come on, let's go. Oh, Tiny, what song would be playing right now?"

"What do you mean?"

"A soundtrack to what just happened, what would it be?" I looked at her and she thought for a minute.

She grinned. "Baby, Light my Fire by The Doors."

"You are something else." I opened the door and looked out, the coast seemed clear. "Okay you go back through the bar and I'll go up here to the kitchen."

I stole one more kiss.

Cooper was standing in the hallway at the top of the stairs. I kept my distance, not wanting him to smell sex and Freddie.

"Hey, where've you been?"

I didn't like keeping things from Jasper, but I needed to figure out what this was before everyone offered up their own opinions.

"I carried some beer down to the bar, it's pretty cool down there. Have you seen it?"

"Yeah it's cool, right. The disco ball is something else."

He stopped and looked at me, his head tilted.

"What?"

He narrowed his eyes. "I don't know."

"Okay, well I'm starving, is this barbecue ready yet?"

"Fuck knows, let's get a drink and find out."

We walked into the kitchen. Brogan and Tate had emerged from their nap and were grabbing some beers from the ice trough.

"Hey! Welcome back to the land of the living." Jasper playfully slapped his brother's face. "Chuck one of those our way please, Sunshine."

He handed them over, silently, still clearly feeling the night before.

"Dude, you need to get on it again, it's the only way you'll feel better." I chuckled.

Brogan held a beer up to my face. "What do you think we're doing with these?"

"Christ you're sorry state." I shook my head at them. "Come on, I want some food."

We walked outside into the sunshine to find everyone gathered on the patio sitting around the garden table, drinking. Tate and Brogan pulled out some chairs as Drew and Dante walked down from the barbecue with plates laden with food.

Jasper clapped his hands together. "Yes, that right there is what I'm talking about." He walked around and kissed Wolfie's head before sitting down next to her.

Freddie looked up and we locked eyes, I watched a pink tint spread across her skin as she sucked in her bottom lip.

This was going to be a long day.

12

COOPER

"I think it's official. I'm the reigning barbecue king." Drew stretched out on one of the giant beanbags we'd set up in the garden.

"It was pretty epic dude, I'll back you for that title." Carter high fived him.

"Yeah. Me too." Murray handed out beers to our little breakaway group.

A couple more of Wolfie's girlfriends had arrived and started talking weddings, which was our cue to leave. We'd pulled the ice trough into the middle of our circle and settled in for the long haul.

Every so often I caught Freddie looking at me and we'd lock eyes until a blush spread across her face. It was the sexiest thing I'd ever seen, I fucking loved it and I couldn't wait to see her naked body glow in the same shade as she milked my cock of every last drop.

If I didn't get a grip tonight was going to be over in an embarrassingly short space of time.

"That girl next to Wolfie is so hot." Mumbled Tate. "Is she a bridesmaid?"

Murray raised his head from his beanbag to look over.

"Yeah, her name's Sophie. She was at school with Franks and Wolf. She's pretty wild. Actually, she'd probably be into you. She always goes for the geeky professor type."

Jasper sniggered into his beer.

"Well, I'll have to see what I can do then." Tate was a sport psychologist and basically looked like Clark Kent, just with more muscles. Something that meant he did ridiculously well with the ladies.

"Jas, what's the deal with the bridesmaids?" Asked Brogan.

My ears perked up, knowing exactly where he was going with this. From the look on Jasper's face, so did he.

"What do you mean?"

Brogan sat up. "Well, who are they and can we hook up with them?"

"It's Freddie, Amy, Sophie and Olivia. And no."

"What? Why?" For a two hundred and twenty pound goalie he whined like schoolgirl.

"Because Cooper will bury you if you go near Freddie." Felix cackled.

True story.

Jasper raised his eyebrow. "Amy is absolutely off limits to anyone. Sophie seems to have been caught in Tate's tractor beam and Olivia is, actually I don't know about Olivia."

Murray sat up and sighed deeply. "Oh mate, I used to have the biggest crush on Olivia when I was a teenager. She was the star of many a wet dream."

Brogan slapped his hand. "What happened?"

He started laughing hard.

"Well, one weekend she was over at our parents' while they were away, and they were all in the pool in these ridiculous bikinis rubbing sunscreen on each other, you know, shit like that. And I was basically walking around with a permanent boner. Anyway, I cracked into my dad's booze and started drinking, because I thought it would help temper my nerves, only at that point I hadn't banked on the late hit you get from hard liquor. And then she suddenly appeared in the kitchen where I was and me, being the fucking player I hadn't yet grown into, thought this was the perfect moment to make my move."

I sat up, looking around. Every single one of us had leaned in waiting for the punch.

"I slid over to her and start talking to her. She looked so good in this tiny, black string bikini she was wearing, she had the perfect pair of tits. You know the type that seem like they can't be contained, like wriggling puppies. If I close my eyes I can still see them." He closed his eyes, then shook his head as if clearing the thought. "And I thought she was definitely into me too, she kept stroking my arm and laughing, but in hind-sight I think she probably thought I was just this cute younger brother of her friend given that she's six years older than me. So I move in to kiss her, but this is the point where the inordinate amount of vodka I'd been drinking decided to make an appearance." His eyes widened and a grin appeared on his face. "And instead of kissing her, this perfect girl who'd been a long term star of all my wank sessions, I puked."

Carter choked on his beer, spraying it everywhere. Felix and Drew were laughing so hard that tears poured down their faces, while the rest were all staring wide eyed with horror. Jasper had started smacking Carter on the back.

"Oh my fucking god." Cried Dante. "Then what happened?"

"Well, luckily I was near the kitchen sink so most of it went in there. But she definitely got splashed and basically looked at me in disgust, screamed and ran out. And I never spoke to her again." He waved his hand out in front of him, indicating the end of the story.

"What? You've not spoken to her since? Never?"

He shook his head. "Fuck no. This is about as far as I get to her."

"Oh dude, you are so fucking funny. Please move to the States and come hang out with us." Laughed Drew.

"I think I'd end up in jail if I hung out with you too much. Vegas was off the charts." He held his beer up and we knocked out bottles against it.

I looked towards the house, the table seemed to have way more people gathered around it than there had been a couple of hours ago. Wolfie appeared at the patio doors with a guy I'd not seen before and watched as Freddie got up to say hi. My fists clenched as he grabbed her for a hug before his hands moved lower, down to her ass which he patted several times, before leaving them there.

Her ass that was currently panty free.

What the actual fuck?

"Murray, who's that guy?" My jaw was clenched so hard, I could barely get the words out.

They all turned to look at the door as Freddie twisted out of his grip.

He rolled his eyes. "He lives next door, he's a bit of wanker. Actually, a massive wanker. But Freddie usually prewarns the neighbours when she's having a party because it always ends up being late and loud. And he always sees it as an invitation."

"What's his deal?" He still had his fucking hands on her. His arm round her shoulder, his grubby fingers were way too close to her breasts for my liking.

The tightness in my chest eased slightly as she moved further away from him.

"He works in the city, I see him around sometimes. Yeah, he's definitely a wanker."

"Have they hooked up?"

I'd be ripping his head off if they had.

"Absolutely no way. He is into her though, he always rocks up uninvited. I've told her to stop letting him in."

"His hand was practically squeezing her tit." I grumbled. "Who the fuck does that?"

Everyone looked at me.

"What? I don't do that. And she's not a bunny. You can't just keep your hand on someone's tit like that. It shouldn't even be there at all." I raged.

Murray gave a sympathy squeeze to my shoulder.

"Do you want us to take him out the back and bury him?" Felix dead-panned.

"Yeah I would actually. Thanks."

I actually would. How fucking dare he?

"Anything for you, Big Guy." He jumped on me, pulling me into a hug.

"Get off, idiot." I pushed him away. "I'm going over there and Murray's coming too because I want to see how close he can get to Olivia before he pukes again."

Everyone cheered.

"Oh fuck yes, we're all doing that." Huck sprang up from the beanbag and everyone followed suit.

"You're all dicks." Murray got up, slinking behind our little gang.

I slapped him on the back as we walked over. "Yeah man. Welcome to the club, we have badges. We're basically pre-pubescent boys who chase girls, but with money and cool cars."

The girls were in fits of giggles, unsurprising given the amount of empty bottles on the table. A couple of the new ones were whispering to each other as they looked over at Dante and Carter.

Brogan, Drew and Felix disappeared into the kitchen, returning with more chairs for everyone except Jasper who'd already dragged Wolfie out of her seat to take it himself before pulling her back into his lap.

I reached over to grab a drink from the table while trying not to stare too much at Freddie, surely this greeting didn't need to go on any longer. He was touching her again. I turned to Huck next to me.

"Dude, get that douche's hands away from Freddie before I lose my shit." I muttered.

He raised an eyebrow.

"Please Huck."

He rolled his eyes before getting up. "Fuck's sake."

He walked over to where they were standing.

"Hey Fredster, what an awesome day we're having." In a move that was as subtle as a bulldozer, he yanked her out of the douche's reach, picked her up and spun her around. "Hey Man, just saw you walk in, so wanted to come over. I'm Huck."

Absolute class.

"Simon." He shook Huck's outstretched hand and it hadn't gone unnoticed to him that Freddie was now under Huck's arm.

I high fived myself in victory.

"How do you know Freddie?" He frowned.

"Oh, we play with Jas." He nodded over to where Jasper was sitting.

"Ice hockey? You all play?" He looked around the group as Huck nodded. "Great. Well, I just came over to say hi, but need to head. Freddie, will you walk me out?"

"Sure, okay."

They walked back into the house and I ran to follow.

"You're losing it, man." Huck called after me.

I flipped him off on my way in, maybe I was but this guy was definitely after Freddie. I heard her open the front door.

"Okay, see you soon, thanks for popping by." She said in a fake, cheery tone.

"Anytime Fred, you know I always love seeing you. Let's have dinner this week when there's less people around."

I walked into the hallway in time to see him pull her into a hug, his hands back on her ass.

Fucking sleaze.

"Jesus Simon, what is the matter with you? Stop fucking touching my arse, you fucking letch." She moved away and pushed him out of the door before he could respond.

She closed the door and turned, startling as she saw me.

"How long have you been standing there?" She glared.

I walked towards her. "Long enough."

Her shoulders dropped. "He's just my neighbour."

"Your neighbour that likes to feel you up." I put my arms around her, pulling her towards the staircase where I sat down, placing her between my legs.

"He's just…"

"Freddie he was fucking feeling you up." I snapped. "You're lucky I didn't knock him out and I would have if you hadn't already pushed him away."

She hung her head.

I tilted her chin up to look into her eyes. "Murray said he was a complete wanker."

She grinned at me, laughing at my use of British phrases. "Yeah, he is a bit."

She was making me lose all sense of control in a way I was still unable to explain.

"Give me a kiss please."

"Coop, what if someone sees us?"

"I don't care." And I actually didn't. "I just need something after witnessing that."

She frowned, searching my face before leaning down and gently pressing her lips to mine.

Gentleness flew out the window, overtaken by a frantic urge and need to taste her. I held the back of her head, keeping her against me as I ran my tongue across the seam of her mouth before plunging inside with an intensity that caused her to fall into me.

Lifting her up so she straddled my legs, I wrapped my arms around her body, gripping her tightly, as our tongues stroked against each other with a desperation I'd never experienced. I started getting hard as she rocked against me.

Carefully grabbing a handful of her hair, I pulled her back.

"Freddie." I groaned against her lips. "If we keep going I'm not going to be able to stop."

I picked her up and put her back down on her feet, straightening out her dress which had bunched up.

Holding her face in my hands I looked at her, her eyes were glistening with lust and I swear she'd got more beautiful since this morning.

She radiated sensuality.

I ran my thumb along her lips and kissed her gently, before moving her away further.

"Shall we kick everyone out early?" She held her hand out for me to take, smirking.

I slid my fingers between hers as I stood up. "Honestly, as long as that douche isn't here anymore I don't care who's around. But the next time we sneak away it's for the night because I'm not stopping at a kiss, and I still have your panties in my pocket."

"How could I forget." She said dryly, dropping my hand as we walked back outside to the others.

13

COOPER

Music was on full volume.

Everyone was wasted, the group mostly dispersed.

Huck and Dante had disappeared with a couple of Wolfie's friends, Tate with Sophie and Brogan was chatting up Olivia in the corner.

"Do you know what?" Slurred Felix as he leaned back in his chair.

"What Clevs? Enlighten us please." Drew sipped on his beer.

"I really like England." The sound of bottle necks clinking filled the air as the boys agreed with him.

"Me too, Clevs. I'm loving England." I looked over to Freddie who was deep in conversation with Molly and Wolf at the opposite end of the table.

My dick punched, reminding me of what he wanted.

You and me both buddy.

It was like he could sense it was getting dark, nearing the time when we could disappear with Freddie.

Since we'd kissed on the stairs earlier I'd been existing in a state of semi-permanent discomfort, barely able to take my eyes off her. She was so beautiful and I couldn't wait to get her upstairs and explore every delicious, mouthwatering inch of her.

As if she could hear my thoughts she glanced up, straight at me, her bright blue eyes burning through me. A sly smile curved up in the corner of her mouth, as her tongue ran along her lower lip. I looked at my watch, it definitely wasn't late enough to start kicking people out.

Fuck.

"Are you going to tell me what's going on?" Jasper slid over into the chair next to me, nudging me in the ribs.

I looked at him, silent acknowledgment passing between us. "I don't know yet Jas, I don't know. I need to figure it out myself."

"Okay dude, well I'm here when you're ready to talk." He leaned over and pulled me into a hug. "I love you, buddy."

I looked around.

Yeah, I was done. I'd stopped drinking about three hours ago and had definitely sobered up. I pulled my phone out and typed a text.

Cooper: *It's time to go, Tiny*

I watched her try to suppress a smile as she read the message.

Tiny: *I thought you were never going to ask*

Cooper: *I didn't ask, I'm telling. I'll meet you upstairs in fifteen minutes. Don't be late*

I turned to our group, every single one of them too preoccupied in what they were doing to notice me leaving. I left them to it, running up the stairs two at a time. I jumped in the shower for a lightening wash, removing all traces of barbecue smell.

On the dot of fifteen minutes I grabbed a couple of condoms from my bag and walked to her room, pushing the door open and silently closing it behind me.

My heart stopped. Tension acute.

She was naked with her back to me, fiddling with some music. I stood still taking her in, waiting for her to turn around. Her hair was twisted up in a knot fresh from the shower and I watched her unclip it, shaking it out across her bare shoulders.

My balls started aching at how desperately I wanted her.

She was absolutely exquisite.

Her soft curves accentuated by toned muscles only worked to contrast with her tiny frame and even in her delicacy she looked like a warrior. My mouth started to water as I scanned my eyes across her body, stopping at those perfect Dimples of Venus. When I'd seen her yesterday in the kitchen after her jog, I'd had to physically restrain myself from running my tongue over them.

She was so fucking sexy and I needed her now.

"Francesca." I whispered into the room and she spun meeting my gaze, her ice blue eyes blazing with fire and hitting me with the force of a hurricane.

I walked over to her, slowly, without breaking eye contact.

She smelt like soap - clean and fresh, with a hint of smokiness left from the afternoon. Taking her face in my hands, I scraped my fingers through her hair and pulled her head back. She stared up at me, so pliant and soft. My heart was hammering in my chest as I gently lowered my open lips to hers, covering her mouth with mine before swirling my tongue around. A moan escaped her and every thought I had screaming through my head was immediately silenced.

I ran my hands down her bare back, cupping her soft, smooth ass, fitting each cheek perfectly into my palms. As I lifted her up against me the remainder of my blood sprinted straight to my dick. I groaned so loudly they'd have probably heard it over the music still thumping in the basement.

She pulled back from my lips, her hands wrapped around my neck, and started licking along my jaw line. It felt so fucking good that it took every shred of self control I had not to throw her on the bed and impale her in one go.

"Coop?" She growled against my skin.

"Yeah, Baby." I rolled my neck back to give her better access.

"Are you going to keep your promise?"

"What promise is that, Tiny?"

"To fuck me like I'd never been fucked."

It was like time stopped. I grabbed a handful of her hair and pulled her up to look into my eyes. A slow grin peaked out from the crook of her mouth.

I don't know why I'd expected anything less.

In three strides I'd crossed the room and flung her down on the bed.

Her breasts bounced as she hit the mattress and I stood silently until she'd stopped moving, trying to memorise every inch of her. She looked like a Herb Ritts portrait, her black hair fanned against the white of her bed sheets, radiating sensuality.

I could feel my dick weeping, desperate to be allowed near this perfect creature, knowing the constraints of my boxers would barely stop me from coming the second I touched her.

Her knees were bent, legs closed and I leant down to open them, stretching her out. A silvery trail of arousal was making its way down the inside of her thigh.

"Do not move." My voice sounding like I'd spent a lifetime smoking sixty a day.

I ran my tongue along my lip. Contemplating. Watching.

I didn't know where to start, I wanted to taste every inch of her all at the same time. I closed my eyes trying to get a grip, before I blew my load. But I was so amped up seeing her like this, seeing the effect I had on her.

I took a deep breath and knelt down, pulling her legs towards me so she was near the edge of the bed. I hooked my arms under her thighs and began running my tongue along the left one until I reached the spot her juices had travelled to, before starting on the other side.

Her ass was hanging off the bed and I grabbed each cheek, using my thumbs to run along the slick path between her slit and her ass. A low rumble escaped her throat, I could feel her legs start to tremble in anticipation and I'd barely touched her.

I hovered my body over her without making contact, breathing her in. I dipped down, my lips the only thing connecting us, and followed a path down her quivering body, nibbling and licking at her soft skin, moving past her rock hard nipples, her breath catching in expectation and need. I got to those four dates marking her skin and ran my tongue over them, absorbing her.

Continuing my torturous journey across her stomach, my tongue dived into her belly button and down across her hip bones, where her quivering turned into full blown shakes, her need for release palpable.

Returning to my starting position between her legs, I could see her lips swollen and dripping, the smell of desire making me lightheaded.

I starved for her like she was my last meal.

"Cooper." She breathed out. "Fucking touch me."

So god damn snarky.

A grin split my face and a throaty chuckle escaped. I held her thighs in place, taking one deep long lick across her slit before flicking her clit with the tip of my tongue.

And that was enough.

She screamed, her back arching as an orgasm ripped through her like a freight train. I watched the power of it take hold as she pulsed in front of me, before dragging her up the bed and sliding two fingers inside her.

"Again." I growled against her, adding a third finger curling it up, not allowing her any reprieve from the tidal wave crashing through her body. "Baby, you are so wet and needy for me."

I pumped into her as sweat started to appear in droplets between her breasts. I bent down to lick them up as another orgasm took hold of her, taking her breath, her beautiful face open in ecstasy.

I pulled my shorts off and ripped a condom from the packet, rolling it on as quickly as I could. She was so fucking tight I needed to get inside her before she came down from the high, minimising the sting which was about to happen.

I spread her legs as wide open as I could and slid inside her in one long, hard thrust, pushing all the way to the hilt.

She was like liquid velvet.

I could feel every single muscle of hers clenching me like a heavenly vise.

And just like that, I was seeing stars.

Jesus fucking Christ.

When I opened my eyes she was staring up at me, her ice blues had turned navy with need and I nearly lost it there and then. I dropped my head, taking her soft lips with mine, stroking her hair.

"Baby, are you okay?" I took in her glazed expression.

"Yes, yes I think so." She breathed out, her eyes widening. "Cooper I need you to move, please move. Now. I feel so full."

I circled my hips to loosen her up a little more and her jaw dropped.

"Oh fucking fuck."

I smirked. "Did you like that?" I did it again and her head fell back as she let out a groan.

"How about this?" I pulled out almost all the way before driving back into her with such force that I had to cover her mouth with mine to swallow her scream.

"More." She gasped.

"You're so fucking greedy." I did it again, our bodies already slick with sweat. "Do you like my cock, Tiny? You like feeling how fucking hard you make me? How desperate your pussy is for me?"

She whimpered again. I was dangerously close to the edge and needed to make this last longer than thirty seconds. I could already feel her thighs trembling under me.

"You need to fucking wait. You come with me this time." I growled in her ear.

I knelt back and switched our bodies up so she was straddling me as I held onto her hips, controlling her movement, grinding her ultra-sensitive clit against my pelvis.

"Kiss me." I ordered and she dropped her mouth to mine, thrusting her tongue into me with the same rhythm as my dick drove into her.

I fisted her hair, yanking it back so she arched against me, giving me access to her perfect breasts. To her nipples that I'd been ignoring until this moment.

I sucked them in, pulling on them with my teeth and she groaned into the air. I don't know how it was possible to make my dick harder than it already was, but she succeeded with every sound that escaped her.

"Coop, I can feel it, I'm going to come again." Her trembling intensified with every thrust I made. "I need you."

My balls tightened at her words and I could feel the pressure building in the base of my spine. I kissed along the column of her throat before I flipped her onto her knees. Pulling her hair back for leverage, keeping her in place, I pounded so deep and hard against her G-spot until she shattered in my arms, her pussy pulsing around my cock. Before she could come down I tossed her onto her back, driving into her over and over chasing my own release.

I exploded inside of her with a ferocity I'd never felt, splitting through my head and stealing my vision, before dropping to the side to collapse, careful not to crush her with my weight.

We lay there, unable to speak and our breathing synchronised as our hearts continued to pound in our chests.

What the fuck had just happened to me? I felt like I'd run a marathon.

I knew without question I'd never experienced sex like that before, I didn't even know it existed. I turned to face her, her eyes closed, her skin pink and flushed post-orgasm and I tumbled over into the abyss, my heart filling up with her.

Kissing her cheek, I eased out, quickly running to the bathroom to chuck the condom away before getting back into bed wrapping her around me. She tilted her head to look at me.

"Wow, Coop. You really keep your promises don't you." She grinned.

I bit her neck making her squeal with laughter. "Cheeky minx. Be careful or you're getting fucked again."

She moved out of my grip and turned so her body was facing me, her expression suddenly serious.

"Coop, how is it like this with us?" A light sheen was still coating her skin. It looked like she was glowing.

I ran a finger across her forehead. "I don't know, baby."

"Will you stay again so we can wake up together this time?" She whispered, her voice filled with a vulnerability I didn't like.

I moved my face close enough to kiss her and brushed my lips against hers. "Just try and stop me."

She grinned against me and I moved on top of her, already hard, my dick frantic to have that connection again. Her legs fell open and I slid through her slick folds, still so drenched for me, her eyes hooded and glazing over. Holding my weight above her, I ran my tongue along her jaw to her collar bone, licking up the saltiness, before gently taking her mouth with mine.

Our bodies pressed together still slick with sweat, I could

almost hear our hearts beating, harmonising with the bass vibrating through the floors below.

"Cooper, I need you again." She murmured into my mouth, grabbing the back of my head and pulling me to her, intensifying our kiss.

She didn't have to tell me twice.

I broke away and knelt back, reaching for another condom, rolling it on with shaky hands.

Why the fuck were my hands shaking?

I pushed her legs wider apart and guided myself inside her, already rippling around me.

"Always so fucking ready for me." I leant down, pressing my lips against hers as I slowly moved my hips.

I could feel every single muscle, she was so warm and perfect. As she groaned I realised I was quickly becoming addicted to her noises.

"It's so good, Coop. Please. I need more." She gripped my ass, trying to push me to move harder.

"Stop rushing. Just feel it, feel how fucking perfect we fit together." I pulled all the way out and slid back in, slower than I had before and watched her mouth slacken. "See. Just like that, baby. You like that?"

She raised her head up to kiss me, but I didn't take it. I wanted her to beg for me, to feel every fibre of my being in the way I could feel her. Holding both her hands in one of mine, I brushed the other down her side and along her thigh, lifting it up to sit around my waist, curling her calf around my back.

I'd never been into missionary before but this was another level. The intimacy overwhelming and yet not nearly enough in equal measure.

Every slow torturous movement, the deep steady rhythm of sliding in and out of her. Watching her face etched in concentration as she got closer to the edge was making my balls ache with urgency.

"Fuuuck Freddie. Can you feel how deep I am? Can you feel how fucking hard your pussy makes me?"

As she started mewing in desperation for release, pressure built at the base of my spine, my balls tightening harder than they'd ever been. Her thighs started to tremble and I knew I couldn't hold off any longer.

I gripped her chin in my hand, forcing her eyes to mine. "Look at me. I want to feel you coming on my cock. I want to watch your face as you milk every last drop out of me. Clench that perfect pussy around me."

Her eyes widened.

"Fucking do it. Now, Francesca."

And with that she growled as a mind-blowing orgasm tore through her, taking me along for the ride, my nerve endings fried. Everything I had was ripped out of me by the power she contained.

I tried to catch my breath, but I was spent. She'd destroyed me. A professional athlete floored by a pint sized, snarky temptress.

Because that's what she was. A temptress.

And I was absolutely under her spell.

Without crushing her, I dropped my body down and moved to her side, keeping her leg around me. Her eyes were closed, her cheeks flushed and her lips swollen from our kisses.

I ran into the bathroom to clean up. I was disgustingly sweaty but I wanted to keep the smell of her on me for as long as I could.

Without opening her eyes she reached out as I got back into bed. I pulled her into me, as close I could possibly get her, wanting to feel her breathing, feel the moment that sleep stole her from me.

I turned off the bedside light, my eyes staying open adjusting to the darkness. It had taken her forty eight hours to completely annihilate every defence I'd built the past thirteen years. And after that performance, she fucking owned me.

An uncomfortable sensation started to seep into my blood. I pushed it away as fast as I could before kissing her head and chasing her into sleep.

14

FREDDIE

L ifechanging.

I'd been awake for the past hour, listening to Cooper's steady breathing, trying to figure out a way to describe what that was last night. And all I could come up with, was lifechanging.

In all my fantasies about Cooper I'd never imagined this.

It had been fucking at its finest.

World class.

Olympic levels.

My body was aching in places I never knew existed. His incredible dick stretching me to the max. I'd been right, it was such stuff as dreams were made on.

What had he done to me?

It was as though he knew what I wanted before I did. As though he knew what my body needed.

And the dirty talk.

So. Fucking. Hot.

How was I supposed to go back to anything else after that? I had been ruined.

I stared at the ceiling, thinking.

Was it because we were friends first?

I tried to go back through all the guys I'd slept with, how many of them had I been friends with first? None.

Friends first. Maybe that was why.

Why I was so comfortable with him.

Why he felt so good wrapped around me.

Why I didn't want him to leave.

He was lying flat on his stomach, his legs tangled with mine. One of his giant arms stretched across me, his face hard against my shoulder. I mindlessly began to trace the geometric patterns which marked his skin, following the lines and edges with my fingertip.

I felt him stir beside me and his hand stroked across my stomach, making my heart race and my pussy throb.

Turning my head I found his eyes open, a sleepy smile curving along his lips.

Fuck, he was so beautiful.

"Good morning, Tiny." He rolled over to his side, sliding his other arm under the pillow and pulled me against him.

I grinned at him, unable to hold it in. "Good morning, yourself."

He leaned over, his lips meeting mine. He began playing with my hair as his eyes closed again.

"Mmmm. This is a wake up I could get used to." He muttered, his head falling back onto the pillow.

"Coop, last night was…"

"I know." He interrupted before I could finish, although I'm not sure I knew how to finish that sentence.

"Do you want a coffee?" I asked.

"I do, but not yet."

"Coop…"

"Shhh, baby." He put his finger up to my lips. "Why are you talking so much, it's still sleep time."

"Oh yeah?" I giggled.

"Yeah." His fingers slowed in my hair as he drifted back to sleep.

I needed coffee. I moved to slide out from under him but he gripped me tighter, not letting me go.

"Francesca, you're starting to seriously piss me off." He grumbled playfully.

"I just want a coffee, I'll be right back."

"No, because then our bubble breaks. We'll go together.

Our bubble? Since when had he ever been cute? It was very un-Coop and I very much liked it. Which was alarming, because mostly when guys tried to be cute with me I puked in my mouth a little bit.

"Okay, I'll wait." I laid my head back down on the pillow and resumed the tracing of his tattoo.

"What time is it?' He asked.

"Just gone ten thirty."

He was silent for so long I thought he'd fallen asleep again, but then he started nuzzling my neck.

"Before we go and make coffee, you've got a decision to make?"

"What decision?"

"Do you want to get fucked in the bath or in the shower?" He growled and the thumping between my legs dialled up several notches.

I started giggling.

Jesus, who was he turning me into? I was not a giggler. Definitely not with men, anyway.

"Tick tock Francesca or I choose." He was planting warm wet kisses across my chest as his thumbs grazed over my nipples.

"The shower." I replied then screeched as I was suddenly thrown in the air.

We were running towards the bathroom.

He wasn't the fastest man in the NHL for nothing.

He walked back into my room, fully clothed and a shred of disappointment ran through me. Cooper Marks' naked body was a sight to behold.

His ass should win awards.

"What's wrong?" He frowned.

"Nothing." I smiled.

"Why the face then?"

Whoops, I didn't realise I'd been that transparent. "You look good naked, that's all."

A grin split his face in half. "Hey you were the one who wanted coffee. I was quite happy staying in our naked bubble."

"Oh yes. I do want coffee." I sighed, making him laugh more.

"What are you doing today?" He rested his arms on my shoulders and pushed his fingers through my hair, causing my head to fall back and look up at him. His eyes were the most strikingly beautiful colour, bright amber rimmed with dark toffee. Warm and inviting.

I swear they changed every time I looked at him.

"I have to go over to my parents'."

"Okay, I'll come."

"Really? You don't want to stay with the boys?"

"No, I want to spend time with you in our bubble." He kissed my nose and my heart skipped a beat. "Come on, let's get you caffeine. I've seen the snarky beast you become and I don't want to stir it."

My mouth dropped open in indignation, his laughter continuing as he pushed me towards the door, smacking my ass.

"I wonder what happened to everyone last night."

"We'll soon find out. Prepare yourself for carnage."

Walking into the kitchen we found Murray cleaning, which meant the carnage would have been at atomic levels.

Tate was drinking coffee and reading the paper, Drew was flicking through his phone.

I could see several people asleep in the garden.

Fuck's sake, was I running a fucking halfway house?

Murray raised his eyebrow at me as Cooper and I walked in together.

"You know, you have your own kitchen." I ignored his face, scanning the scene in front of me. "And you two have a very nice hotel to stay in."

"We're going, just need to call a car to collect us. We've been in the same clothes since Saturday." Drew mumbled without looking up from his phone.

My lips curled up in disgust. "Disgraceful."

"What happened last night?" Cooper pulled out a chair as I grabbed some mugs.

Murray leaned against the counter. "Not much, everyone was pretty fucked by the end of the night. The girls went home. Brogan went back with Olivia I think."

Woah, that was good gossip.

"Has Murray told you about his history with Olivia?" I smirked, looking at Cooper. "Not the finest moment of his life but a favourite of mine."

He grinned. "Yeah we were talking about it yesterday. Brogan was asking Jas which bridesmaids he could hook up with."

I pursed my lips. Of course he was.

Murray rolled eyes. "Calm down, Jas said no one. But that's when I segued the Olivia story."

I placed a coffee in front of Cooper. He looked up at me and winked. "Thank you, Tiny."

"Franks, can you make me one please?" Murray begged as he sat down.

I shook my head at his sorry state and handed him the other one before starting the machine up again.

"Have you seen Wolfie and Jas?"

"No, they're still in bed I think." Replied Tate.

I took my coffee from the machine when it finished and sipped it. Ahhh sweet caffeine.

I looked at them all. "Have you guys eaten?"

"No, we were waiting for you." Muttered Drew earning him a back-handed slap to the arm from Cooper.

I was right. A fucking half-way house.

"God, you're all so fucking lazy. This is exactly why a hotel was booked for you. You're supposed to be there, being waited on. Not here."

"Franks, you're awfully stroppy this morning. Drink your coffee and you'll feel better." Murray looked at me innocently as Cooper smirked into his cup.

I narrowed my eyes at them both and walked into the pantry. I put together a tray of breakfast items including yoghurt, berries and cereals, placing them on the table, along with a loaf of fresh sourdough and preserves.

"See, look at how amazing you are at this." Murray grabbed some bowls and plates from the cupboard as Wolfie and Jasper walked in, making a loud entrance.

"Good Morning, everyone." Jasper sat down at the table, pulling Wolfie onto his lap. It was like they didn't even see the other chairs.

"Why are you so perky?" Asked Tate.

"Because I'm marrying the love of my life in five days."

"Awwww baby." Wolfie turned in his lap and kissed him full on the mouth, with tongue.

We all grimaced and looked away.

"Too fucking early for that." Grumbled Drew, saying what we were all thinking. "Tate, where's this car?"

"Hey, I'll kiss Wolfie whenever I want. Why are you being so grumpy?" Shot back Jasper.

"He still can't find that girl." Tate answered for him.

"What girl?" Asked Wolfie and I in unison.

Drew's ran his hands through his hair, his shoulders dropping. "I met a girl and lost her number."

Fucking hell. These boys. Although I'd never seen them ever get bothered about losing a number, they'd just go and find another one.

"Where?" I buttered a piece of toast and bit into it.

He sighed. "In Vegas."

"Oh Drew, you're not supposed to get the strippers' numbers." I teased.

"She wasn't a fucking stripper." He shouted at me.

Woah.

Everyone turned to look at Drew. That must be some hangover he was sporting. I'd never seen him in a mood before.

"Hey, don't speak to her like that, you dick." Snapped Cooper.

And now they were looking at Cooper.

"It's okay." I held my hands up. "I'm really sorry, I was only joking." I walked over to Drew and gave him a hug.

"I'm sorry, Fred. I didn't mean to shout at you." He hugged me back, then noticed Cooper scowling at him and quickly dropped his arms.

"Who was she? What was her name" Asked Wolfie gently.

"I met her in the hotel, I can't remember her name because I called her Lucky. My phone had died, so when she left she wrote it on my arm with her number but I was so tired I fell asleep again and it rubbed off. I've been trying to find her through photos on Instagram but I can't. And I don't know where she was staying because she came back to mine."

Wolfie and I stared at him, not really knowing what to say. He was always so jovial and the life of the party. This sad, mopey Drew was unnerving.

I rubbed his arm, trying to comfort him. "Well, what do you know about her?"

His face dropped and he shrugged. "Not much, but she

was so incredible. We didn't really spend our time talking if you know what I mean."

"Yes, we all know what you mean." Cooper drolled.

"She was fucking hot, actually." Offered up Murray, unhelpfully.

Wolfie got up and walked over to him, pulling him into a big hug. "Honestly Drew, if it's meant to be, you'll see her again. Look at what happened to Jasper and me."

"Yeah thanks. We'll see, I guess. Vegas is pretty far from New York though." He sulked.

I briefly wondered if these boys had ever not been able to have something they wanted.

"You can't think like that. If it's meant to be, it will be. Do you know anything other than her name?"

"No, I just have a picture of her and that's it."

"Let's see then." I held my hand out and he passed me his phone.

Wolfie stood next to me and peered into the screen. It was a picture of the two of them cuddling and laughing at the camera. She was very, very pretty. Auburn hair, turquoise eyes with golden flecks and a face covered in freckles.

"She's beautiful."

"Yeah." He sighed.

"I know it sucks, but you'll find her. Just believe it. Come on, we'll cheer you up today." Wolfie put her arm round him again. "Do you want to look around London? Jas and I can give you the tour."

He managed a weak smile. "Yes, that sounds fun. I need to shower though, so let me go back and get clean clothes then I'll go."

Wolfie clapped her hands together. "Great, we can all go."

"Actually I can't, I need to go over to the barn." I said.

"Me either. I'm going to help Freddie." Cooper announced. Everyone turned to stare at him but he remained completely unfazed.

"We can meet you guys later, we can be quick." I looked at Wolfie.

"Okay great, sounds like we've got a plan then."

Jasper stood up and headed out to the garden to let the sleeping beauties out there know what was going on. One by one they all got up and walked into the kitchen.

"Has anyone sorted a car?" Carter stretched his arms above his head and I caught a glimpse of his washboard stomach. Not as impressive as Cooper's, but good none the less.

"Yeah, they'll be here in five." Replied Tate.

"Awesome work, my man." He grabbed a piece of toast off a random plate.

I picked up the car keys from the bowl as Cooper stood up. "Okay, we should probably head out. Then the sooner we're back."

"I just need to grab my phone, I'll be two seconds." Cooper tapped me on the ass before running upstairs two at a time.

I opened the front door and walked to the car.

"Hello beautiful Freddie."

I turned around to find Simon standing behind me and gave an internal groan. I'd never met anyone so unaware and irritating.

"Oh, hi." I turned back to the car boot as it opened dropping the bags inside, shifting away from him.

"Have you got a minute to talk?"

"Not really, I'm heading out." He stepped closer to me, almost blocking me between the car and his body. "Can you move?"

Cooper, hurry the fuck up.

He leered, running his hands down my arm. "Come on Fred, I just wanted to chat about yesterday. I get it, last night you were with your friends, but they're going to be gone soon. We've been dancing around this for so long. We need to finally take advantage of the fact we're neighbours. And I think we could have such fun together."

Puke.

"I'm not interested Simon, I've told you." I snatched my arm away.

"Come on Freddie, don't play hard to get. I know you're interested, I can see it." He moved as though to stroke my hair.

I ducked out of his reach. "You can see nothing. Stop fucking touching me."

"Freddie, you're a tease, I know you're playing hard to get." He moved closer.

I'm going to knee him in the balls in a minute.

"What the fuck is going on? Get your grubby hands off her." Cooper roared, making Simon jump back.

He was standing at the front door with Huck and Drew flanking him, Felix coming up behind. They were just missing Jasper and Brogan and he'd have the starting lineup of the New York Rangers bearing down on him.

"Freddie, get in the car."

Oh god, this wasn't going end well.

"Freddie, get in the fucking car."

I ran around to the passenger side without arguing, jumping in the seat as they all stormed over to Simon. I pulled down the vanity mirror to watch them.

Fuck, they were intimidating.

Cooper was towering over him, his face contorted in rage, while the rest of them just stared at Simon. I could see Cooper pointing right at him, gesticulating, before he crossed his arms over his chest and waited while Simon walked back into his house.

The four of them watched him disappear, then huddled around talking as two cars pulled up. The three boys jumped in one, followed by Tate, as the rest of them ran out of the house into the other car before it drove off.

I shut the mirror as Cooper opened the door and got in, his woody amber man scent filling the car and sending my senses reeling.

His jaw twitched while we sat in silence and I tried to decide if he was mad or upset. On a scale of one to the time he was in the penalty box, this was around a six, but there was something else crossing his face.

I put my hand in his lap and he lifted it, tapping the tips of my fingers on his lips, before opening my palm and placing it against his. It was so tiny next to his giant hockey hands.

"Coop…"

He turned towards me, his eyes filled with confusion and discomfort. "What is it about you?"

"What do you mean?"

"It drives me crazy seeing anyone touch you." He frowned.

"Why?"

He took a deep breath, his shoulders dropping. "I don't know."

"You're the only one touching me."

"Damn fucking right." He growled. His eyes dropped to my lips. "Give me a kiss please."

I leaned over and he cupped my face, brushing my hair away from my forehead. He dragged me against his open lips, slow and intense, his tongue gently pushing into my mouth, swirling inside and stroking against mine.

I pulled back slowly. "What did you say to him?"

He shrugged. "He won't be bothering you again."

I didn't want to push the point because, quite frankly, I didn't care, so I changed the subject. "Hey, did you notice I didn't argue with you about the driving?"

He smirked. "I did notice, which bodes well for you. You're finally learning I'm in charge."

I grinned at him.

"Oh and Tiny, we're not hurrying back. We're staying in our bubble today." He pulled out into the road one hand on the wheel, the other firmly between my thighs. "Okay baby, hit me with the music."

Prince belted out of the speakers as we drove away.

15

FREDDIE

We drove straight around to the barn and hopped out. He took my hand as we walked over and stood in the entrance, peering in. The event team had been working overtime to get this place ready and it was really starting to come together.

There was a bustle of activity as everyone darted around in their various roles. It might have looked chaotic but it was a well oiled machine and every single one of them knew exactly what was happening and when.

The old beams criss-crossing the roof had been covered in ivy. Blossom trees had been strategically placed around the room, the long tables snaking around them. Glass bottles, soon to contain tea lights, were hanging down from the branches. At the far end, the barn's wide doors were open and I could see the marquee had already been erected, which is where the after party would be. Four burly men were currently carrying the dance floor through.

It was definitely going to be awesome.

"Freddie, have you done this?" Cooper turned to me, his tone holding more than a little reverence.

I looked up. "Well, the team has, but it's my conception based on what Wolfie wanted."

"It looks incredible."

"Thank you." My cheeks began heating up.

Normally I didn't care so much what outsiders thought, as long as the client was happy then I was happy. But a compliment coming from Cooper felt different. As though I wanted him to see what I could do and be impressed, especially as he'd taken none of my suggestions for his house.

"Has Jas seen this?"

I shook my head. "Wolfie gave him a virtual tour last week, but he's not been down yet. They'll come down day after tomorrow when they move here before the wedding."

"Is this what you want?" He asked quietly.

"For a wedding?"

He nodded.

"No, this is Wolfie's dream, not mine. I've never been that fussed about getting married. If it happens it happens but I think I'd rather elope and have a massive three day party somewhere hot, where all our closest friends are hanging out, having the time of their lives eating, drinking and listening to amazing music."

He looked at me, his eyes searching mine as if he wanted to ask me a question but wasn't sure what it was.

Our moment broke as Carrie came running over.

"Hello." She ground to a halt in front of us, slightly breathless.

"Hey Care, this is looking great."

But she wasn't listening to me, she was full on staring at Cooper, her mouth slightly open. An unfamiliar feeling of discomfort ran through me.

I tried to push it away.

"Carrie?" I snapped my fingers in front of her.

"Oh yes, sorry." She focused back on me.

"Carrie, Cooper. Cooper, Carrie." I begrudgingly made introductions.

"Hey." Replied Cooper and her staring started up again.

And was she blushing? I began to feel raged.

What the fuck was going on with me?

"Carrie can you stop gawping for a moment and update me please?" I snapped, then felt guilty.

Fucking Cooper, I shouldn't have brought him.

"Oh god, sorry, sorry. Everything is looking good, come on." She led the way and we followed.

Cooper tried to take my hand and I snatched it away. He raised his eyebrow at me, the corner of his mouth curling up in amusement.

"Tiny, don't get jealous, I can't help it if I'm irresistible." He whispered.

"You definitely aren't." I grumbled.

He laughed out loud before throwing me over his shoulder and smacking my ass in one swift movement.

"Put me down." I hissed. "How am I supposed to have any authority if you're throwing me over your shoulder. I'm the boss."

He put me down without breaking stride but held onto my hand. "But Tiny." He bent down to my ear. "As I'm the boss of you does that make me the boss here?"

"You are not the boss of me."

"We both know that's not true." He winked.

Dick.

"Okay, so the floor is going down in here tomorrow." Carrie pointed down as we walked into the marquee. Workmen were scattered around the room, trying to erect the ceiling cloth which would look like a starry night once the lights were on. I was suddenly aware of a large group of mostly women all holding various pieces of foliage. And that they were all staring at us.

And by us, I meant Cooper.

"What's this room going to be?" Asked Cooper, oblivious to the scene he was causing.

"It's the after party." I replied. "The DJ is set up over there. Dance floor is going to be right here. There's a little lounge area over there next to where one of the bars will be. The other will be there." I showed him around, pointing out all the different spaces to him.

"And where are the hook up areas going to be?" His voice lowered.

I rolled my eyes at him.

"Come on, show me." He tugged on my arm.

"No."

"If you show me, I might have a surprise for you." He raised his eyebrow at me.

I crossed my arms over my chest. "Is it your dick?"

"It might be."

"No thanks, you're annoying me."

"Just for that you're definitely getting my dick later. Hard." He growled in my ear, sending goosebumps across my body.

I shrugged, not wanting him to see how affected I was. "Meh, maybe."

And walked off to where Carrie was.

"Freddie, who is that guy?" She whispered.

"The best man."

"Wow." She sighed.

I scowled at her, my mood darkening.

"Hey Carrie." Cooper called. "Where are these hook up areas Murray requested? He wants to make sure they're going in."

She giggled at him, like she couldn't believe he was talking to her. Any shred of professionalism seemed to have evaporated.

Jesus.

"They haven't gone in yet. We'll figure it out later in the

week, when we start on the outside."

"Make sure there's a super secret one for Freddie and me, okay." He gave her such a massive smile I was half expecting a cartoon sparkle to hit one of his teeth with a little bell sound.

"Oh sure. Yes, yes sure." She stuttered looking back and forth between Cooper and me.

"Oh, for fuck's sake. I'm going over to the house."

I stormed out and was half way across the field before Cooper caught up with me. He pulled me into his arms, wrapping them around my waist.

"Care to explain what that was?" He looked down at me.

"No." Because I didn't know.

And whatever it was, I didn't like it.

"Bébé." He said in his sexy French, bending down and kissing me.

"Get off me." I tried to push him away.

"Nope." He smirked and kissed me again, nuzzling against my neck until I couldn't hold it in any more.

I burst into laughter.

"That's better." He cupped my face in his hands and brought his mouth to mine. He traced the outline of my lips with the tip of his tongue and I opened up, granting him access. Warm and wet, our tongues danced together and I began melting against him.

He was so fucking perfect and dreamy.

And I had zero resistance.

He nipped me as he pulled away, before quickly smacking his lips against mine once more.

"Come on, let's go and find your parents."

"Actually, we need to get the car." I winced at my childish behaviour, turning back towards the barn. I'd stormed out and completely forgotten about it.

He held the door open and I jumped in. As he got in his side he looked at me before starting the engine.

"What?" I asked.

"Tell me what's wrong."

"I'm not bloody bringing you again, productivity drops to zero."

He chuckled. "Now tell me the real reason."

Urgh, how is it impossible to lie to him? He's so fucking annoying.

"I didn't like everyone staring at you. Like they wanted a piece of you." I mumbled.

He reached out and pulled my face round to his. "Baby it doesn't matter who stares, I only have eyes for you." Cooper Marks being cheesy, never thought I'd see the day.

But, the fact that he was also being entirely sincere made my heart skip and a pulse start up between my legs.

"I'm not used to feeling like this."

"Like what?" He pressed.

"Like I need you." I sighed.

He brushed his thumb against my cheek. "It's the same for me. And I'm not used to it either."

"How has this happened so quickly?"

"I don't know."

"Coop, is it real?" I whispered.

He looked at me with a deep frown and kissed me again, before starting the engine. "Come on, let's get you fed. The beast is waking up."

It didn't go unnoticed by me that my question remained unanswered.

"Hello darling," My mum pulled me into a hug as I walked into the kitchen. "I thought I saw you drive in earlier."

"Hello," I kissed her cheek before she let me go, turning to Cooper and bringing him in for a hug too. My parents had been over to New York so many times since Jasper and

Wolfie got engaged that they'd almost taken Cooper on as one of their own too.

"Hello Cooper, darling. How are you?"

"Hi Diane, I'm good thanks." He hugged her back.

"And you all got here okay, Freddie's house is okay? She's looking after you all?"

"If I'm honest I could do with less of her snarky attitude, but she's been a fairly decent hostess." He grinned, winking at me. "A firm three stars I think."

Cheeky fuck.

I walked over to the dogs in the basket, stroking their heads in hello.

Mum laughed, like it was the funniest thing she'd ever heard. I'm pretty sure I'd never seen this side of him before, this jovial teasing and joking. It was unnerving, mostly because I liked it.

A lot.

"There she is." My dad walked in and gathered me into a hug.

"Hi Pops."

He slapped Cooper on the back, before also hugging him.

My dad loved a good hug.

Growing up this house had been a chaotic thoroughfare of the four kids and all our friends. Yet Jack and Diane wouldn't have had it any other way. I'd been lucky to grow up surrounded by all their love.

"How are you kids doing? We checked out the barn earlier, it's looking good Franks. You've done a good job." He ruffled my hair, like I was still sixteen.

"She has." Cooper smiled as he looked down at me.

A blush rose through my cheeks. "Thank you."

"We're about to leave for Alex and Jamie's, what time are you heading back to London?" My mum asked as she picked out some peaches from the fruit bowl and put them in a bag. No doubt for my niece, who loved them.

"Not sure, not late. What time will you be back?"

"We'll probably stay there, so make sure you lock up properly." Dad picked up the car keys.

"Yeah, yeah. I know."

I got reminded every single time, like it was me who'd left all the doors and windows open when we'd gone away one weekend. Obviously Murray. We'd returned home to find the next door farm was missing some sheep, who'd then been discovered in residence at ours. The place trashed.

"Okay bye, give a kiss to the kids for me. We'll see you in a couple of days." I followed them out to the driveway.

"When are you all coming down?"

"I'm coming Wednesday but Jasper and Wolf will be here tomorrow with Patti and Bram." Jasper's parents were flying in.

"Okay darling, see you both then." She gave us a final hug before leaving and we heard the tyres crunch on the gravel as they drove out.

Cooper pulled me into him. He bent down and rested his head against my shoulder, taking in a deep sigh.

"Are you okay?" I frowned.

He looked at me, his eyes serious.

"No." He shook his head. "If I don't get inside you in the next five minutes I think I'm going to burst."

"You're an idiot."

"Come on, I want to see the bedroom of the teenage Francesca Danvers and all the trouble she used to get into."

"Hey, I was a good girl!"

His pupils dilated and I could feel him getting hard against me. He rolled his lower lip and ran his tongue along it. "We'll have to make up for lost time then won't we?"

My knickers immediately flooded.

Fucking hell.

For the second time that day he threw me over his

shoulder and smacked my ass. It was fucking painful so I wasn't sure why it was making me laugh so much.

"Francesca, where's this bedroom of yours?"

"Top of the stairs, turn left, end of the corridor." I tried to keep the excitement out of my voice as he moved as fast as possible.

He pushed the door open with his foot and kicked it shut.

My room had remained much the same since I'd left home following university. The white walls were covered in framed drawings I'd made as part of my final year at art college. Photos of my parents, childhood friends and family were scattered around while piles of records sat in the corner with my old field hockey sticks next to a huge bookshelf filled with art and photography books.

Cooper sat on the bed and put me down between his legs, running his big hands along the backs of my thighs and up to my ass. Thick fingers pushed underneath my t-shirt and inside my bra as he started kissing my stomach. His tongue circled my nipple, a throaty groan escaping as he trapped it between his teeth and began pulling hard, sending sparks straight between my thighs.

It was like he knew every single button he needed to press to get me hotter and wetter. I was burning up and my knickers were soaked.

"Francesca." He mumbled into my belly button as his tongue continued tracing around. "Think very carefully how you answer the next question."

He looked up. I could see the fire burning in his eyes, the amber flickering like a flame.

"Okay."

"Have you ever had sex in here?"

I suppressed a smile, trying very hard not to laugh.

The amber darkened. "I'm not joking, answer me."

I ran my hands through his hair. "No Coop, I've never had sex in here."

It was almost the truth. Heavy petting with Nick Lucas after school prom didn't count, right?

"Correct answer." He growled and yanked my shirt over my head taking my bra with it, his eyes widening as my boobs came into view.

He leant back on the bed, running the pad of his thumb back and forth across his lips as he contemplated his next move, like he meant business. His eyes started glazing over, the thick outline of his cock, hard and heavy, pressing against his shorts.

Never had I wanted someone more than I wanted him. It was like our bodies were meant to be together.

Like he was made to touch me.

The throbbing between my legs intensified with every second longer he stared at me. I was so wet I could feel it seeping through.

"Take off your jeans and get on the bed." He ordered.

Nervous excitement started to course through me as I unbuttoned and pulled them off climbing onto the bed, staying up on my knees. He moved away from me and pushed the pillows against the headboard sitting back against them, his eyes never leaving mine.

And then I realised he was expecting a show.

"Spread your legs."

I did.

"Now tell me how wet you are." His voice was husky and filled with lust.

"Very." My voice was shaking in desperation.

"Show me."

My heart rate kicked up. How had I lived until now without him in my bed?

My fingers slipped under the elastic of my knickers and circled my clit. I was so sensitive there was a good possibility I might explode any second. I felt a deep, broken moan creep up my throat escaping in a sound I've never heard before.

I rubbed myself again, my breath shallowing.

"Show. Me." He sounded as close to the edge as I was.

I drew my fingers out, my clit crying at the lack of friction, and held them in front of him. They glistened with my arousal. He leant forward and guided them into my mouth, forcing me to suck on them before he pulled them out with a loud pop.

Grabbing the back of my head he slowly ran his tongue along my lips, pushing into my mouth, caressing it, swirling around, tasting me. A deep growl rose from his chest.

He sat back.

Holy fuck, I was mesmerised.

This was off the charts sexy.

His eyes were running down my body, the amber now almost black with need. The outline of his cock had become more pronounced against his shorts, so big and thick I ached to run my tongue around the rim.

He whipped off his shirt, his chest and abs rippling. He was so insanely beautiful, I couldn't stop staring as he sat back again, the tip of his cock peeking out from the waistband of his shorts. He slid his hands under the elastic, pushing them down and chucked them to the side letting himself spring free. And spring he did.

My very own Jack-in-a-Box.

I watched as he spread his legs before he gripped his cock and started stroking himself, hard.

My mouth filled with saliva, I wanted those hands on me. Desperately.

A dark smile crossed his face. "Do you want my cock, Francesca?"

I nodded.

"Then earn it. Show me how you touch yourself." He growled.

If I couldn't see how much he wanted me I'd be swimming with nerves, but the lust in his eyes gave me the confidence to give him what he was asking for. He was as turned on as I was, his need acting as a powerful aphrodisiac.

Who was I becoming? I'd definitely been having sex with the wrong men. As though everyone I'd ever been with before had been a poor audition for this moment.

Slowly running my hands across my stomach up to my breasts I palmed them, squeezing them together. I watched his jaw relax and I knew he was thinking about pushing his cock between them.

I tweaked my nipple, yanking it, feeling it harden even more than it was. He was so close to the brink, his breathing in bursts, his tongue tracing back and forth along his lip. He followed the path of my fingers, his eyes hooded.

How far could I push him before he threw me in the air and pounded straight into me?

I spread my legs wider, moving the edge of my knickers to the side so he could watch and inserted a finger deep into my pussy. My head fell back. This was turning me on so much, I could feel myself fluttering and tried hard to stave off the sensation. I wanted to come on him, on his cock.

"Fuuuck, Coop. I'm so wet."

"Another one, Francesca." He could barely speak.

His strokes were getting harder, pre-cum dripping off the end, running over his fingers.

I added a finger and began pumping them inside me.

I met his gaze.

"Coop, have I earned it yet? Is it my turn for your cock?" I whispered. My clit was swollen and I wanted him so badly I'd started shaking.

His eyes narrowed. "I think you have."

And in my next breath I was on my back, my knickers ripped off my body as he rammed into me in one swift movement. The burn seared through me as I adjusted to his size, the sting feeling so fucking good.

I squeezed my eyes shut, trying to stop the shockwaves

running through me. Trying to stop the explosion hitting me at warp speed.

"Motherfucker." His snarled into my neck.

My breath had turned to whimpers, I could feel my orgasm building to atomic levels. He lifted his head and looked at me. His body hovering over mine, his biceps bulging with tension. I could see the little divots at the top of his shoulders deepening as he held himself away from me.

"Coop, I can't hold it off. I need you to move. I'm going to come."

"No baby, you need to earn it like you earned my cock. Clench that tight pussy of yours. Make yourself come." His words rumbled through his chest, low and fraught with arousal.

Jesus, the dirty talk.

I was having an out of body experience.

He ran his thumb along the edge of my lip, pushing it inside my mouth.

"Clench." He ordered, his hooded eyes boring into me.

I started clenching his thick cock as he stayed still, watching me. My lips still wrapped around his thumb.

"Fais le plus dur." He groaned. "Harder. Do it."

"Fucking hell." I screamed as wave after wave crashed through me, I'd never made myself come like this. And suddenly, as though the electricity flowing through me shocked him into life, he rose above me spreading my legs as wide as he could, hooking my knees under his arms. Before I'd had a chance to come down from my orgasm he started pounding into me and I could do nothing except hold on and let him.

"Coop..." I lifted my body up as close as I could get to him. Wanting his mouth, wanting his lips on mine.

"I fucking love how wet you get for me. I want it all again. You're going to come. I want you coming on my cock. I want to feel your perfect velvet pussy gripping me over and over." His voice was hoarse with need.

He pulled all the way out before sliding back inside me with a ferocity I'd never experienced. I could feel his cock swelling more with every stroke.

He moved my legs up to his shoulder, holding them straight against his chest, the pace never slowing. "Oh fuck, Francesca. You're so fucking tight. I can feel every single ripple."

I couldn't speak, I was so close to bursting again.

"I can't hold off any longer, I need you to come right now." He reached between us and started pinching my clit, making by back arch off the bed as another orgasm ripped through me, stealing the air from my lungs. He bent down, licking a nipple before sucking so hard across my chest I silently screamed as the pain fought against pleasure.

Stroke after punishing stroke, he pushed harder and harder inside me until he cried out and collapsed sweaty and breathless. I could still feel him pulsing inside me as he slowly lifted his head, taking my mouth in a white hot kiss, his tongue twisting against mine until our heartrates settled.

He pushed my hair back from my face with a tenderness in his touch and gathered me up into his arms.

"I think it's safe to say you've had sex in here now." He sniggered into my hair.

I looked up at him with a grin. "I don't know what that was, but it wasn't sex like I've ever experienced."

He chuckled and kissed the top of my head. "You might be correct. That was indescribable."

He moved to pull away from me and a look of terror filled his face.

"What? What's wrong."

"Oh my god. Freddie, we didn't use a condom." He whispered, rubbing both hands over his face.

I held his jaw. "Hey, it's okay, I use birth control."

"I'm so sorry." He sounded so pained. "I've never gone bare before. I'm clean, I promise."

"Cooper, it's okay. We're both safe. We're good." I leaned up and kissed him, taking his mouth in mine, brushing my tongue against his lips.

He shook his head. "You make me lose all sense. Fuck, no wonder I couldn't last." He sighed right before his eyes widened.

"What?" I followed his line of sight and looked down in horror to find red and purple marks dotted across my chest.

Hickeys!

What were we, fifteen?

He'd fucking branded me.

I looked at him, a smirk curling his lips.

"You had better pray the neckline of my bridesmaids dress covers these." I snarled.

The bastard didn't even look sorry.

"Well if they don't, at least I won't have to bother telling everyone you're mine." He shrugged nonchalantly.

"If they don't, you won't have the chance because I'll have murdered you."

He laughed so hard I nearly murdered him then and there.

At this rate I wasn't sure we'd even make it to the wedding.

16

COOPER

The park was getting busier as we ran around the lake for a second time. We were already pushing eight miles and I was starting to lag.

The air was heavy.

"Dude, I'm done." I called to Jasper who was slightly ahead of me, both of us drenched in sweat.

I held my hands on my head as I sucked in as much air as I could. It was too warm to be running long distance, not as warm as New York would be at this time, but still too warm. I could see clouds rolling in on the horizon, almost like a storm was brewing.

"Thank fuck. I've been waiting for you to cave the last three miles." He stopped in front of me.

I shook my head. "You're lucky you're pretty, because you're a dick."

"Awww Bae. You think I'm pretty." He grabbed my head and kissed me.

I pushed him away, laughing, suddenly desperate for caffeine.

"Let's walk back and pick up a coffee."

"Good plan." We headed towards the exit. "You know, I

kind of enjoy walking around here. No one knows us and no one bothers us. We're totally anonymous."

It was true. People were paying no attention to us. If we'd been in Central Park we'd have been stopped a dozen times for selfies and autographs before the end of our run. We loved our city and they supported us in an amazing fashion, but it was kind of nice to blend in with the crowds.

"Yeah, I know what you mean. It's kind of peaceful, like it would be if we had a different job."

"But then how boring would that be?" He pushed my shoulder.

"I dunno, Murray seems to manage it." I laughed, knowing full well Murray's life was anything but boring.

"Yeah right. Murray is exactly like us, without the hockey. He probably fucks as many girls as Clevs. He definitely has some stories from Vegas, I'm not even sure Wolfie and Freddie realise what he's like."

I could imagine. He'd slotted in well with our group, something not many outsiders did.

"Hey, did you know he's looking for an office in New York?"

"No, that would be awesome. Good for Wolf too. How'd you know?"

"Freddie told me." I replied and his eyebrow raised.

He was just about to make a comment when his phone rang. Saved by the bell. And coincidently we were right by a coffee shop.

Happiness washed over him as he answered. "Hey Wolf Cub."

I motioned to him that I was heading inside and he nodded. I ordered coffees, then turned to watch him through the window while I waited for them to be made. The smile never left his face.

It suited him.

He looked so damn happy and I briefly wondered if I would ever look like that.

Sex and easy women had always been my lifestyle choice. Zero fuss, zero commitments. I just wasn't sure I wanted it anymore.

I collected the cups, noticing a phone number on one. I looked up, the barista giving me a coy smile as she fluttered her eyelashes.

I walked out without acknowledging her. Her blatant come on leaving a sour taste in my mouth, one I hoped the caffeine would wash away.

Jasper caught my eye as I walked back outside.

"Yeah baby, we'll be back in an hour." He looked at his watch. "Is that good? Yeah okay, I'll tell him. Okay, I love you more."

"Tell me what?" I handed him his coffee and a banana muffin.

"Thanks bud. Oh, Freddie had to go and see a client or something. She's working but she'll be back later."

We started walk again. "Oh okay. I'm gonna see Murray's this afternoon anyway, we're going to the pub."

"When are you coming down?"

"Tomorrow. The guys wanted another day in London." I dropped a piece of muffin in my mouth.

He eyed me. "And that's the only reason you're coming down tomorrow?"

No. No, it wasn't.

I wanted a night with Freddie where no one else was around. Where she didn't have to try and be quiet as I fucked orgasm after orgasm out of her. Being skin to skin with her, I'd never imagined something could feel so good. I'd quickly become addicted to the noises she made every time I slid inside her.

I loved making her scream for more and I didn't want to stop.

"Dude, just ask." I sighed.

"What's going on with you and Freddie?" He sipped his coffee, his eyes scrutinising.

I stopped walking and faced him, running my hand through my hair. "I wish I knew and could explain it. But I can't."

"What do you mean?"

I shrugged. "I don't know. She winds me up so much, she's fucking infuriating. And she's always getting pissed at me for ridiculous reasons. But then she looks at me as though I'm the only man on earth and I'm a goner. It's like I've only just realised I've been missing something my entire life."

I sounded like such a douche. I needed a slap to the face.

"Woah. Shit man, I didn't realise."

"Yeah."

We started walking again, in silence.

"Have you told her?" He asked.

"Told her what?"

"Um, how you feel?"

How I feel. How I feel. How do I feel?

"I don't know how I fucking feel. It's been five days." I grumbled.

He let out a loud gaffaw. "Coop, man. It's not been five days. You've been into her since you first met her. Why do you think the guys are always winding you up about her?"

"Because they're dicks." I sipped my coffee and grimaced. This was not New York coffee.

He scoffed. "Yes. But also because they're trying to push you into doing something about it."

Fuck's sake.

I rolled my eyes.

"Have you tried making a move? I'm pretty sure she wouldn't turn you down."

I stopped dead, then turned and stared at him, incredulity

spreading across my face. Had we really not been obvious? It felt like I could barely keep my hands off her.

"You already have?" His voice filled with confusion.

I slapped him on the cheek. "Jas. I'm not talking about sex with Freddie."

"YOU'VE ALREADY HAD SEX?" He bellowed and several people turned around, looking at us in disgust.

"Can you keep your fucking voice down? I don't think the old lady across the park heard you." I hissed.

"Sorry." He mumbled. "But what the fuck, man. Why didn't you tell me?"

"Because I didn't know what was going on? I still don't, really." I shrugged.

He finished up his muffin, stuffing the remainder in his mouth. "How did this happen?"

"You remember when we landed and I went with her to run errands?"

"IT HAPPENED THE DAY WE LANDED?" He shouted again.

Jesus fuck. What was the matter with him?

I gritted my teeth. "Jas, seriously. Do that one more time and you'll find my fist in your face. And I'll explain your black eye by telling Wolfie you got into a fight with a kid on a skateboard."

Or something equally lame.

"Sorry." He frowned.

"We were collecting suits and bumped into that fucking chump, Stuart."

Fucking Stuart.

"The guy she went on a date with?"

Even thinking about it still wound me up. "Yeah, she kissed me to try and stop him from noticing her."

Jasper cracked up, laughing right in my face. "Oh man."

"I know. She's a dick."

We turned out of the park gates and onto the street. I was

following Jasper, not entirely confident he knew the route we were going.

"Wait, why was she in such a rage when you got back to the house?"

I joined in his laughter, remembering how mad she'd been. "Because I was pissed. And I told her how pissed I was that she did it, plus I wouldn't let her drive. You know she ignored me until after The Killers?"

"Oh dude, you are in trouble. She's so fucking surly, she's absolutely going to make your life difficult."

"Tell me about it."

She was difficult in more ways than one. Mostly because I couldn't stop thinking about her when we were apart. But it only got worse when we were together and I couldn't touch her because too many people were around.

I wanted her to myself.

"So it happened then?"

I nodded. "Yeah."

"And?"

We'd never been shy about sharing stories before, but this was different. In the same way I'd never ask about him and Wolfie.

"I'm not giving you details about sex with Freddie."

He shook his head as he looked at me. "Not what I'm asking, Man."

I thought about his question, knowing the answer he wanted. Unsure I wanted to admit it.

I sighed again.

Fuck it.

"Best I've ever had. Mind blowing. Like nothing I've ever experienced."

He slapped my face before kissing my cheeks, like we were in the Godfather and he was Marlon Brando. "Welcome to the club."

"Fuck off." I grinned.

"When are you going to tell her?"

I frowned. "Tell her what?"

"That you love her."

I sipped my coffee and choked on it, coughing into my hand as I tried to speak. The words catching in my throat. "What? It's been five days. I do not love her."

Wait, did I?

Denying it out loud sounded wrong.

No, I didn't.

I couldn't.

"Okay, you keep telling yourself that."

Tension started building in my head as I thought about what he was implying. Thought about the implications.

"Stop Jas, you know what happened last time. I'm not doing it again. I can't do it again. I can't have another whirlwind romance and divorce under my belt."

I'm not a fucking Kardashian.

Jasper stopped walking again. At this rate it was going to take us longer than an hour to get home.

"Coop, why would you even think that? That was thirteen years ago."

"Because it's been five days." I threw my hands in the air in frustration at not being able to articulate how I was feeling. "It's the literal definition of a whirlwind romance. How do I know it's even real? How do I know I've not just got caught up in everything going on around right now? How do I know it's not because we're in London and everything is intensified?"

He stared at me. His eyebrows raised at my outburst.

"Dude. It's not been five days." He argued again. "You met her nine months ago and you've been into her ever since, whether you want to admit it or not. You speak every day. And how do you know? I don't know. You just do. When you know, you know."

"Thanks, that's really helpful." I dead-panned, my palms

pressed to my temples.

"Look, I've never seen you get worked up about any woman the whole time I've known you. Have you even ever spent the night with one?'

I shook my head.

I hadn't. It wasn't something I did. I leave as soon as it's over.

"But with Freddie, you see red if she's even talking to another guy, so that's got to mean something, right?" He squeezed my shoulder. "And a year ago, I'd have said the same. The bunnies were easy, but when I met Wolfie it was like I could suddenly see in colour and I realised how much she added to my life. I can't bear to be apart from her. She makes me a better person, Man. That's how I know."

I chucked my coffee cup in the trash can. While his words were wildly unhelpful, I did find them slightly comforting.

"Thanks Buddy. I dunno, I guess I'll figure it out."

"Yeah you will." He curled his palm around the back of my neck. "Seriously though, just remember she's going to be my sister-in-law. So, you cannot fuck her over otherwise I will have no choice but to let Wolfie fuck you over."

I laughed at him. "You're such a pussy, how you're captain of our team is always a wonder to me. I'm not going to fuck her over. I promise. I just need to figure some shit out. Hey, can you do me a favour and not say anything to Wolf until Freddie has told her?"

"Yeah okay." He looked at his watch. "Fuck, we need to get a cab. We're so late and Wolfie will have my balls if we don't leave on time. She's already had a melt down about whether or not it might rain and we need to get my parents from the airport."

Whipped.

He was one hundred percent whipped.

And for the first time in my life, I kind of wanted to be too.

17

COOPER

"Here you go, Mate." Murray came back from the bar and placed a pint in front of me.

We were sitting in a beer garden of a busy pub in Notting Hill. It was exactly like a movie set. Although I'd imagine that's what people thought when they came to New York.

"Thanks, Dude." I took a sip. "Hey, this isn't bad."

"Yeah, London IPA. Not like that watered down shit you drink." He shot at me.

I eyed him. "Yeah, if you were a professional athlete with a strict dietary regimen you'd drink what you were told to."

"No way, no one tells me what to do." He smirked.

He was so like Freddie.

Except when I told her what to do, she did it. Most of the time. Okay, when sex was involved.

I shifted my jeans against my crotch, they grew tight as I thought about what I'd told her to do this morning. She'd been on her knees, her lips wrapped around my cock taking me right to the back of her throat.

I exploded in less than a minute.

She'd destroyed any control I used to have.

I shook my head, pushing away my XXX thoughts while I

was sitting with her brother. "Hey, Fred told me about New York. What's the deal?"

"Jamie wants to open up an office over there, so I'm the obvious choice to run it."

"Man, that would be so cool." I took another sip of my beer.

He picked up a coaster and started spinning it between his fingers. "Yeah, I'm going to head over in a couple of weeks and scout out some spaces which the realtor has found."

"Do you need to find more clients?"

"Yeah, but we already have a lot of US based ones so it makes sense for us to be over there."

"Well, let's chat when you get over. I've been thinking about getting a new money guy." I looked up at the sky, it was alarmingly dark for two in the afternoon.

He frowned. "What are you looking at?"

"Not sure, feels stormy."

His eyes followed mine, looking up. "Yeah it does. Hey, where's Franks?"

I shrugged. "Dunno, I think she's at home. Or she's going to be home soon, she had to work this morning. Why?"

"She doesn't like storms."

Big droplets of rain started to fall on us. "Come on, let's go inside and I'll text her."

Cooper: Hey baby, where are you? xx

Tiny: Just getting home. Where are you? x

Cooper: Are you okay? I'm with Murray, I'll see you soon. Don't forget we have a whole house to ourselves so you'd better be naked xx

"She's just getting home." I told him as we found another table. "What's the deal with the storms?"

He was just about to answer when we noticed two women standing right by us. They had the unmistakable predatory bunny vibe about them.

This should be interesting.

"Well, hello ladies. How can we help?" Murray smirked, but they were looking at me.

"Are you Cooper Marks?" They asked in unison, the one on the right twirling her hair in her fingers.

I grinned at Murray, as he shook his head.

"Yes, I am."

"Could we get a photo?" The one on the left asked as she shoved her tits very close to my face.

Yep, there was no fucking way I was having a picture of me on the internet with Tits McGee and her sidekick.

I shook my head. "Not today ladies. Another time, but thanks for coming to say hi."

If she was disappointed she hid it well, instead trying a different approach for my attention. She ran her hand up my arm and pouted. "Okay well here's my number if you're staying here. I know you're all over for Jasper Jacobs' wedding, so let us know if you need a tour guide or anything. We're both happy to help any way we can."

I watched Murray's eyes pop, a grin spreading across his face.

"Oh my god." He mouthed.

"Sure, thanks."

She held her number out, putting it on the table when I didn't take it.

"See you around." She winked at me and walked off purposefully swaying her hips, begging to be noticed. Instead I looked out of the window, the rain was hammering against it.

I picked up the number, ripping it up and shoved it into the neck of an empty beer bottle. Murray was still grinning as I finished my pint.

"What?"

"Women walking up to you in the middle of the afternoon and offering you a threesome. Man, I wish I'd been a hockey player." He grinned.

"You do alright." I shook my head at him. "Weirdly I was saying to Jas this morning how nice it was to be anonymous in London. Guess the cat's out of the bag. At least we're heading out tomorrow."

"Yeah."

All the lights in the pub turned on making me realise how dark it had become. And then the thunder started, the humidity of the last few days finally breaking.

"Hey, what was that about storms?" I asked, causing him to frown.

"Did you say Franks was at home?"

I nodded.

"You need to get back. Come on, I'll drive."

We ran out. By the time we got to the car we were drenched, it was raining so hard we could barely see out of the windscreen as we drove away.

"This weather is crazy." I was having to shout as the rain was so loud. "Anyway, can you please explain why we need to get back?"

"Franks doesn't like storms." His hands were gripping the steering wheel trying not to skid on the newly greasy road, windscreen wipers on full blast. "When her parents died, she was at our house. It was a really stormy night and the car they were driving was hit by a telegraph pole which had been struck by lightning. It careered off the road into the river. They think that her parents had already been knocked unconscious by the pole, but her little brother drowned."

"Holy fuck. That's horrendous." An icy chill ran through my bones. "God, poor Freddie."

And then it hit me, what the four dates were under her heart.

"Her tattoo?"

"Yeah, it's their birthdays and the day they died."

Another flash of lightening filled the sky.

"Fucking hell, Muz. This is literally the worst thing I've ever heard." I actually felt nauseous. Horrified at the pain she'd suffered.

Desperate to protect her.

"I know. She'll tell you about it, but I just wanted to give you the heads up. It stuck with her for a long time, whenever there was a storm as a kid she'd have nightmares for days. She's had a lot of help for it but when the storms are really bad she can have a relapse. And this is a bad storm."

It felt like it was right on top of us.

"Also, let's hope this passes to save ourselves from a raging Wolf. She's going to go apeshit if the wedding is rained out."

"Jasper can deal with her." I mumbled, although I wasn't really paying attention, I was thinking about Freddie and getting to her as quickly as possible. I picked up my phone and called her. It rang out.

"How far away are we? She's not answering her phone."

"Not far, just about to pull into the road."

I looked down at my phone as a message came through.

Jasper: Are you with Freddie? Wolfie can't get hold of her.

Cooper: She's at home. Getting there now.

He stopped in front of the house. "Mate, she'll be fine. Don't worry, just that today might be a bit rough, just watch a movie or something. It's just better if she's not alone. Anyway, you'll figure it out. I'll drop the car back tomorrow."

"Yeah cool, thanks. See you tomorrow, Dude. Thanks for the heads up."

I let myself into the house, every single light was on. Somehow, I knew it was because you couldn't see the lightening when all the lights were on.

"Freddie, baby. Are you here?" I shouted, walking from room to room.

Nothing.

"Francesca? Where are you?" I turned and ran up the stairs two at a time, just as another loud rumble of thunder hit.

I found her in bed. Or more accurately, when I walked into her room, I could make out a lump under her duvet. I dropped to my knees at the side of the bed and pulled back the covers.

She was shaking uncontrollably as tears poured down her face, her eyes screwed shut, her hands over her ears.

I'd never seen anyone so scared in my life.

"Baby." I cupped her face and tried to wipe away the tears. "I'm here, it's okay."

"Make it stop. Please." She sobbed.

And my heart broke.

I climbed into bed next to her, scooping her up and pulling her into me. Her heart was racing. I wrapped my arms around her tiny frame as tightly as possible, trying to get her shaking under control. I held her head, kissing her, stroking her hair. My shirt became wet with her tears.

"Ça va, ça va aller." I whispered to her over and over.

It's going to be okay.

The rain was smashing so hard against the windows I thought they might break. I tried to keep my breathing even to calm her, but every time the lightening struck and the thunder crashed her shaking got worse. She was clammy and beads of sweat had broken out on her forehead.

All I wanted to do was take her pain away.

How the fuck do I fix this?

Maybe I needed to call Molly. She'd know.

The rain was so loud I could barely think. Suddenly I had a brainwave.

"I'll be right back." I kissed her head.

Slipping out from underneath her, I ran into the bathroom turning on the two big showerheads. I stripped down to my boxers and went back to Freddie.

"Baby, I'm going to take off your pants." I said, running a thumb across her cheek.

"No, Coop. I can't right now." She mumbled.

I tried not to get angry at the fact she thought I'd want to fuck her while she was in this state.

"No, we're not having sex. I'm taking you to the shower." I peeled off her yoga pants, leaving her vest and panties on, lifting her into my arms.

Her shaking was still going strong as she clung to me, her head against my chest.

I stepped into the shower and sat down under the hot water, cradling her in my lap. I held her tight as the water flowed over us, soothing us, blocking out the sound of the rain.

"Baby, it's okay. I'm not going anywhere." I stroked her head, slowly rocking back and forth, holding her as tightly as I could. I placed her hand against my chest. "Feel my heartbeat, I'm here. I'm right here."

I don't know how long we stayed under the water, steam filling the bathroom, our bodies going pruney. But slowly, as our breathing synced, so her shaking began to subside. Out of the window I could still see the rain lashing down, although the lightening appeared to be less frequent and I hadn't heard thunder in a while.

"Coop?" Her voice so quiet, breaking through the sound of the water cascading over us.

"Yeah baby?" I held her tighter.

"Thank you for being here."

"You're welcome." I kissed her head. "I'm not going anywhere, but we are going to have to get out of this water soon."

"Okay." She whispered as I kept stroking her hair.

"Francesca, listen to me. I'm going to wash us, then dress us. Then we're going to go downstairs where I'm going to make some pasta and we're going to snuggle under the blankets and watch a movie. Okay?"

"Okay."

I stood us up and placed her on her feet. Lifting her hands up, peeling off her soaking vest my breath caught as her chest came into view. I'd almost forgotten I'd done this to her, something I should have felt guilty about but didn't. Little purple marks were dotted across her creamy skin and she'd never felt more mine than she did right in this moment.

Mine.

I could feel myself getting hard, my body instinctively drawn to hers, and I pushed it away as quickly as I could.

"Turn around, baby." And she turned as I pulled down her panties. I couldn't be that close to her pussy without wanting to taste it.

I grabbed the soap and started lathering up, running it across her back, down her legs, between her thighs, then gently spun her around and washed her front. I ignored every compulsion I had to suck her rock hard nipples between my teeth but as I got to the dates below her heart I dipped down, kissing them.

Glancing up, fresh tears filled her eyes, making them seem even bluer than usual.

"Baby, I'm so sorry. I'm so sorry for what you've been through." I brushed my thumb across her cheek, pressing my lips to hers as briefly as I could. Any longer and I'd be fucking her in the shower, and I wasn't willing to break my promise no matter how much I wanted to.

I stripped out of my boxers, quickly washing myself before turning off the shower and wrapping us both in thick, warm towels. Leading her through to the closet, I sat her down on the chair and started looking for clothes.

She was so quiet, watching me rifle through her drawers until I could find what I was looking for.

"Baby you're gonna have to help me out with these." I held

out a pair of panties in front of her and saw a little smile peak out from the corners of her mouth as she took them from me, slipping them on.

"Arms up." And she complied, so unlike the Freddie I knew. I pulled a vest down over her head, then handed her another pair of yoga pants which she put on.

"Okay, follow me."

We walked into my room where I put her in one of my hoodies. It was so big on her, but I wanted her in it, wanted her wrapped up in me as much as possible. I threw on some sweatpants and another hoodie, before taking us downstairs where I led her to the big sectional in the corner of the kitchen, covering her with a blanket.

I flicked through the TV and found some old re-runs of Friends.

"We'll stay here while I'm cooking, then go downstairs and watch a movie. Okay?" She nodded as she settled in. "I'm going to get you some water."

I looked at the clock, it was five pm. We'd been in the shower for nearly two hours. It was still very dark outside, but the storm had passed, the rain lessening. I felt like I could breathe again and finding a bottle of whiskey on the side poured myself a glass, knocking it back, trying to steady my nerves.

Jesus Christ. What the fuck had happened today?

Her eyes were closed when I placed a bottle of water next to her, she'd fallen asleep. I brushed strands of hair away from her face and kissed her temple. Her eyes were still slightly puffy but she looked peaceful for the first time since I'd left her this morning.

I took the opportunity to run back upstairs, grabbing my phone to shoot a few texts off to Murray and Jasper, letting them know Freddie was okay.

Heading back into the kitchen I marched straight into the pantry to see what I had to work with. It was impressively full, there were even the ingredients to make pasta from scratch if I had time, but I wanted to get her fed as quickly as possible, to help with the shock she'd experienced. I took what I needed from the shelves and fridge, turned the oven on and got down to making the best mac and cheese in existence.

While it was baking, I sat on the sofa and pulled her on top of me, her chest rising and falling in a soothing rhythm.

This was not how I'd expected the day to pan out.

So much had gone on I didn't know where to start, as an almost overwhelming tidal wave of emotion crashed through me. Seeing her like that had scared the shit out of me. The strong, feisty, vibrant woman I knew had been so vulnerable and I'd felt completely helpless as she sobbed in my arms.

Aside from my family and some the guys I'd never felt the urge to protect someone before, never wanted to look after another human being in the way I wanted to with Freddie. The instinct to shield her from pain, so strong.

I tried to remember the conversation I'd had with Jasper that morning. He was convinced I loved her.

Did I?

Is that what this feeling was?

I thought I'd loved the women I'd married but that wasn't like this. This was all consuming. How could I trust what I was feeling when I didn't know what it was?

Had it always been like this?

The timer on the oven went off, stirring her awake. She lifted her head up to look at me.

"Hi there Tiny, you want some mac and cheese?" I stroked her face, pulling the hood back where it had fallen down.

Her eyes opened wide. "You made mac and cheese?"

"I did and it's the best mac and cheese you'll ever have." I moved from under her as the timer went off again. The rain had stopped, the sky brightening up.

172

I took it from the oven and spooned it into two bowls, the cheese still bubbling on top, and took it over to her.

"Hope you're hungry."

She sat up straight, taking it from me. "Coop, this looks so good. Thank you."

"You're welcome, baby. Now scooch over."

We ate in silence, Friends still on the TV. My heart warming as she started laughing at Chandler and Joey. She was slowly coming back to life, her cheeks flushed against her pale skin. When we'd finished I stood up, taking her empty bowl and placing them on the counter.

"What movie do you want to watch?" She asked as I sat back down and moved her into my lap so she straddled me.

"Whatever you want to watch, I don't mind." I answered truthfully, I'd only be watching her over any film.

She ran her hands over my scruff and through my hair. "Coop, thank you. I'm really happy you're here." She leant down and kissed me, her perfect lips covering mine, her tongue exploring my mouth.

God, I wanted her so much my body ached for her.

My dick started to stir and I pulled her back, we weren't ready to have sex no matter how much he disagreed.

She looked at me, confused.

"Baby, when you kiss me my dick gets hard and I really need him to not make an appearance right now." She started to speak and I stopped her. "I want us to watch a movie and curl up next to each other, then have an early night. And maybe, if you let us do all those things I will allow you to make my dick hard."

"You'll allow me?" She raised her eyebrows at me and I felt Freddie returning to me.

"Maybe." I stared at her. "Come on, let's pick a movie and snuggle."

"Can we have popcorn and wine?" She asked.

"You can have whatever you want." I stood us up and

placed her back on the floor kissing her on the head. "You get the wine, I'll get the popcorn."

I carried her up the stairs after she'd fallen asleep on me for the second time that day and placed her on the bed. I took her pants off as she curled up on the pillow and went into the bathroom to get my toothpaste.

Brushing my teeth as I walked through the house turning off all the lights, I found her in the bathroom when I arrived back upstairs. I sat on the edge of the bath, watching her as she washed her face.

She was so beautiful, like nothing I'd ever seen before.

She could outshine the sun and stars.

She caught my eye in the mirror, watching me watch her. Turning around, smiling, she walked over to stand between my legs, pushing her hands through my hair.

Her nails scraped my scalp sending shivers down my spine in more ways than one. Running my nose along her jaw, inhaling her clean, citrussy scent, a shot of lust hit me straight in the groin.

The bullet carved with her name.

"Coop?"

"Yes Tiny." I pulled her further into me.

"You know how you promised to let me do the things that make your dick hard?" She gave a lopsided grin.

I raised my eyebrow at her. "I definitely didn't promise."

She tilted her head. "Well, you did a little bit."

"Francesca…"

"Coop, don't treat me like I'm made of glass." She said angrily, her mouth set in a hard line.

I pulled her in tighter, keeping my voice as soft as possible. "Baby, I'm not, I'm treating you like a human being. You went through something today and it was terrifying. Terrifying for you and for me. I didn't know how to fix it."

"I don't need you to fix me."

"Today you did." I looked at her and watched her face fall. I tilted her chin back up. "Look at me and answer me this. Is this," I gestured between us. "Just sex to you?"

Please say no.

She shook her head and frowned. "No. It's never just been sex. You know that."

"Good, because it's not for me either. So, trust me when I say I know what you need right now. And it's not sex. That doesn't mean I don't want it, believe me. Saying no to you is literally the hardest thing I've ever done in my life. Because you are smoking hot."

A grin broke through the scowl.

I cupped her face. "I know we have to talk about what this is and we will. But it's been a long day and now is not the time."

She sighed. "Okay."

"Now, for one night only, will you please come to bed with me and let me spoon the shit out of you all night long." I stood up and held my hand out to her.

She shrugged. "I guess."

"A fucking shrug." I shook my head at her and she grinned again.

She took my hand and led me to bed.

18

FREDDIE

The dogs shot ahead in the field, chasing an invisible rabbit, disappearing out of sight.

"Those fucking dogs had better not get lost again. Or they can find their own way back this time." Wolfie kicked through the grass in frustration.

We had gone for a walk to escape the craziness of our parents. Or more specifically, our mother and her future mother-in-law. Wedding psychosis had officially peaked and after Wolfie had forbidden them from going anywhere near the barn, following a floral rearrangement incident, they'd started on the flower girls and page boys.

We'd left them debating the merits of whether they should walk down before or after Wolfie in church and whether they needed to have another practice session in, even though there had already been three this week. I could have easily answered with a 'Hell no, we're already having to bribe them into behaving as it is' but chose not to.

Instead, we'd walked out grabbing a bottle of wine on the way, and it was unlikely they'd even notice we were gone.

Three days of sun had dried the ground following the

storm and the warmth of the summer had made an appearance once again. William returned with a giant stick in his mouth dropping it at Wolfie's feet.

She picked it up, throwing it and he ran off to find it.

She looked around at the debris of fallen branches. "That storm was pretty heavy."

"Yeah."

What a day that was. It had changed so much.

Tension was building in my temples from all the thoughts whirring around in my head. Thoughts that had been on a steady increase for the past week, ever since the boys had landed.

"Are you sure you're okay? You still haven't told me what happened." She took a swig from the bottle, the classy girls that we were.

I picked a leaf off a branch and started rolling it between my fingers as a distraction. Where to start with this conversation.

"Fred?"

"Yes?"

"Tell me."

I scratched my nails across my scalp. "Do you remember when we were doing finals and there was that massive storm that wiped out all the electricity? And I had a full melt down that ended up in you taking me to hospital because I couldn't breathe?"

Her eyes widened. "Yes."

"Well, it wasn't as bad as that." I smirked taking the bottle from her.

"Oh god, idiot." She pushed me into a hedge, making me laugh. "But were you okay? I was worried when you didn't answer your phone, but Cooper told Jas you were okay."

"Yeah, it wasn't pretty but I was okay. Actually, I haven't had a melt down like that in years."

I'd thought a lot about it and decided it was down to stress. Stress of all the change happening.

Of Wolfie leaving.

Of Cooper arriving.

Of not knowing.

He had me feeling completely out of control. Which was ironic, seeing as he liked to take it all anyway.

"And it was just you and Cooper?"

I nodded, biting the inside of my mouth.

"Oh god, I bet he didn't know what to do."

"Well, he did actually."

She looked at me, her eyebrow raised in question. I blew out my cheeks, knowing now was the time. I couldn't get away with not telling her anymore, especially as I was sure Jasper knew.

"In a nutshell, he found me in bed and couldn't stop me crying. So he took me into the shower and sat with me for two hours so I couldn't hear the rain or the thunder, then he made me mac and cheese, and we watched movies."

"Cooper?" She clarified, picking up William's stick again. Rookie had arrived to join in the throwing game.

"Yeah."

"Holy shit."

"I know."

I looked into the field, watching the dogs try to find the stick we'd thrown.

"Spit it out." She turned towards me and I could sense her staring. "I know there's more to this."

I squeezed my eyes shut, about to admit to her something I'd been terrified of admitting to myself.

Of saying out loud.

But I was certain.

"I think I'm falling in love with him."

She gave a gasp, almost choking on the air she'd inhaled.

Which was quickly replaced by a shit eating grin spreading across her face, mainly because she'd thought been right.

I nudged her, hard. "Oh shut up. And don't say anything to Molly."

"I won't, but think you best start from the beginning."

I told her everything, starting at Stuart and finishing with the fact that we hadn't spent a night apart this week. That he had so many sides of his personality and I couldn't decide which one I liked best.

The dominant Cooper who owned my body and made me beg for more until my voice was hoarse and my throat sore.

Or the fun, teasing Cooper who made me laugh more than any man I'd ever met, the one who pulled me from my bad mood and deflected any crap I gave him, who matched my temper and didn't back down when any man before had.

Or the Cooper who'd held me as I sobbed and shook, who'd protected me from my own spiralling thoughts and grounded me against my demons. It was something no other man beside my brothers or my dad had ever done or seen before.

And he'd taken it all in his stride.

Like no other man.

Wolfie was still staring at me, unblinking.

"Are you going to say something?" I asked.

"I'm kind of speechless."

"I'm sorry I didn't tell you sooner, there's been a lot going on this week."

She pulled me into a hug. "You don't have to apologise, I could see something happening but figured you'd tell me when you were ready. I was not expecting this though."

Yeah, you and me both.

"I know, it's a lot."

She thought for a second. "Does Jas know?"

I shrugged. "I don't know, wouldn't he have told you if he did?"

"Not if Cooper had sworn him to secrecy. Although he's terrible at keeping secrets from me, so I'm not sure. What's the sex like?"

I tilted my head at her, pursing my lips.

"Oh come on, you have to give me something. All I've talked about all week is the wedding." She whined.

I couldn't hold back the smile that threatened to burst out as a visual of Cooper's naked body invaded my brain.

"It's intense, the best I've ever had. Like he knows what my body wants better than I do. And he's a machine. Look at this." I pulled my t-shirt up over my bra. His personal branding was still very visible even after four days of fading.

"Fucking hell! Oh god, that's so sexy." She shrieked before her eyes darkened. "Although I'll murder him if you can see it in your dress."

"You'd need to get in line behind me. You can't though, I've checked." I tucked my shirt back in the waist band of my shorts.

"Well, fuck."

"I know."

We started walking again. Rookie had joined us, bored of the stick game.

"What are you going to do? The boys leave in a few days."

"I don't know, we haven't even talked about it. It's like we've been in a bubble. We said we would, but we haven't yet."

We'd agreed this was more than sex between us. It definitely was for me and he'd said it was for him too, but there would soon be an ocean between us. I pushed away the niggling feeling which surfaced every time I thought about him leaving.

"What do you want to do?"

My face scrunched. "I'm not sure what I can do."

"You can work anywhere, you don't need to be based in London."

"I know."

"So move over."

"Wolf..." I rolled my eyes at her. She'd conveniently forgotten the meltdown she'd had when her and Jasper had been trying to figure out their relationship and being apart.

"What's he like with you?"

"What do you mean?"

"Like, when you're together, what's he like. Is he tactile? How do you think he feels?"

I thought about it for a moment.

"It's like he's going to die if he can't touch me. It doesn't matter what mood he's in, he has to be touching some part of me. And even when we're all together as a group if he's not next to me I can feel his eyes on me."

She stopped us walking, her expression serious.

"Fred, I've never seen Cooper with another woman, I've never even heard him speak about one. He's always at ours and I heard Felix grumbling to Drew a few weeks ago that even when Cooper goes out with them it's like he's not present."

"What does that mean?"

"I don't know, but do you think he feels the same way you do? You've always had the chemistry, this has been a long time coming. Even from the first day you met, remember at the pool?"

I thought back to my first trip to New York, when Wolfie was living there. We'd watched their game on the TV and he'd been sent off. The camera had panned in on his face, he'd been so angry and intense, the muscle along his chiselled jaw visibly twitching. I remember being drawn to him even then, wondering what sex would be like.

The next day I'd met him in person at a pool party, which

remains one of the only times in my life I'd been lost for words. My power of speech stolen by his beauty.

However, there were always too many bunnies, clinging on for his attention. So while we might have always had a connection, I hadn't wanted to acknowledge it.

Until this week, when it had been unavoidable.

"Do you think? Murray said something similar."

She pulled a face, looking pissed off. "Murray knows?"

"Not really, he knows about the Stuart incident because I was in a bit of a spin after that happened and I came down here to get some space. But I haven't spoken to him about anything else. He just reminded me about New Year last year."

"Oh yes, he went mental at that guy."

"He really doesn't like men near me. He's kind of possessive. Actually, not kind of. Very. He said that he didn't care if people saw this," I waved at my chest, "because then he wouldn't have to explain to everyone that I was his."

"Fuck." Her eyes widened. "Maybe there's your answer then. If he didn't feel the same then he wouldn't care who you spoke to."

"Maybe."

I was still not quite convinced.

Rookie started barking and we turned to look at what. The air caught in my throat.

Jasper and Cooper were walking towards us.

It didn't matter how many times I saw him he still absolutely took my breath away.

While Jasper was perhaps an inch taller at the most, Cooper seemed wider, his muscles straining against his soft, white t-shirt, his shorts hanging low on his hips.

My body pulled towards his as though he was my own personal magnet and I could feel the familiar warmth running through me, ending deep inside my thighs, my knickers damp. It had become the norm whenever I was around him, my blood on simmer. My arousal bubbling like lava, never far from the surface.

"Fuck, they look so good." Wolfie whispered under her breath so only I could hear.

A noise that sounded a lot like "hmmmmmm" escaped me in agreement.

"There she is." Jasper pulled Wolfie into his arms, kissing her. "In twenty-four hours you'll be my wife."

Their goofy grins mirrored each other and I glanced at Cooper from the corner of my eye. But he was also looking at them, his expression unreadable.

I clenched my fists to compress the itch to touched him.

"What are you guys doing here?" Wolfie pulled her mouth away from Jasper, the rest of their bodies still pressed together.

"We saw your moms." Answered Cooper with a grin.

She slapped her hand to her head. "What's the issue now?"

"Nothing, everything is perfect. Come on, let's go back and talk to them." Jasper kissed her again before picking up the now empty bottle of wine hanging from her fingertips.

"What time is everyone coming over?" Cooper was looking at me, his eyes mischievous.

Our parents were hosting a pre-wedding family and friends barbecue later this afternoon and the gang would be arriving shortly.

"In a couple of hours." I replied.

He turned to Wolfie and Jasper. "You two go ahead, we'll catch you up." He took my hand in his. "Can you take the dogs?"

I watched Jasper and Wolfie smirk to each other. Yeah, Jas knew and I briefly wondered what Cooper had said and how he'd said it.

I'd get it out of Wolfie later.

"Yeah, sure Man. See you in what? Five minutes?" He laughed out loud.

"Fuck off." He gave me a slow once over that made heat curl down my spine. "Make it two hours."

"Yeah, right." Cooper looked at his watch. "You have ninety seven minutes." He put his arm around Wolfie. "Come on, Cub. Let's leave these two to…" He grinned. "Sorry, what was it you needed to do?"

Cooper stared at him, not taking the bait.

"Jas, stop being a dick." Wolfie dragged him away. "See you guys in ninety seven minutes."

"I'll show you a dick." I heard him say to her before they were out of ear shot.

I looked at Cooper. "So, they know."

"I don't care." He grinned. "Hello."

"Hello." I grinned back, licking my lips in anticipation as his arms wrapped around my waist, pulling me in.

His lips descended on mine, his tongue gliding through my mouth staking a warm, wet claim, like he did every time we kissed. Hungrily stroking against me, it sent an explosion of shivers straight through from my toes to my brain, freezing it in the way a scoop of Ben and Jerry's would, but way more delicious.

I could feel him getting hard.

"Come on." He sucked on my bottom lip, bringing me with him as he moved back. He took my hand, pulling me away towards the forest.

"Where are going?"

"The nearest surface I can fuck you against." He growled in my ear.

And a fresh flood of wetness hit my knickers as though his voice had a direct line to my vagina.

Ding Ding Ding.

We kept going until we reached a small clearing where he pushed me against the trunk of a tree and stood back, studying me, his tongue running along his lip. "Those shorts are obscene."

They really weren't but if it meant he looked at me like he was about to eat me, I didn't care what he said about them.

Please eat me.

"Really? These? Maybe I should take them off." I started to unbutton them.

His eyes flared as he watched me very slowly pull the buttons apart, the twitch in his jaw moving double time as he ground his teeth in frustration.

"Stop." He ordered. "I'm doing it. You're too fucking slow."

I hid a smirk as he fell to his knees. Ripping my shorts open, he yanked them down along with my knickers.

"There you are." He jerked my legs apart and buried his nose against my groin, inhaling deeply.

Holy shit.

I definitely shouldn't have been as turned on as I was.

He was absolutely outrageous.

Lifting my leg over his shoulder, he cupped my ass, squeezing it hard as he pulled me against his face. He ran his thumb through my folds, circling my clit, rubbing my juices everywhere. It was almost embarrassing how wet he made me.

"Jesus Fuuck." My eyes rolled back in my head the second his tongue flicked against me, before he took a long, hard lap.

And then another.

And another.

I could feel myself getting addicted to his tongue.

Maybe I already was.

"You. Taste. So. Fucking. Perfect." He punctuated each word with a flick and by the end of his sentence I was doubled over as he started stabbing inside me.

My legs were shaking.

The pressure of an impending orgasm began building in the base of my spine, until a blast of air hit me as he pulled away leaving me crying out for the friction.

"Watch me." His caramel eyes burned with desire as I looked down.

He pushed two fingers inside me, before adding another twisting it and curling it up against my G-spot. My head fell back as I grabbed a handful of his hair, trying to push myself onto him.

"Francesca, open your fucking eyes. I want you to watch me make you come in my mouth." His pink tongue darted out and flicked against me, making my entire body throb in desperation for release. My hips started grinding against his face in rhythm with his fingers. My breath coming in bursts. I could barely hold myself up as he continued teasing, edging me closer. Knowing full well he wasn't giving me the exact pressure I needed.

"Please…" I begged although it was more of a groan than a word.

"How badly do you need it?"

"So badly." I gasped.

He gripped my hip and trapping my clit between his teeth sucked so hard it felt like I'd been ripped in two as my orgasm tore through me, making my knees buckle. He held onto me, keeping me standing, and he lapped me up while wave upon wave crashed onto his tongue.

"Hold on tight, Baby." And in one smooth motion he stood up, lifting me with an arm under my ass while the other undid his shorts, setting his perfect dick free.

I wrapped my legs around his waist as he held onto my hips, ramming me down onto his thick cock and sliding into me in one long thrust. Even with how drenched I was I could never get over the sting of the first time he entered me, feeling him inside me, filling me up.

"How do you feel so fucking good all the time? So tight." He moaned into my neck, pushing me against the tree, the rough bark biting into me under my t-shirt.

I scraped my nails through his hair, pulling his head back and bringing his mouth to mine.

I could taste myself on his tongue as I roughly plunged inside him, wanting more. Wanting to devour him so badly, it was primal.

Because I starved for his touch the second he let go of me.

He nipped my lips as a groan escaped him, so guttural that it sparked the fuse burning though me. I clung onto his shoulders, running my hands across his giant biceps as his grip on my hips tightened.

"Lift your shirt up, I need skin." He ordered as he pulled almost all the way out of me, frantic to feel my touch but his need to control my hips winning.

I freed my boobs, watching his eyes widen as he drove back into me at the same time as taking a nipple between his teeth and biting down. A low groan travelled straight up from my clit.

"Fuck yes." He breathed into my other nipple as his pace increased.

My first orgasm never had the chance to properly subside and I could feel it still fluttering through, building to the next one. His hips started pistoning into me with brutality, fucking me so hard his cock swelled more with every thrust.

He was as close to exploding as I was.

"Mouth." He growled and I fell onto his lips, his tongue ravaging me in desperation.

I swallowed his panting.

"Tiny. Fuck. You have to come, I can't hold it."

His words were my undoing and I shattered around him, sending him into a spiral of his own surrender. I could feel him quivering and pulsing inside me as he slowed his thrusts, holding me up as I collapsed against him. Aftershocks ran through me as our breathlessness subsided, oxygen replenishing our lungs.

Both sweaty from exertion, I clung onto his shoulders

pressing my face into his neck, soaking him up, inhaling his musk.

I never wanted to leave.

It would never be better than this.

I could hear him softly humming into my skin before a deep sigh escaped as he squeezed me harder.

"Baby, I need to put you down." He lifted my hips up, breaking our connection, and took a long lingering breath against my lips as he placed me on the mossy floor.

He picked my shorts up off the ground and held them out for me. I stepped into them and he pulled them up, leaving me to button them as he put his own on.

I could feel his thick cum leaking into my knickers.

"By the way, you're not wearing those shorts to the barbecue later." He looked at me, daring me to challenge him.

But I was never going to be wearing these anyway, so I let him think he'd won which I would use for points later.

Cunning like a fox.

"Okay baby, I won't if you'd rather I didn't." I smiled at him.

He narrowed his eyes and scrunched his nose. "You weren't going to wear them anyway, were you?"

Bollocks.

"I hadn't decided." I glared at him.

"Good job I decided for you then, isn't it?" He chuckled, knowing he'd caught me in a lie.

He checked his watch. "Well would you look at that, fifty three minutes."

He pulled me into his arms, bringing his forehead to mine, and I giggled, because that's who I was now.

He brushed a piece of hair away from my face tucking it behind my ear and kissed me on the nose.

"Can't say I've ever had woodland sex before, but I think I'm a big fan. And it was definitely needed to get me through tonight."

I frowned. "You love a barbecue."

"I do. But when it's taking me out of our bubble, I'm less keen." He sulked, pouting his bottom lip.

Who was this guy?

"Come on, cutie." I took his hand and led him back towards the house.

19

FREDDIE

The barbecue was in full swing. Drew and Dante had already taken over, arguing about who was king.

I was sitting at a table with most of the girls - Molly, Amy and Sophie. Olivia having slunk off somewhere with Brogan. Across the garden I could see Wolf and Jasper deep in conversation with our mothers, something I did not want to get anywhere near.

In the distance, every so often, I could hear the knocking of a cricket ball against a bat followed by a lot of shouting. Murray had taken the boys into the field, teaching them how to play, although I wasn't optimistic of the outcome.

After taking themselves on a full tour of the garden area and scoping out the options, the dogs were sitting underneath my feet, having put themselves in prime position for any dropped food.

"Those two might be king of the barbecue but they're the worst at the service." Sophie looked over at the boys, her hanger making an appearance. "I've barely eaten all week and I'm famished."

"I think that's the secret. Everyone's starving by the time they get the food that it tastes amazing. I'm going to get us some snacks before my stomach starts eating itself." Amy stood up and walked away.

I topped up everyone's glasses with the last of the champagne on our table. "She has a point. Also, I'm going to be too drunk to eat soon."

Molly rested her chin in her hands, her elbows bent on the table, looking wistful. "I can't believe Wolf and Jasper are getting married tomorrow."

Sophie nodded. "I know, it feels like only yesterday when she called to tell us she'd bumped into a giant, god like man who spilt coffee all over her."

"Yeah, hot coffee guy." I snorted.

Amy returned with crudites, placing them on the table, before the World's Slowest Barbecue made an appearance. We dived in, munching carrot sticks and hummus in silence.

I could sense his presence before I saw him.

His body a tractor beam for mine.

I looked up to see him walking through the garden gate, Murray's arm around his shoulder laughing at something undoubtedly stupid.

He glanced my way our eyes locking and the grin fell off his face, instantly turning dark and predatory. As a dropped match would follow a trail of gasoline, the burning from the fingerprints he'd left on my hips ignited and travelled straight to my groin.

I turned back to the girls.

Sipping from my glass, quenching my suddenly parched mouth, I tried to distract myself from the near incessant need I had to throw myself at him and fuck him on the closest surface whether it was available or not. As though it had been days, not hours since he was last inside me.

"I'll tell you," Carter pulled me out of my daydream and flopped into the chair opposite, "I am both a professional athlete and an intelligent man, but cricket? No."

Sophie smirked. "Take it you didn't win then?"

"There were no winners or losers in this game." He replied in a huff.

"So you lost?" I asked.

"He sure did." Laughed Murray as the rest of them walked over. "Hey, we need drinks."

"I've got them." Felix arrived with a few more bottles of champagne and started filling everyone's glasses.

"No thanks. I don't want to be hungover tomorrow." Molly covered her glass with her hand.

"Mol, that's exactly how you're supposed to turn up to a wedding." He sat down next to her, putting his arm around the back of her chair.

She pulled a face, making him laugh.

The chair next to me moved.

"That's my seat." Cooper shoved Huck out of the way and sat down. He lowered his voice. "Hi Tiny. Fancy seeing you here. Nice dress, although I'm not sure it's really any more appropriate than those fucking shorts. You are a god damn minx."

His fingers grazed along my thigh, bunching the silk in his fist and a flush ran over me. I'd changed out of my shorts and put on a high necked, long dress. High necks being all I could manage this week. So, I'd deliberately worn something cut low on the back, as well as the side to purposely drive him crazy knowing he'd want to touch the patch of skin by my breasts.

"Final night as a single man, Jas." Felix called to Jasper and Wolfie walking over, holding hands. "Not too late to back out, you know. Wolf, sure you wouldn't rather marry me?"

"Watch it." Jasper slapped him on the back, as he reached over and poured two glasses, handing one to Wolf. "You know you're only here because Wolfie needed a clown to watch the kids tomorrow."

I turned to her. "Hey, did you sort everything out?"

She sat down next to me. "Yeah, they can have what they

want. I just want to marry Jas, I don't care about anything else."

"Oi! You better bloody care about the reception. I've slogged my guts out for that."

And it was looking fucking epic if I did say so myself.

I'd gone back over to see the team after Cooper and I walked home, although I'd banned him from coming with me after last time. There had still been jobs to finish.

She tipped her head. "Obviously, apart from that."

I felt a movement in my lap and looked down to find Cooper's hand resting near the top of my thigh. He was facing in the other direction, talking to the boys at the other end of the table.

Turning back to Wolfie, her eyebrows were raised and her lips rolled in silent response to our earlier conversation.

"Food's ready." Drew yelled from the buffet table, his arms outstretched. "King of the Barbecue once more."

"Finally." Sophie was the first up returning with a plateful, although no carbs seeing as we all had to squeeze into very unforgiving dresses tomorrow.

The rest of us swiftly followed suit, tucking in. I had to hand it to them, the boys knew how to cook.

Drew leaned back in his chair. "What have you girls got planned for tonight?"

"Massages." Replied Olivia, who'd returned with Brogan, a rosy tint in her cheeks.

"You already look pretty relaxed to me." Felix eyed her, earning himself a slap around the head from Jasper.

"What are you guys doing?" I asked.

"Drinking." He downed his beer.

No big surprise there then.

"You know Felix, one of these days I'll see you without a hangover and won't recognise you." Molly drolled.

"Maybe, Mol. But my charm ain't going anywhere. And if I'm this pretty now, you won't be able to keep your hands off me when I'm really giving it one hundred percent. I mean, I know it's hard for you already."

"It's really not." She shot back.

Huck picked up another burger, biting into it. "Relax, we're in the English countryside. It'll be an early night."

I watched a sly grin peak the corner of Murray's mouth. "Yeah, you say that but Coop was offered a threesome in the pub the other day."

"What?!" Molly, Wolfie and I all screeched at the same time.

Cooper dropped his head, shaking it, narrowing his eyes at Murray who was still grinning.

"Yeah, they were gagging for it." He was such a fucking shit stirrer.

"Fuck seriously? What happened?" Dante asked.

"We were having a pint. They came up to our table and said they knew he was in town for the wedding and they'd be 'happy to show him around and help him with anything he needed'." He air quoted, his grin still steadfast.

"Brilliant."

"I know."

"Oh Murray, shut the fuck up." I shouted at him.

"Gross, who does that?" Wolfie's indignation was admirable considering Jasper hadn't exactly been a wall-flower before they'd met.

I felt his hand sneak back into my lap, trying to provide some reassurance. He dropped his voice. "Tiny, it was nothing. I didn't even speak to them."

"Okay." There wasn't anything else to say, but that.

I willed away the nausea now sitting in the pit of my stomach. Hating it.

My blue eyes had turned green.

"Okay, Wolf Cub. I'll see you at the end of the aisle. Don't be late okay." I heard Jasper say as I walked past them towards the house.

It was time to go separate ways for the night.

We were heading back to the country hotel the entire wedding party had been booked into. I had no idea what the boys were planning for Jasper, but given what I'd heard out of Vegas I imagined him to be in bed by ten pm. With any luck Cooper would be too, well out of the way of any tempting offers and skanky girls.

A hand wrapped around my wrist and pulled me to the side of the house.

Strong arms snaked around my waist, soft lips descended onto mine, catching my mouth in his. The faint taste of beer was on the tip of his tongue as he ran it against mine, sucking on it, taking it with him before moving to his next target.

His fingers travelled up my ribcage, his thumbs burrowing under the fabrics and brushing my nipples.

The touch of his skin scorching me like a brushfire.

His lips trailed along my collarbone, nibbling my pulse point, moving up before unleashing an assault back on my mouth that made my knees so weak he had to hold me up.

He pulled away, a chuckle rising up his throat before looking up at me with serious eyes.

"I know a much better form of relaxation than that massage you're about to go for."

I lifted an eyebrow. "You do?"

"Yes I fucking do." He growled into my neck, pressing his whole body against me, his cock hard and leaving little to my imagination.

The heavy feeling I'd been carrying lightened. He sighed against me and lifted his head.

"I'm sorry about what Murray said. Please don't be mad at me."

"I'm not, really."

He gave a half smile. "Because you know you're the only one my dick gets hard for."

"Wow, that's the most romantic thing you've ever said to me." My eyes rolled as my hands moved around his neck.

"What can I say, it's what the ladies want. Now, kiss me please before I have to go a whole night without you. Something I'm not too happy about by the way."

He grabbed the back of my head, his mouth capturing mine once more.

20

COOPER

S leep wasn't happening.

The full moon was shining through the window, lighting up the room as bright as day. This was the first night in a week I hadn't gone to sleep with Freddie beside me and my bed felt very empty. I'd slept alone for thirteen years and now after a week of being with her I was wide awake because she wasn't curled into my side.

Fuck this.

I got up and flung some shorts on, grabbing her spare key card from the bedside table. Five minutes later I let myself into her room. She was fast asleep on her front, arms above her head. The covers had slipped all the way down her naked body, resting on an ass more round and juicy than any peach. I slid in next to her, pulling her into my chest, her breathing settling me as I followed her into sleep.

It was barely light when I woke her up, my head between her legs lapping at her, pushing my tongue inside her velvety warmth.

I'd never tasted anything so perfect.

Drinking down her intoxicating nectar I listened to her soft, sleepy mewing consume me. But who was I kidding, she been consuming me for the past seven days, wrapping around me like ivy, crushing my lungs until I couldn't breathe.

The only reprieve I had was when she was close by.

My head was a fucking mess.

Her back arched as she came in my mouth, her body relaxing further, falling back into the sleep it hadn't fully emerged from. I was so fucking hard that my entire body ached as though I'd just gone twelve rounds.

I was shaking with desperation to be inside her.

Reeking of it.

Instead, I got up and dressed.

"See you later, Baby." She barely stirred as I brushed my lips against hers and walked out of the door without looking back.

Knowing that the second my dick slid into her tight, wet pussy I'd have stayed there all day and fought off anyone who tried to tell me I couldn't.

I didn't recognise the person staring back at me when I caught sight of myself in the mirror as I arrived at my room.

I didn't know who I'd become.

21

COOPER

J asper opened the door, a t-shirt covering his junk, sweat running down him. We were t-minus three hours and twenty-seven minutes.

"Dude, I could have been anyone." I closed the door behind me as he walked off.

"You could, but I knew it was you. There's a peep hole." He swapped his shirt for a robe.

"Fair point." I fell back on the sofa. "How're you doing? Did you go for a run? I would have come."

"I couldn't sleep so went out early. But I'm good, yeah, I'm okay." He scratched the stubble on his chin, which he'd be shaving off very soon.

I stood back up, taking two glasses from the bar. "Really? Because you look like you're about to take the deciding penalty for the cup final."

It was a special day and special days needed to start with a special drink. Opening the box of Louis XIII cognac I'd brought with me I removed the stopper and poured it out, handing one to Jas.

"Thanks man."

We sipped in silent reverence.

"This is good stuff." He tipped his glass and looked at it.

"I know."

Only the birds in the trees were making noise right now. I thought about Freddie, knowing how much she hated them waking her up. She was not a morning person. I wondered what she was doing right now.

No prizes for guessing she was with Wolfie.

"Fuck Dude, you're getting married."

"Yeah." He was still staring at his glass.

"Have you spoken to Wolf this morning."

His whole face lit up. "Briefly, but she had to go, too many people turned up to dress her or whatever."

"Man, why do girls need so much and take so long?"

"Beats me. I'd be happy marrying her in sweats."

"Yeah." Freddie was always most beautiful first thing in the morning. Or when she'd just stepped out of the shower.

I checked my watch. "So, we have at least two hours before your hair and make up arrives. Come on, let's get out of here for a bit."

There was a loud bang at the door, followed by another one, as though someone was throwing themselves at it.

"Let us in." I could hear Drew's muffled yelling from across the room.

"We should have left earlier." I shook my head, opening the door just as Felix launched himself at it and missed, falling forward and landing on the floor.

The rest of them piled in, stepping over him before he had a chance to pick himself up.

Tate walked over to Jas, hugging him. "Big day, man. You feeling okay?"

"I'm good."

I looked at Jasper, he appeared a little grey around the edges. His nerves were definitely starting to show.

We needed to distract him.

Carter picked up the cognac and sniffed it. "Coop, did

you bring this?"

"Yeah. Pour it out." I passed him the glasses from the drinks' cabinet.

Drew flopped down in pole position on the sofa, taking a drink from Carter handing them out. I sat on the arm as everyone else took theirs.

"This is good stuff." He echoed Jasper's earlier comment. "Where did you get it?"

"I was shopping with Freddie this week and found it."

He tilted his head. "What's going on with her?"

I didn't have the time nor the inclination to unpack that question, so I ignored him and turned to the group.

"Okay team, listen up. Today is a big day for all of us. As big as the Cup Final. The day we let our Captain fly free and he finally becomes a man."

Jasper rolled his eyes as everyone else sniggered.

"And while he might be the one getting married, we're still a unit and we're all responsible for getting him down the aisle. So, we have two hours to fill before we need to get dressed and look pretty."

"I vote mini golf." Shouted Dante.

"Dude, why are you shouting?" Drew lifted his head and looked at him.

He shrugged back.

"Nah, I'm not playing mini golf." Jasper walked back into the room, changed out of his bathrobe and into sweatpants. "You can go, but I'm going to stay here."

"I'm happy here too, we have to be at the church before you guys. Plus, I need to rest myself for this evening." Felix put his arms behind his head as he got comfy on the other sofa. "In fact, check the drawers under the tv." He nodded towards it. "Mine had an Xbox. Let's fire it up."

I opened the drawer and pulled it out. "Bingo. Okay who's playing this, who's going for golf?"

Five minutes later only Felix, Drew, Jas, Tate and I

remained. I found it weird that grown men who didn't play fully sized golf on any given day, considered knocking a ball through a windmill an acceptable way to spend time.

"Okay. Usual teams. Me, Jas against you two. Tate can pick the team he's on, but we all know he'll choose ours. Best of five." I said, as Tate topped up our glasses.

"You're on."

Our team won, like there was any doubt. In eight years of playing against them, Felix and Drew were yet to beat us.

We all walked towards the door ready to get the show on the road.

I slapped Jasper's face. "See you in an hour. I'll try and make sure I don't look prettier than you."

We arrived at the church on schedule, exactly fifty minutes before Wolfie was due to make her entrance. Jasper had been getting quieter by the second.

Felix, Drew and Tate had already started handing out wedding programmes to the guests who'd arrived, while Murray and Jamie were showing people to their seats. There were a lot of hats.

Bram, Jasper's dad, came over to the car as we got out and pulled him into a hug before handing us both a mini flower arrangement for our buttonhole. A white one for Jasper, a green one for me, matching the rest of the boys in our navy suits.

He fixed Jasper's flower for him. "How're you doing, buddy?"

"I'm good. Good." Which was pretty much all he'd said since we'd got dressed.

I spun him to face me, holding the back of his neck. He was as pale and as nervous as he'd been before our first ever game. "Jas. Look at me. Do you need to puke?"

He shook his head.

"Then take a deep breath. It's all good, she'll be here bang on time and you'll get married, then have a perfect life and loads of babies. Okay." I reached into my pocket and handed him the hip flask I'd filled. "Here."

"Thanks man. I appreciate it, you're the best." He squeezed me into a hug, before taking the flask and a giant glug.

I took it back before he ended up getting married while wasted, something Wolfie would have my balls for. "You know it. Come on, we need to get inside. Wolfie said you're supposed to mingle."

He glared at me. "Fucking mingle."

"I know, Dude. I know." I slapped him on the back and we walked towards the church.

As two of the more prominent players in the NHL, with thousands of meet and greets under our belts from over a decade of being at the top of our game, a simple 'hello' to the congregation shouldn't have been an issue. But we soon learnt a wedding meet and greet was a whole different ball game.

One no one had warned us about.

Sexual harassment by elderly relatives should be a thing, because I'd definitely been felt up by more than one old lady. Along with a handful of phone numbers I'd been slipped, which I needed to bin before Freddie found them.

I checked my watch, we had ten minutes to go.

I leaned into him, interrupting his chat with another person he'd never met. "Jas, we should get up there."

"Yeah, okay. Let's go." He thumbed to the alter. "It was great to meet you, enjoy the day."

We walked away.

"Fuck me." He mumbled.

Jasper and I stood at the front of the church, nervous excitement passing between us as we counted down the minutes. And on the stroke of one, music started up announcing the arrival of the bride. I knew Wolfie wouldn't be late.

I squeezed his shoulder. "It's show time, buddy."

The page boys and flower girls appeared at the doorway holding hands, to a collective 'Ahhhhh' they started walking slowly down the aisle.

Suddenly my palms were clammy as it dawned on me I was about to see Freddie for the first time since I'd left her sleeping. My heart began beating out of my chest as I waited for her turn to arrive at the door, my neck straining for a peak. Amy came down first, followed by Sophie and Olivia.

Then there she was.

My mouth went dry and my breath caught, which was appropriate as she looked absolutely breathtaking. She was wearing a long, silk dress of navy blue which hugged every lethal curve of her body, curves I longed to touch.

Ached to touch.

I could feel my need for her pooling in the base of my spine, suppressing a grin as I took in her high neckline, knowing exactly what was underneath.

Mine.

As she neared the alter our eyes locked, the navy turning her icy blues even bluer, heat radiating through us. Then she winked and all my blood rushed straight to my groin.

Was it illegal to get hard in a church?

I heard Jasper sniff.

I'd been so engrossed I hadn't even noticed Wolfie walking towards us. Just as I had been desperate to get to Freddie, Jasper couldn't wait any longer and marched towards Wolf who was still only half way down the aisle. She had the biggest grin on her face as she brushed away one of Jasper's tears, laughing as she took his hand and they walked back to the alter together. She handed her flowers off to Freddie, who stepped back next to the rest of the girls.

I'd like to say I took in everything the vicar said, listened attentively to the vows and performed my duties as best man and keeper of the rings with aplomb.

But it would be a lie.

I paid zero attention to anything except Freddie. Like memorising a play before a game, I memorised every inch of her.

The way a strand of hair had come loose from the twisty thing at the base of her slender neck, my fingers itched to run it through them before tucking it back behind her ear.

The way the pout of her lips deepened as she sung the hymns. Lips I wanted to taste on mine, to watch as they wrapped around my cock until I hit the back of her throat.

The way her dressed pulled against her exquisite body as she swept it away every time she sat down.

The way she wiped away her tears, just as I'd done when she'd sobbed and shook in my arms.

She was so beautiful it hurt to look at her.

My daydream was rudely snatched away from me by a loud cheer erupting throughout the church as Jasper and Wolfie were officially pronounced husband and wife. The music started up and they made their way out into the warm sunshine.

Finding myself next to Freddie as we walked behind the happy couple I reached down entwining her fingers with mine, unable to keep my hands to myself any longer.

I dragged her away to the side, the second we exited the church. "Come here."

I didn't care who was watching as I cupped her face. I restrained myself from pulling her hair back and plunging my tongue into her, no matter how much I craved to.

Instead I gently kissed her perfect mouth, careful not to spoil her make up, before tucking the loose strand of hair behind her ear, knowing it wouldn't stay. But I didn't care, I would do it all day.

"Hi." I smirked, staring at her. "You look absolutely phenomenal. I held myself back for as long as I could."

I watched her blush as a smile peaked out. "Thank you."

"Oh baby, don't thank me. Tonight you're going to get absolutely ruined." I promised, making her grin. The minx I knew so well replacing the coy bridesmaid she'd been a moment ago.

I held my hand out and she took it. "Now come on, let's go and resume our duties before I drag you off for the rest of the day."

We walked back towards the party our fingers still linked together. She tried to take her hand away but I held fast.

"Nope. Everyone is going to know you're mine today." I expected an argument and got nothing.

She looked up, batting her long, thick lashes. "Best kiss me again then, so I don't forget."

Fuck me.

I touched my lips to hers just as we arrived at our little group, amongst the throng of wedding guests milling in the churchyard. Felix was staring at me, so I kissed him too. Just because I knew how much it would piss him off.

"Who the fuck are you and what have you done with the grumpy shit I play hockey with." He grumbled wiping my kiss off his mouth. "Although I see he's finally grown a pair of balls."

I booped him on the nose. "Clevs man, we're at a wedding. I'm all about the love today."

"Seriously. Cut it the fuck out." He swatted at my hand as our attention was drawn away by a man clapping very loudly, while holding a clipboard under his arm. I heard my name being called.

"What's all this?" I muttered.

"Photo time."

I groaned. This was as bad as the church meet and greets.

I looked around for Freddie, she'd wandered over to Wolf

and the rest of the girls as they hugged jumping up and down, happiness beaming out of her like sunshine.

I was wrong, this wasn't so bad.

An hour and twenty minutes and three photography locations later we finally had drinks in hands, standing near the barn. A band was playing as larger than bite sized appetizers were offered around, Jasper's single contribution to the wedding planning. I searched around looking for Freddie, but I'd lost her to the girls.

"How are you feeling about the speech?" Felix pulled my attention back.

"Good, it's going to kill."

He grinned. "Have you put props in like I told you to?"

God, he was a dick head.

I silenced him with a look while he stuffed a slider into his mouth as Drew walked over, halting the waitress in her tracks relieving her of the entire board.

I took one from him.

Felix stole three bottles of beer from a passing tray, handing them to us. "Where've you been?"

Drew brought the drink to his lips. "I went to look in the barn and check out the seating plan. It's so good in there. Have you seen it? It looks like a sparkly forest."

"Yeah, I came on Monday but haven't seen it since."

Fuck. Was that really only five days ago? It seemed like forever.

He raised his eyebrows. "Freddie did the whole thing?"

I nodded at him.

"She's awesome. I asked her to do my house."

An internal conflict was waging battle between trying to suppress a smile at how hard she'd worked and how proud of her I was, and absolutely not wanting her anywhere near Drew and his house.

"What's wrong with you, you look constipated."

"Nothing." I sipped my beer.

Felix rolled his eyes. "You're such a dick. I saw you kissing her."

"You kissed?" Drew's face lit up in amusement.

"Yeah and they were holding hands after they emerged from the side of the church, looking a little rumpled."

"We did not look fucking rumpled. I barely touched her." He smirked at me like he'd caught me in a lie. "What? I'm not denying anything."

"So, what's going on?" They asked in unison.

I shrugged. "I don't know." I took another slider off Drew's platter putting the whole thing in my mouth to buy me some time while they stared at me.

"Coop, come on. You like her right?"

"What do you think?"

They continued grinning at me as I frowned.

Huck and Dante walked over with Carter, followed by Brogan, Olivia and Freddie who I pulled over to stand next to me, brushing my fingertips against her palm. I looked down and winked.

As we turned back to the group all eyes were on us.

"Why are they staring?" Freddie asked me while she pulled a face at them.

I grinned at them all. "Because they're dicks. Just ignore them like I do."

"Hey! It's the happy couple." Shouted Dante loudly as Jasper and Wolfie join in our little gathering.

He picked Jasper up in a big hug just as Murray and Tate arrived along with several bottles of champagne they'd scored from the bar, popping the corks and filling up glasses for everyone.

"What a fucking awesome day we're having." Tate held his glass high the air. "I fucking love love."

I felt Freddie's hand slip into mine and squeeze it.

I suddenly felt drunk and it wasn't from the champagne.

22

COOPER

"So, on behalf of my wife and I." A huge cheer filled the barn. "We want you to fill your glasses, raid the bar, dance your asses off and live to tell the tale of the best night ever. But before you do, be kind to Coop as he's been working his ass off on this speech. I assure you only the good bits are true." He smirked at me before sitting down, kissing Wolfie one more time.

"Coop, Coop, Coop, Coop, Coop, Coop." The team table chanted as I stood.

Not sure why I expected anything less. Idiots.

I held my hands up until silence filled the room again.

"Thanks Man, I love you buddy." I turned to Jas before facing the crowd. "For those of you who don't know me, my name is Cooper Marks and I'm the best man. And by man, I obviously mean player, something which has been widely written about and acknowledged among sports journalists and hockey fans. Isn't that right, Jas?" I put my hand on his shoulder and he shook his head at me. "Now he wasn't wrong when he said I'd been working my ass off, mostly because anything really good to tell you is under NDA and legally I'm not allowed to discuss it. So, if the lawyers ask, everything you hear tonight is factually correct and all parties involved have agreed to the terms and anything outside of that is alleged and cannot be stated otherwise."

"Wey Hey." Yelled Felix to the room.

A rumble of laughter echoed off the walls.

"But before we begin I have a little gift for you all, to start you on your journey this evening." I nodded to the guy at the back of the room and twenty wait staff walked in each carrying a tray of espresso martinis, which they started handing around.

"In case you don't know the origin of how Wolf and Jasper met, get comfy and settle in for a story."

Time flew by.

I definitely been getting more laughs than I was expecting and without props. Fuck you very much, Felix. I'd also managed to avoid Freddie's gaze up to now, I hadn't wanted to see her and lose my train of thought because that would one hundred percent happen.

"At the beginning of every season, Jas delivers his team speech supposedly for the rookies, but we all know it's really because Clevs needs reminding on a regular basis."

I watched as Drew smacked Felix over the head.

"His one rule, call him before Coach." I nodded over to Coach Campbell who grimaced back at me. "You'd thank us if you knew, Coach. He is an exceptional Captain and this is because he loves his team. He puts us first."

Another massive cheer went up from the table.

"Wolfie hasn't just married Jasper, she's married us too. Jas, if you're half as good a husband as you have been our Captain then Wolfie is one lucky girl and you have this marriage locked down from the start. We all learn from you every day. We thought we knew the meaning of sacrifice but in the past year we've seen how far from the truth that was because every day you work to be the best you can be for us and for Wolfie. And she's taken us all on in her stride. We all hope we're only so lucky to meet someone as perfect for us as Wolf is for you." I finally glanced to where Freddie was sitting, my eyes meeting hers, wet and glistening with emotion, before they darkened as lust blazed through them.

My cock stirred.

I turned back to Jasper. "We're proud of you buddy, we love you." I held my espresso martini up, which I'd not had the chance to drink yet, and waited for everyone else to do the same. "To Jas and Wolf."

It was almost two am with only the hard-core crowd of wedding goers and relatives left on the dance floor. The DJ still going strong, currently playing a remix of Jason Derulo. I knew this because I could see Freddie shouting his name over and over at Wolf. They were on the dancefloor, along with Molly and Drew, all of them jumping up and down.

She was so ridiculous and I couldn't tear my eyes off her.

Her hair had come loose from the twisty thing it had been tied in, falling across her face and I longed to push it back.

I'd barely touched her all night.

She'd spent the evening talking to every single person in the room and I'd left her to it after jealousy had begun creeping through me with each minute I'd had stolen by someone else wanting her attention.

It weighed heavy in my chest and I didn't like it.

I was supposed to be leaving in two days.

I leaned against the bar, my eyes still trained on Freddie. Jasper was next to me, watching Wolfie. The pair of us silent.

The barman placed another round of drinks next to us. I turned to pick one up, my concentration breaking.

"Fucking married, Dude. And this dickhead for a brother in law." I thumbed to Murray who joined us, standing in the middle.

"I think you mean Legend." He downed another espresso martini in one.

I'd lost count after the eighth, the three of us were both wasted and highly alert.

"And don't pretend you don't want to be related to me too." He grinned.

"Nah, I'm not getting married again."

Was I?

"You were married?" Something flashed across his face. At least I think it did, I couldn't be sure given how much we'd drank.

"Briefly. Biggest mistake I ever made." I muttered.

Jesus did these martinis have truth serum in them?

Murray pinned me with a glare I couldn't read. "What happened?"

I shrugged. "Got carried away."

"Fuck Coop! You should join, just fucking look at how lucky I got." Jasper swung his arm around me, we all continued to stare at the dancefloor.

I didn't disagree.

"Anyway." I raised an eyebrow. "What are you even doing here? I thought you'd be off in the bushes somewhere."

"I haven't been with you all night." He winked.

I shook my head, grinning. "And you just left her?"

"Mate, it's still early doors. Gotta build up the anticipation, makes it less vanilla. She'll be gagging for it soon, then I get whatever I want." He was practically leering.

"Christ. Have you been reading The Felix Cleverly Playbook on How to Get Women?" I smirked.

"I have no need for that, my friend." A dark smiled curled up on one side of his lips. If he had a moustache he'd be twisting the ends.

"Speaking of, where is Clevs?"

"He disappeared a while ago with some blonde chick." Drew walked over, taking a drink from the ever-flowing bar. "Yo, your ladies are like the Energiser bunny. I need to lie down."

I dropped my head and smirked, thoughts of a naked Freddie flooding my brain. Christ, I couldn't keep her out.

"Hey, you guys know there's a firepit outside right?" He continued, knocking back a shot.

We all stared at him.

"What? It's really cool. No one's out there."

"Yeah, why not, let's go." Said Murray. "Still got a few hours to kill anyway."

Drew leaned over to the barman. "Hey man, we're gonna take this outside with us. 'Kay?" He picked up the ice trough filled with beer and carried it outside.

We all slumped down on big squashy sofas surrounding the firepit, the flames taking the chill off the midnight air.

In the distance I could see two figures emerge from the field.

"Where is everybody?" Asked Brogan as he and Olivia reached us.

"Mostly left, the girls are still on the dancefloor." Jasper relaxed against the pillows, rolling his sleeves back up.

We'd lost our jackets and ties hours ago.

Murray shifted uncomfortably as Olivia sat down near him, I grinned and smacked him on the arm. "Pussy." I mouthed.

"Fuck off." He muttered at me under his breath.

"Oh my fucking god. Yes." Drew jumped up and we all turned to see him run towards a waiter walking our way with a huge tray of bacon sandwiches.

"This is exactly what I needed." He took it, stuffing a sandwich in his mouth, before placing it down in front of us. We all dived on them.

"Excuse me." Jasper called to the waiter's retreating back. He turned around. "Could you let my wife know we're out here with these?"

"Wife." I smirked.

"I know." He held his left hand up, the ring on his finger shiny and new.

Two silhouettes appeared in the doorway. My breath stuck in my lungs, a reaction I was becoming used to.

"Hello." She slurred as she fell into my lap.

I wrapped my arms around her, running my nose along the column of her neck inhaling her citrussy, woody Freddie scent. She let out a soft moan as she leant back into me, making my dick uncomfortably hard.

"I like being here. You're very comfy." She yawned, her voice dropping low as she fell asleep.

I looked up to find everyone staring and rolled my eyes. "Show's over. Someone pass me a drink."

Drew took a beer out of the trough and handed it to me, smiling as he took a seat next to me.

"Thanks man." I frowned questioning his expression.

"You look good together." He said. "She suits you."

What? Like she was my favourite hoodie?

I peered down at her sleeping softly and brushed her hair away from her face. When I looked back up, Drew was still staring at me.

"What?"

"Nothing, just it's nice, is all."

I didn't disagree.

And found myself smiling too, because it was nice. "What's going on with you? I thought you'd be off with Clevs somewhere."

He sighed. "Nah, I'm not really feeling it right now."

"Is this about that Vegas chick?"

"Maybe, I dunno. She was cool, you know." He sipped on his beer. "Can't really get her out of my head."

"Yeah, I get it." Freddie's breathing had fallen in sync with mine as I mindlessly twisted her hair through my fingers. "The girls were right though, if it's meant to be it will be."

He raised his eyebrows at me.

"Yeah, I know. Sorry." I definitely wasn't myself right now.

He gave a quiet chuckle as Jasper stood up. "Right, I think I need to get my wife to bed so I can rock her world."

I looked at Wolfie, who was fast asleep in his arms. Not sure there was going to be much rocking.

"Yeah. Let's go." I stood up too, picking Freddie up with me, whispering in her ear. "Tiny, we're going back."

"What a fucking awesome day." Tate yawned right next to me, making me jump.

"Jesus. Where did you come from?" I scowled.

He grinned at me.

Freddie stirred and I put her down. Still wobbly from sleep, I wrapped my arms around her.

"Come on, we're all going back." I brushed my lips against hers.

We walked out of the barn, empty except for two unidentifiable people going at it on a chair the corner.

"See." Tate nudged me as we exited into the open air and got in the waiting cars. "Fucking awesome day."

I swiped the keycard against the pad on her door. She flopped onto the bed and I followed, pulling her in to face me. She stared at me, her big blue eyes glittering with emotion and my cock started to swell again.

An eyelash had fallen onto her cheek, I brushed it off and held it in front of her. "Make a wish."

She closed her eyes and blew it away.

"What did you wish for?"

She giggled. "I can't tell you that. It won't come true."

"You can if it was 'I wish Cooper gives me a really good

dicking' because that's definitely coming true." I nuzzled into her neck until her giggling turned to full howling.

The air crackled, I'd become so hard my balls felt like they were about to burst. The toll of the day, of watching her from afar, of not touching her, taking hold.

It was suddenly a frenzy.

I ripped her dress over her head, shedding my clothes as she reached behind and unfastened her bra, throwing it to the side. I sucked a nipple between my teeth, biting down on it making her cry out.

I was desperate to get inside her.

Reaching between us, slipping into the lace of her panties. Pulling them off, I stabbed my fingers up through her dripping pussy and I thumbed her clit until she was panting.

"You're so fucking wet for me, every single time." I growled into her mouth and grabbed her ass, rolling my hips against her clit, providing the friction she badly wanted. "You don't get a warm up this time, Francesca. You're coming on my dick first."

I positioned her over me, pushing her down as I thrust upwards, impaling her in one swift motion. Her back arched and she screamed into the air. I could already feel her walls fluttering around me.

"You're so tight. You squeeze my cock so good. Clench for me, I want to feel it again." I held onto her shoulders, leveraging her against my pumping hips.

She was so fucking hot, it was no wonder I felt like I was about to come the second I drove into her.

She was smooth velvet, wrapping around me in a perfect fit.

Her lips fell onto mine as I thrust inside her, she swallowed a groan so deep it felt like it had come from my ever tightening balls.

"Ohmygod," She cried out, riding me harder and harder,

our bodies slick with sweat. "Fuck, I need to come. Please Coop."

I flipped her, hooking her legs over my shoulders and pounded into her, again and again. Her back arched and I felt my cock pulse, my orgasm flying down my spine and ripping my balls apart just as she shattered beneath me. Her entire body convulsing around me as she screamed my name, clenching me from her core as I pumped inside her until I had nothing left to give.

I rolled to the side to collapse without crushing her, keeping her body as close to mine as I could get it. Every time I expected this intensity to lessen, but it just got stronger, smothering me until I couldn't breathe. I held her until our breathing settled and we moved in rhythm.

I slipped out of bed and ran to the bathroom, warming a washcloth to clean us up. I swept it between her legs.

"Don't wipe too hard, I want to feel you inside me." Her head was already on the pillow, her eyes barely open.

I climbed in beside her, dragging the duvet over our naked bodies, spooning against her.

"Sleep tight, baby." I kissed her head.

"Sleep tight, Coop. I love you." She mumbled.

My body stilled.

Did I just hear that right?

She loved me.

She said I love you.

She loved me.

My heart started beating in my ears as the darkness of the room consumed me. An overwhelming awareness of déjà vu flooded my senses and sent my synapses reeling.

Did I love her too? Is that what this tightness in my chest was?

We hadn't spent a night apart, the intensity of the past week finally catching me. Reality seemed to stand still because I'd lost all grasp of it.

She turned in her sleep, facing me. She was so perfect, her features soft and delicate.

I don't know how long I stayed there watching her, watching her lips as she softly inhaled and exhaled.

I watched until I couldn't watch any longer.

I shut my eyes, willing sleep to take me away.

23

FREDDIE

The sun was shining right onto my pillow contributing to my already pounding head. I groaned, throwing my arm over my eyes and turned away from the blazing light smacking my face against Cooper's shoulder.

I took a deep breath, almost tasting his musky scent on my tongue. In the course of seven days I'd gone from sleeping alone and wanting my space to waking up next to Cooper as my new favourite thing.

The past week had made my head spin.

The intensity he possessed almost compelling. Never in my life had I experienced this level of attraction to another person.

I'd become used to the feeling of my body being drawn to his, automatically dialled into his frequency, sensing him whenever he was near.

He knew what I needed before I did, so attuned to my body that it drowned out any reservation I'd ever felt before. His jealousy a novelty, his need to be near me a powerful aphrodisiac casting a spell over me, obliterating all common sense.

I pulled my face back, his giant biceps coming into focus.

His arm was behind his head, emphasising his sculpted muscles and massive chest.

I leaned up onto my elbow, so I could study him, drool over him uninterrupted but as I levelled up next to him I realised his eyes were open. He was staring at the ceiling, a line etched between his brows.

I ran my finger over it, smoothing it out.

"Good morning."

He caught my hand as I started to move it lower, holding my palm against his lips. Kissing it.

"Hi Tiny." He replied, still staring at the ceiling.

My brows creased. "Are you okay?"

He turned his head to face me, his eyes travelling over me as though he was trying to commit me to his memory. "Yes, all good."

Something started clawing inside me.

He sat up and got out of bed, silently walking to the bath-room. When he came out his boxers were on, his arms pushing through the sleeves of his shirt.

"Where are you going?" I sat up, clutching the sheet to my chest.

"We have the brunch, I need to go back and get dressed." He sat on the bed, tucking my hair behind my ear but not quite looking at me. "I'll come and get you to head over, okay?

"Okay?" I don't know why it came out as a question but there was something off.

He leaned in and kissed me on the head. It was a move so innocuous and one he'd made many times.

Yet why did it feel like a death knell?

Because he never missed an opportunity to bring me to orgasm, as though he was in competition with himself. Or taste my mouth. Or just be wrapped around me naked.

He walked out of the door, quietly clicking as it closed behind him.

What the fuck just happened? Apart from the fact that Cooper had lied to my face.

I slunk down into the bed, anxiety curling through me until my stomach knotted. I shut my eyes, every memory I had from yesterday playing through my mind like an old movie.

The wedding.

The kiss behind the church.

The feel of his eyes following me wherever I went.

The way he wrapped himself around me by the firepit.

The desperation to be inside me.

The declaration of love.

Fuck.

I told him I loved him.

Did I?

Yes, I loved him.

I was in love with Cooper Marks.

And when I told him, he'd run away.

And he hadn't said it back.

Pain lanced through my chest, squeezing my heart. Humiliation burning me like liquid nitrogen.

I shook away the tears before they threatened to spill and sprinted to the shower. If he wanted to avoid a conversation, then so would I.

I pulled up in front of my parents' house, the dogs sitting in the doorway their tails wagging in greeting.

"Hello darling," My mum brought me in for a hug. "How are you feeling? Do you want something to eat before everyone arrives."

"Just some coffee please. Where's Pops?"

"Doing something in the garden." She handed me a coffee as I sat down.

"Thank you." I blew on it before taking a sip, the scorching liquid warming my throat and settling the nausea in my stomach.

"Where's Cooper?"

I frowned. "I don't know."

"Oh, I thought you'd be with him. You seemed to be joined at the hip this week."

"No we're not." I grumbled. "He was just helping me out, we had a lot of wedding jobs to do."

She raised an eyebrow at my attitude, which I chose to ignore. I didn't want to talk about Cooper.

"What time did Jas and Wolf say they'd be here?"

"We're here." They floated in holding hands, smiling and so in love.

The nausea returned.

"Hey Francesco," Wolfie kissed me, squeezing me tight. "Where's Coop? Is he here?"

"I don't know. I'm not his fucking keeping." I snapped, pushing her away.

Everyone was staring at me. Understandably.

"I'm taking the dogs for a walk, I'll be back later." I stormed out shoving on my headphones, whistling for the dogs as I left.

William ran ahead, Rookie trailing behind. He was getting a bit old for chasing. I turned left through the gate, watching the birds startle and flitter around the trees.

I sat down on an old log, swallowing the urge to burst into tears, instead breathing deeply and allowing calm to wash over me.

William continued racing around as Rookie came and sat by my feet.

I lay back on the moss, turning up Fleetwood Mac as I stared at the sky watching jet trails draw patterns across the cloudless expanse of blue. I used to come to this spot as a teenager, when I needed to get out of a chaotic house and just think. It helped me tap into my creativity, sometimes I'd draw, sometimes I'd paint. It helped me feel closer to my parents, without feeling guilty about everything Jack and Diane had done for me.

A shadow crossed over me as a hand pulled my head-phones off. I jumped out of my skin and fell off the log, hitting my head on the ground.

"What the fuck are you doing?" I looked up to see Wolfie peering down at me.

"I came to find out why you stormed off." She held her hand out and I took it, getting to my feet. The sun hit her diamond wedding band and sparkled in the light, reflecting on my shirt.

"I didn't storm off." I grunted and her lips pursed.

"Here then, maybe this will put you in a better mood." She handed me a warm croissant, wrapped in a napkin.

I smelt it, it was my favourite chocolate and almond. The centre was all gooey.

"Thank you." I started the peel the layers of pastry away, dropping them into my mouth.

The dogs joined us, slobbering for a piece of croissant. They weren't getting mine, but Wolfie broke off bits of hers, feeding them as we sat in silence.

I waited to see how long it would take her to ask again. Less than a minute, it turned out.

"Are you going to tell me what's wrong? It's clearly something to do with Cooper."

"I told him I loved him." I mindlessly licked melted chocolate off my hand.

"But that's great!" She cried, flinging an arm over my shoulder.

"It's not. He couldn't get away from me quick enough."

Crease lines crossed her forehead. "What? What does that mean? What happened?"

"I told him last night as we were falling asleep, this

morning he could barely look at me. Got dressed and ran out of the door." I turned to her. "He kissed me on the head."

She looked horrified.

"I know."

Her face scrunched up. "I don't get it. I've seen how he is with you, I've seen how he looks at you. Maybe he just freaked out?"

"Maybe. Still made me feel like shit though." I sighed. "It doesn't matter, he has to leave tomorrow anyway."

She finished up her croissant, wiping her fingers on the napkin. "Have you talked about you two and what you're going to do?"

I shook my head. "No. We said we would but we haven't."

Silence took over again, although I could practically hear the cogs whirring in her brain.

"Fred, it doesn't make any sense. He loves you, I know it. I can feel it in my bones. Maybe he's just worried about leaving you. It's been a big week."

Big week was an understatement.

"Yeah, I know. It's been too much, but maybe that's all it's been, just a way to occupy his time. He was just so different this morning, I've never seen him like that. It made me think I'd imagined everything."

"You haven't." She turned to face me, shaking my shoulders. "Fred, you haven't. Everyone's seen it."

The feeling of dread stayed firm.

"Well, something's happened."

She squeezed my leg. "Just talk to him, I'm sure he's just worried about leaving and how things will be moving forward. It'll be hard to be apart."

"I know. But it would be nice to have a conversation about it instead of the decision being made for me."

"Look, when I left Jasper and came back here, I genuinely thought I was doing the right thing. But I wasn't. I'm sure that's all it is. Just talk to him, it'll be fine."

I let out another deep sigh and laid my head in her lap.

"This is shit. I don't like feeling like this."

It was like my emotions were on the rollercoaster ride of their life. I couldn't remember ever having such highs or lows in such quick succession.

She stroked my hair, soothing me. "Don't forget that you're also hungover and tired, which is going to make you feel much worse. I know, it seems totally shit. But, it's also quite exhilarating."

I groaned. "Give me a break. No, it fucking isn't. You're just in love."

She nudged me. "True. But so are you."

"Yours isn't unrequited." I shot back.

"Neither is yours. Come on, we need to get back before they send out a search party." She stood up, pulling me with her.

We walked back through the fields, passing the barn. I thumbed to the entrance.

"I just want to go in here, see if the clear up crew has arrived."

Her nose wrinkled up. "Okay. Do you mind if I don't come? Because I don't really want to see them tearing my wedding down."

"No, I'm good. I just need to check on them. There's a lot for them to do."

She hugged me. "It's going to be fine, just talk to him."

"I'll see you in a bit."

She walked off toward the house as I headed into the barn.

I'd always marvelled at the speed with which an event break down would take place, but seeing it this morning filled me with a sadness I couldn't articulate. The adrenalin I'd been running on finally crashing down to an abrupt stop.

It was all over.

My hard work.

The week.

Everything.

And on Monday we'd move on with our lives. A stabbing pain shot through my heart at the thought and I held back the tears which threatened to fall.

The tables had already been removed, men on ladders were pulling down the starry ceiling. A mini fork-lift truck was taking out the blossom trees. The florists were dismantling the floral arrangements, hundreds of stems laid out on the table, their summer scents mingling together and filling the air. They would shortly become bouquets and delivered to the house for everyone at the brunch to take home.

The hundred thousand fairy lights were being packed up, taking me back to the day I'd dropped them off.

The day I kissed Cooper.

"Where the fuck have you been?" He snarled and I spun around to find him storming across the floor towards me.

Okay, so I was getting angry Coop.

He had a fucking nerve.

"I beg your pardon." I blinked at him.

He stopped in front of me, close enough to send my senses into overdrive but not quite close enough to touch.

"I've been searching everywhere for you. I've called. I said I'd come back and get you after I changed."

"Right." I stared at him, anger flooding my veins.

"Well?" He stared back.

"Sorry, I'm confused. Could you just explain if you meant you were coming back to get me after I said I loved you? After you could barely look at me? Or after you couldn't run out of the door fast enough?" I counted the points out on my fingers.

His face paled and dropped, guilt marring his perfect features.

"Freddie…" He reached for my hand, but I snatched it away.

"We'll talk about this later."

He was still standing there as I stormed off towards the house.

"Oi, Freddie. Where do you think you're going." I turned around to see my cousin, Jack, leaning against the doors leading into the garden.

He was a sight for sore eyes. My anger diminished and I suddenly felt lighter than I had since I'd woken up.

He looked like he'd stepped straight out of Hollywood, via a rugby pitch. Only twenty-two, he'd just finished university and his boyish good looks worked like a charm, for women of all ages, causing havoc in its wake and getting him whatever he wanted. I'd yet to find someone who said no to him.

He was just like Murray had been, and still was, and therefore idolised him. During his school breaks they could usually be found getting into trouble together somewhere.

I flicked my hair away from my shoulders, facetiously. "You know, places to go people to see."

He pushed off the doorframe and pulled me into a massive hug, lifting me off my feet. "I barely saw you yesterday. Where were you?"

I laughed. "I was around, but every time I saw you there was someone else hanging off you and I didn't want to interrupt."

True story. Jack was a magnet for all sexes, I'd not seen him alone all night.

"Yeah, you know it. But as my favourite person in the whole world, you always take priority with me."

I rolled my eyes. "Think you can put me down now?"

"Yes, but only if you come and sit with me and tell me everything you've been doing." He placed me on the ground, pulling me to the nearest table to sit down next to him.

"I say, who's that rather scowly chap over there? And why

does he look like he wants to rip my head off?" He said, looking over my head.

I didn't need to turn around to know he was talking about Cooper.

Fucking Cooper.

"Tall, dark hair, massive muscles, face like thunder?"

"Yep." He was still looking over my head, as though in a stare down.

"He's Jasper's best friend. He was best man."

"Really? He looks different not in a suit." He winked and it wasn't at me.

"Yeah." I grinned, because I knew how much that would have pissed him off. Not many people took on Cooper and came away unscathed, but Jack was a cocky shit at the best of times.

"What's the deal? He looks like a wanker."

I sighed. "He is a bit. Today anyway. But you should know, he's one of Murray's favourite people."

He scoffed.

"Seriously, he is. And he's not that bad, we just had an argument earlier. He has a thing about other guys around me. He's protective."

His eyes jerked to mine.

"What? You're in a relationship with him? Are you joking?"

I shook my head. "I don't know what we're in."

"Fred." His voice filled with concern as he pulled me in and kissed my head. So different to the one I'd been given earlier, this one brimming with warmth and compassion. "What was the argument about?"

My shoulders dropped. "I told him I loved him. And he didn't say it back. Actually, he left."

Pain once again flooded my chest.

His fists squeezed my legs. "What the fuck, Freddie. What

a prick. You know what, fuck him. You deserve so much more than that."

"Thanks Jackie. While I appreciate your outrage, it's not quite that simple."

If only it was.

"Of course it is, he should be worshipping you. You're amazing."

Out of nowhere a blonde hurtled herself at Jack.

"Jackie!" Wolfie screeched as she sat on his lap. "How are you?"

She'd definitely been getting stuck into the mimosas.

"Hey Wolfie girl. Just chatting to Fred here about that bellend." He nodded to Cooper.

She ruffled his head, destroying his perfectly unperfect styling. "Ah, he's not bad, Jack. He loves Freddie, without a doubt. I've decided he's just struggling to come to terms with it. He's a bit of a broody one, that one."

I leaned back in my chair, fidgeting. My mind going into overdrive with everyone's opinions.

He turned back me, his expression stern. "Freddie. You don't need someone to come to terms with being in love you."

Wolfie clutched her hands to her heart. "Oh Jackie. You're such a romantic."

"And you're drunk. What time's your flight? They won't let you on the plane if you're too pissed."

"We're flying private." She took Jack's beer, drinking it as if to prove a point.

Jack looked at me, rolling his lips as his eyes widened. I suppressed a smile.

"Is my wife drunk again?" Jasper arrived with a plate of food and some water before he sat down to eat.

"Drunk on love." She smirked, holding onto him to pull off Jack's lap and into his. He rolled his eyes but I knew he secretly loved it.

"Cub, can you eat this please?" He asked her before turning to Jack and slapping his shoulder. "Hey man, how are you? Have fun yesterday?"

"Yeah, fucking awesome day Mate. So, so good. Where are you guys headed later?"

"It's a surprise." He winked at Wolfie who was grinning like a buffoon.

"Nice."

I stood up, stretched and rolled my shoulders trying to ease the tension I'd been carrying around.

I needed some breathing space.

"What are you doing?" Jack looked up at me.

"I need some air."

He stared at me in confusion, "We're outside."

"I know, I'm tired. I just meant, I need to go and clear my head." I turned to Jasper and Wolf. "What time are you going?"

"Soon. Or as soon as she's more sober." Answered Jasper.

"Hey!" Protested Wolfie

"Okay I'm going to take off now then. Wolf, say goodbye to me please." I pulled her up, holding her tightly. "Have the most magical time. Stay off your phones. I don't expect to hear from you until you're back, okay."

"Okay, but you need to let me know what happens with Coop." She kissed me as Jasper joined the hug.

"Don't be too hard on Coop, Fredster. You have him by the balls right now." He whispered.

What the fuck did that mean?

24

FREDDIE

I stepped out of the shower and wrapped a towel around myself letting it absorb the water dripping down my body.

Taking some oil from the counter top I slathered it everywhere, inhaling the calming lavender as I padded into my room ready to get into bed. Exhaustion had hit me in an overwhelming fashion and I was desperate for the day to be done.

I heard a soft click.

I didn't need to turn around to know he was standing behind me. He'd let himself in with the spare keycard he'd kept.

He looked up at me as I turned. "Hey."

My stomach flipped and I willed myself to stop shaking from the adrenalin snaking through me. He was too fucking good looking for his own good. My body betraying my want to stay cool and collected.

"Hi."

He gestured me forward. "Freddie, come here."

I stayed where I was crossing my arms as I leaned against the desk, very aware I was still in my towel.

He sighed and walked over to me. Before I could stop him, he pulled me into his arms. I kept mine crossed, the closeness too much.

He tilted my chin up, forcing me to look into his eyes. "I'm sorry. I'm so sorry."

"What are you sorry for?"

"I'm sorry for today, I'm sorry for the way I behaved."

I relaxed against him by a single degree. "We need to talk, Coop. This week, it's been a lot."

A twitch started up in his jaw.

"But I meant what I said, I love you."

He winced, his jaw tightening.

And the pain of witnessing that one reflex seized my internal organs like an iron fist. I clung onto everything I could to stay stable on the outside, while my insides were crumbling.

I stepped away from him.

I tried to keep my voice steady. "Cooper, how do you feel about me?"

My heart rate was on the incline and he was silent for an eternity.

"I don't know." He mumbled, looking at his feet. "I don't know how I feel about you."

Was he for real?

Annoyance started to replace the shame I was feeling.

"You don't know how you feel about me?" I repeated for clarification.

He didn't say anything.

"Okay, let's try this. You know enough that you don't want anyone else to have me. Enough to demand no one else touches me. And you go ape shit if anyone else even talks to me. I was talking to my fucking cousin and your eyes were popping out of your head. Is that right?"

He thrust his hands into his pockets. "We're going to be on different sides of world."

"That wasn't an answer to my question."

"Freddie, it's been a week. An intense week, but a week none the less. And I have to go back and you'll be here. You're this perfect, beautiful, vibrant woman and men fall at your feet. I've seen them. And I hate it." He growled.

Rage swept over me as I thought about his words.

I gritted my teeth. "Are you saying you don't trust me? Are you serious?"

He opened his mouth to speak.

"YOU HAVE FUCKING BUNNIES." I seethed.

"That's different." He argued without meeting my eyes. He stepped towards me and I moved further away from him.

"No, it fucking isn't."

"Freddie, I've done this before." He stared at me, his amber eyes piercing straight through to my soul. I could see the colour draining from his face.

My brows pulled together in confusion. "Done what before?"

He rubbed his hands down his face. "Thought I'd fallen in love in a week. And it backfired."

What the fuck did that mean?

"How so?"

He took a deep breath. "I ended up divorced two months later."

"You were married?" It came out as a whisper. I could barely manage to say it without feeling like I was going to be sick.

He looked so ashamed. "Yes."

"And that's what you think this is?"

He shrugged. "I don't know."

"Right. Just like you don't know how you feel about me."

His shoulders dropped but he didn't say anything.

"So, let me get this straight. Once upon a time you married a woman you'd known for a week and then you got divorced. And because that happened you now assume it'll

233

happen again. And I'm being punished for something I have no control over because you don't trust me enough to not cheat with all these men that are throwing themselves at my feet."

"Freddie…"

"Give me a fucking break. The way you've been all over me this week, ordered me not to speak to people, demanded I give you my full attention. Wanted everyone to know 'I'm Yours.'" I air-quoted aggressively. "And now you're leaving because you don't trust me. A lack of trust I have done absolutely nothing to earn. Do you know how humiliating that is?"

"Freddie…" He reached out to me again.

I stumbled, trying to get away from his touch.

"Fuck you. I'm done with handing you the control. This possessive bullshit has ceased being sexy. You're just fucking selfish. You knew exactly what you were doing. You made me fall in love with you," My voice broke as the rage spilled over, "you selfish, selfish fucking bastard. And now you spit me out because you're too much of a coward to see if we could have something real."

"It's not like that." He pleaded.

"It's exactly like that." I spat back. "You don't know how you feel about me. But you know what, it should be fucking obvious how you feel about me. I know how I feel about me and I know I deserve better. So just fuck off and leave me alone."

"Freddie, please…"

"FUCK OFF." I screamed, spittle flying through the air.

My chest caved as tears poured down my face.

He tried to pull me into him and I recoiled further. I knew the second he touched me I would crumble.

His eyes bored into mine, his face pale and contorted in sadness.

I ran into the bathroom, slamming the door behind me. I

couldn't hold it back any longer, the pain barrelling up my throat in a loud sob.

Stepping into the dry tub, I curled up into a ball, the iron casing causing shivers to run up and down my spine, exacerbating the cold sweat that had already broken out.

I stayed there until I couldn't stay there any longer.

I slumped out of the bathroom and found a sleeping pill in the bottom of my wash bag. Swallowing it, I climbed into bed and pulled the duvet over my head, letting the darkness I felt through to my soul take me.

I woke the next morning, cold and groggy. The bed empty for the first time in a week. The memories of the night before prickling my skin and injecting me with shame.

I showered, packed and dressed on autopilot.

I just wanted to be home.

A knock on the door jolted me out of my misery and I ran to open it without thinking. My heart begging and pleading that it had all been a bad dream and I'd find him standing outside. But it was Drew.

He frowned, giving me a once over. "Hey Fred. Are you okay?"

I nodded, not able to speak.

He tilted his head, pondering. "What happened with Coop?"

"What do you mean? Did he say something?" I could feel my eyes getting hot with the impending onslaught of fresh tears.

"Not exactly. But I just called him and he's back at home."

"My home, why would he go there?"

"No," He narrowed his eyes. "His."

Blood started whooshing through my ears.

"What?"

"He's at home in New York. He flew out last night." He stared down at me. "Freddie, what happened?"

But I wasn't listening. My throat thickened as a sob tried to escape. My guts twisting as I grasped onto what he was saying.

He left. He actually left.

Left me.

Left my country.

Left my broken heart.

25

COOPER

My feet kicked against the end of the pool as I spun, powering through the water for another lap. I'd been in here an hour and was yet to exhaust my body to the point I needed it. The point that would take me to sleep.

But every time I closed my eyes I saw hers. Pale blue piercing through me, rimmed with pain and brimming with unshed tears.

Haunting me.

I was going on fifty hours.

Fifty hours since I'd slept.

Fifty hours since I'd had Freddie curled up next to me.

Fifty hours since I'd felt a semblance of happiness.

Fifty hours since I'd fucked everything up.

My legs powered through the water as my thoughts drifted back. I knew I'd made a mistake the second I boarded the plane. By the time I walked through my front doors the bile was churning inside me so badly I'd barely made it to the bathroom where I puked until I dry retched.

I'd left her.

She told me she loved me and I'd left her.

We were over as quickly as we'd started.

And now it was too late.

As I'd walked back through my house it had hit me. Jasper had been right. It hadn't just been a week.

My house was filled with her. Her imagination, her creativity, her vivacity.

And I loved her.

I'd picked up my phone, the texts I'd sent her had gone unread. I'd pressed her number to call, but it cut out before the ring started up. I'd looked at it, trying the number again and the same thing happened.

Cooper: *I'm so sorry, Baby. I'm so sorry. I need to speak to you, please call me. xxx*

I'd watched for the message to deliver, to see if she'd read it straight away. I stood there waiting, but the second tick never appeared. Two hours later it still hadn't. Nor five. Nor fifteen. I'd tried calling her again and again.

But it never rang.

After eighteen hours I realised she'd blocked me. And I'd thrown my phone against the wall in rage at my stupidity.

And what I'd lost.

I'd left the shattered pieces on the floor as a reminder.

A football hit the water as I reached the end of the pool. I stood up, looking around for where it had come from.

"How the fuck did you get in?" I scowled at Drew and Felix, both standing over me, their arms crossed on their chests.

Felix grinned. "We know the gate code."

"Well I'll be changing it immediately then." I pulled myself out of the pool and grabbed my towel from the sun lounger. I turned to them. "Want to tell me exactly what you think you're doing here?"

Felix narrowed his eyes at me. "You look like shit. When was the last time you slept?"

I towelled myself dry, ignoring them.

"Coop?" He asked again.

"What?" I snapped.

"When was the last time you slept."

I ground my jaw, glaring at them.

They glared back, like they were a pair of fucking cops trying to intimidate a witness.

Dicks.

"You don't fucking scare us, so you may as well spill because we're not leaving until you do."

Fuck's sake.

"Saturday night. Happy?"

"You haven't slept since Saturday?" His eyes were wide open.

I shook my head, dropping it.

"Oh buddy." Drew put his hand on my shoulder, squeezing it.

I suddenly felt so overcome with emotion and tiredness that my vision became blurry with moisture. I pinched the bridge of my nose, trying to rid myself of the ache which seemed to have travelled back from the U.K. with me.

"I'm fine." I stalked towards the house, Good Cop Bad Cop in hot pursuit.

"Coop? What the fuck happened, Man?" Pressed Drew, as we walked into the kitchen.

I took three beers from the fridge and opened them, sliding two across the island. I looked at him to continue.

He sipped his beer. "What the fuck happened with Freddie?"

"What do you mean?"

"You know what I mean. Why are you here and why was she sobbing in my arms yesterday morning?"

My fists clenched.

He fucking touched Freddie.

"What?" I glared at him.

"Oh fuck off. After I called you, I went to find out what happened and she had no idea you'd come back here. I think she was hoping it was you at the door, because her face fell when she saw me. And when I told her where you'd gone she wouldn't stop crying. What the fuck did you do?"

My brows knitted. "She didn't tell you?"

"No, but you're going to."

I'd never seen Drew get angry with me. Never really seen him get angry off the ice, period. And even then it was more part of a role he played. He was always the diffuser, never the instigator. Not that he couldn't flatten a person with one punch when he wanted to.

I gave a deep sigh. "She told me she loved me."

"And?"

"And I didn't say it back."

"Why the fuck not? You clearly do."

"Because I didn't realise I did until I got back here."

"So phone her up and tell her, you fuckwit." He shouted, like it was oh so simple.

"I can't!" I shouted back.

"Because of that?" Felix pointed to my phone, lying in pieces on the floor. The indentation on the wall where it had struck, clearly visible.

I pulled my hand down my face and sank onto the stool at the counter. "No, because she fucking blocked me."

"Use my phone." He held it out, ready to dial.

"No!" I shouted. "She blocked me. She doesn't want to hear from me."

"Coop…"

"Look, I just need to figure it out. But I'm so fucking tired, I can't think straight."

Drew rounded the counter and squeezed my shoulder again. "It's okay, this is fixable. Go to bed and sleep, we'll talk about it when you wake up."

My head slumped down on my hands. "I'm not going to be able to fucking sleep."

"Just do me a favour you grumpy shit and humour me. Because we have nothing else to do and we're not leaving.

The pair of them were staring at me, daring me to defy them. But I was too fucking tired to argue.

"Fuck, you're annoying. Fine." I stomped off up the stairs to my bedroom, like a petulant child.

Turning the shower on I stepped under the steaming water washing off the chlorine, trying to induce a shred of relaxation. I started getting hard as my mind filled with Freddie once more.

Memories of her perfect pink lips wrapped around my cock, taking me deep in her throat as she pulled on my balls. I started stroking myself, my dick swelling to painful proportions. My hands were no match for her soft skin. Her warm, wet mouth. Her dripping, velvety pussy.

Fuck, I missed her.

This had been the longest we'd gone without speaking in nine months.

I missed her as much as I would miss a limb.

I gripped my cock harder, pulling it faster through my soaped up fist. Freddie's face flashed before my eyes, full of ecstasy as she rode me, her back arched as she came hard on my cock, clenching around me over and over. My orgasm punched through me with Mach force, my hand against the shower wall holding me up against the power of it.

I watched my cum pathetically drain away.

I needed to fix this.

I dried off and slipped between my sheets, naked. I didn't hold out much hope of sleeping. Not without her next to me.

I looked at the clock as I opened my eyes. I'd been asleep an hour, but it was better than nothing.

My stomach rumbled.

Light headedness hit me as I stood up and walked to the bathroom for a piss before heading downstairs.

"There's Sleeping Beauty." Felix barely looked up from

playing Xbox, his thumbs moving at lightening speed across the controls. "Feeling better?"

"I was only gone an hour." I opened the fridge and started pulling out food, laying it on the counter. "I told you I wouldn't be able to sleep."

"What?" Drew glanced up from his phone.

Suddenly starving, I twisted the cap off a protein shake and downed it in one.

I took a chopping board from the cupboard and placed it on the counter. Picking up a sweet potato, I began slicing it.

"I said I told you I wouldn't be able to sleep."

He frowned. "You haven't been asleep the whole time?"

"I've been gone an hour."

"You've been gone twenty-five hours." Felix shouted from the sectional in front of the TV, his eyes still on the screen, his fingers never slowing down.

I stopped what I was doing and looked at them. "What?"

"It's Wednesday. You've been asleep a whole day."

"Fuck off." I rolled my eyes and went back to slicing up vegetables.

"Dude. It's Wednesday." Drew held his phone up so I could see.

What the actual fuck. Twenty-five hours?

"I've been asleep?" My voice laced with incredulity.

He smirked. "Yeah and snoring away like the princess you are."

"And you guys have been here the whole time?" I waved my knife through the air, pointing at them.

"Yes, we said we wouldn't leave."

I looked at him, gratitude flowing through me and sticking in my throat. "Thanks buddy."

He shrugged like it was nothing. "Yeah, you'll owe us. Now what are you cooking?"

I tossed him a pack of steaks. "Here, get these on the grill."

He walked outside and I turned on the oven, throwing in

the sweet potatoes. Felix pulled out a stool and sat down, replacing the Xbox controller with a giant bag of chips.

"Pass the dip from the fridge, will you?"

I grabbed it and slid it over to him.

"What've you two been doing while I was asleep?"

"Xbox mostly. And a workout." He stuffed a handful of chips into his mouth.

I grabbed a handful myself and threw them in my mouth. I watched Felix as he chewed, dreading the answer to the question I was about to ask.

I took a deep breath. "Did either of you hear from Freddie?"

He shook his head. "We can try her though?"

Drew walked through the black, steel-framed glass doors that stretched along the back wall of the kitchen and lead out to the backyard. They were the same as the ones Freddie had in her house, they'd been her suggestion.

"Dude, text Freddie." Felix turned to Drew as he sat down.

"You want me to?" He raised his eyebrows at me in question.

"Yes, see what she has to say. I have to start somewhere at making this right."

He pulled out his phone. "Do you want to write it?"

I took it from him, then gave it back. "No, you do it. She doesn't want to speak to me." I rubbed my finger and thumb across my brow, trying to ease the tension. "Tell her I'm sorry and that I need her to call me. That I'm miserable without her. That I love her."

"Not that last bit. You can't tell her you love her for the first time on text." Said Felix. "Or the miserable bit. You sound like a sad bastard."

He had a point.

"I fucking am." I muttered.

"Just tell her that Coop really needs to speak to her."

I nodded and watch Drew type it out.

His phone pinged almost immediately. He picked it up and looked at it, grimacing before handing it to me.

This was going to hurt.

Freddie: *Tell him to go fuck himself*

My stomach churned as a wave of nausea hit.

"Coop…"

I picked up the heavy wooden chopping board I'd been using and flung it as hard as I could across the kitchen, smashing a vase in its wake.

"FUCK."

My chest was heaving with adrenalin. My heart pounding.

I turned back to the boys.

Drew looked at the mess. "Well, this is going to be harder than I thought." He offered, dryly.

I didn't disagree.

26

COOPER

I startled as my phone pinged indicating a message and threw myself across the sofa grabbing it off the end table, praying.

The waiting was slowly driving me crazy.

Drew: Pick up game in an hour, then beers.

My skin flushed red and I gritted my teeth so hard I could hear the crunch. Taking a series of deep breaths, my anger began to subside. Anger which had been at volcanic levels the past few weeks exploding with no warning. I managed to hold back from launching another phone across the room in fit of rage.

I'd been back in the States for two and a half weeks, two of which had been spent trying to get hold of Freddie in any manner possible. Something that had proved more of a challenge given that I couldn't text or call her.

I'd tried Murray but he'd said I needed to figure it out myself.

So, I'd emailed my apologies.

And sent more with flowers, every day.

Drew had suggested writing it on a cookie. Which I did,

because I was getting desperate. Even though it was the lamest thing I'd ever done in my life.

I'd said sorry a million times.

I'd told her why I'd left.

I told her I needed to talk to her.

Needed to hear her voice.

Needed to see her face.

I'd told her everything except that I loved her. Because the first time I said that to her wasn't going to be anything less than in person.

She'd responded with nothing but her silence.

I was as twitchy as a junkie needing a hit. Except I couldn't buy my drug of choice off a street corner.

In its absence the hole in my chest was slowly filling up with hatred laced rage.

What more did she fucking want from me? I was practically on my knees begging for her forgiveness.

And I knew I'd stay there until it worked.

The last two weeks had been the emptiest of my life. I hadn't realised how closed off I'd been until Freddie.

How much I'd shut out.

How much she'd smashed through with her boundless energy, snarky attitude and giant heart.

She'd become my anchor.

I fucking loved her. Loved her so much that the thought of not being able to hold her one more time was causing me physical pain.

I looked at my phone as it went off again.

Clevs: *You best be getting dressed*

I groaned. He was right, I couldn't sit around and wait for a message to come through. I tried hard not to think about what I'd do if it never came at all.

The smell of the ice filled my lungs, bringing a sense of calm. I laced my skates and jumped over the boards, scooping up the puck before hurtling it towards the back of the net. Rounding the goal, I picked up another repeating the process. Before doing it again.

And again.

Each time hitting it harder.

This was better than any punching bag.

"There you are." Drew skidded to a halt in front of me. "I was waiting in the locker room."

"Just throwing some pucks." I started bouncing one on the end of my stick.

"You doing okay, Man?" He looked at me.

I shrugged.

"Have you heard from her?" He held his stick out to me and I flicked the puck to him. We knocked it back and forth like a tennis ball as we skated down the rink.

"No. Nothing. I don't know what to do. I can't get hold of her. Have you heard anything?" I looked at him, a shred of hope flickering in the depths of my stomach.

He shook his head. "No, sorry man. Nothing." His face was filled with empathy.

The flickering died and I let out a deep sigh.

"Okay ladies, let's play some pick up." Felix led a couple of rookies onto the ice.

We used pick up games as an informal way of trying out new players who'd been traded or were being brought up from the farm team for the coming season. It was a good way to stay ice fit during the off-months as well as try out any new plays and lines.

"We're playing three on three. And boys, watch out for Cooper. He bites."

I rolled my eyes, such a dickhead. Although given the mood I was in, he wasn't wrong.

Drew called time and I stole the puck before the rookie in

front of me could blink, skating off faster than a bullet, flinging it into the net. I took my time getting back to them, every single one staring at me.

"You need to be quicker than that." I winked before turning to Felix. "You were right, this is fun."

An hour later I peeled off my pads, sweat pouring down my body. I must have skated eight miles up and down the rink. No one else got near the puck. My heart was still pounding and I should have felt good from the adrenalin rushing through my body, but I didn't.

I felt flat.

Felix pushed open the doors to the locker room. "Well, that was more of five on one, than three on three."

I stripped off the last of my kit and grabbed a towel, walking into the shower. I stood there, letting the scalding water run over my body and soothe my aching muscles. I don't know how long I was in there, but it was enough for a fully dressed Drew to come and find me still under the water.

"Coop, how long are you going to be, man? I'll wait for you."

I turned off the shower and started drying myself. "You go. I'm not in the mood to socialise."

He followed me into the changing room. "Coop, come on. This isn't doing you any good. You need to get out. You can't stay at home and mope forever."

"I'm not fucking moping."

I was.

"And I'm not in the mood to go out with a bunch of rookies I don't know."

He sighed. "Okay, dude. I'll catch you later."

I opened my locker door and checked my phone screen.

Blank.

It was dark outside.

Another day nearly done.

Another day of Freddie's silent treatment.

A movement in the shadows caught my eye as I reached for the half-drunk bottle of whiskey on the counter. I really needed to change the code on the gate. Or at least lock my front door.

Drew and Felix strode through the kitchen like they were on a mission.

"Get dressed, we're going out." Felix ordered taking the glass of whiskey from my hand, drinking it himself.

"Where?"

I already knew the answer.

He stared at me, leaning against the door frame his arms crossed over his chest. "You need to blow off some steam."

What I needed to do was forget, so I didn't argue.

"Fine." I walked upstairs.

"We'll wait for you in the car." He called after me.

The driver pulled up at the top of a dead-end alley way. A place of total insignificance to the untrained eye.

But we'd been here before.

Many times.

Hidden cameras monitored us as we walked down and an unmarked, black steel door swung open allowing us to enter.

"Clevs. How you doin' man?" Felix was pulled into an embrace by an enormous security guard. Enormous even by our hockey playing standards. His voice deep and low like a foghorn.

"Linus, good to see you." Felix slapped him on the back. "How are you? How's life?"

"All good, you know how it is. Haven't seen you in a while. You got yourself a girlfriend?" He laughed at his own joke. Everyone knew Felix was never getting in a relationship.

"Nah, man, we've been in England for Jas' wedding."

"Oh yeah, I saw some pictures." He turned to us. "So, what're you looking for tonight, gentleman?"

Drew hugged my shoulder. "Coop here needs cheering up. His heart's been broken."

I scowled, shrugging him away. "Fuck off."

Linus patted me on the back, the force of which almost pushing me forward. "Don't worry, Coop. You know you've come to the right place."

"Thanks." I was starting to sober up and I definitely needed to be way more drunk. "Linus. No brunettes."

"You got it." He reached behind him and pressed an invisible button. "Okay fellas, you know the drill."

We held our arms out and he passed a scanner over us before handing our phones to him for secure lock up.

Membership to the club was by invitation only and no guests were allowed. A myth to anyone who'd never been granted entry, members included those from the highest echelons of New York society. It had no name, but given we had to enter through a black door, that's what it became known as.

Secrecy and security were honored by everyone who entered and no one put up a fight because the stakes were too high, plus Linus would break your bones without blinking.

The slow thump of the music filled the soundproofed entrance we'd been standing in as a wall slid open, revealing a woman on the other side waiting for us.

She was dressed in a black corset and matching, low cut panties. Aesthetically she was incredibly beautiful. Her long legs and hour glass curves would be the envy of any Victoria's Secret model.

She smiled at us through full and glossy red lips, her big almond shaped eyes sparkling above sharp cheekbones.

"Gentlemen, if you'll follow me."

Her taut ass swayed as she walked in front, thick hair bouncing as she moved.

I heard Felix groan. "Fuck, I'm already getting hard."

My brows tightened. She was doing nothing for me.

Nothing.

We walked along a dimly lit corridor, closed doors down the left-hand side each one barely visible against the black walls. She stopped outside one and unlocked it, holding it open.

As we'd done many times before we walked through into a dark room, a heavy musky scent hitting us.

The smell of sex.

Just like the rest of the club the room was dimly lit and built with sex in mind, three of the four walls lined with soft, deep red leather. The other side overlooked a stage where two naked girls rubbed oil over each other with a third walking over to join in.

Private balconies from the closed doors we'd passed all faced the stage. There was no outside socialising with other members.

Discretion was utmost.

Another beautiful girl was waiting for us, our preferred drinks choices on the tray she was holding.

"Kendra will be your server for this evening, let her know if you need anything at all. I'll send your girls through shortly. Enjoy the show, gentlemen." Our hostess walked out, closing the door behind her.

We took our drinks.

Drew downed his in one. "We're going to need more of these."

We'd spent so much time here over the years and my body used to buzz in anticipation every single time.

For first time ever I felt nothing, even with the orgy currently taking place on stage.

Kendra brought over a tray of shots and I knocked four back one after the other, needing the buzz to return.

The slow, steady beat of Massive Attack's Angel played out. The melodic bass providing a seductive rhythm for the girls performing.

One of the two side doors of our room opened and we turned to look. Three blonde women entered, each more beautiful than the last, all wearing nothing more than a thong and the skimpiest bra.

Their bodies honed to perfection.

The club catered to members with a lot of money and these women looked like they were worth every cent of the ten thousand dollars they made each night.

"Hey Coop, how're you doing? It's been a while." Amber, the last one to walk in, ran her fingers over my chest.

We had history together.

This wasn't the first time I'd seen her naked.

As well as private booths this place held luxury suites upstairs. Members weren't allowed to leave the premises with any of the girls, but the suites provided an opportunity to extend time with them. And on a few occasions we'd taken advantage of that.

"Okay."

"Well let's see what we can do about making things a bit better than okay, shall we." She took my hand and silently led me over to one of the large club chairs in the corner, pushing me down.

I watched Felix walk out of the back door with one of the girls, already gone for the night.

I leant back in the chair as Amber started gyrating over me, her body moving in sensual rhythm. It was easy to see how she was one of the most requested women in the club.

She picked up my hands in hers, moving them around to her back, unhooking her bra. It slowly dropped and her tits were in my face, nipples tight. I'd never been able to figure out whether they were real or not, but I'd always thought they were fucking fantastic.

Until now.

I wasn't even hard.

In fact, my dick was practically crawling inside itself.

She slid her hands across my body and arched her back, pushing her tits towards me again, her hips rocking on my lap. She started moaning and I knew from previous experience she was getting off and trying to take me with her.

I felt sick. The alcohol mixing with the bile which had been sitting in the pit of my stomach for too long.

Her touch wasn't right.

Nothing about this was right.

She was too tall.

Too blonde.

She wasn't Freddie.

"Stop touching me." I leant as far back in the chair as I could get, trying to put distance between us.

"Coop…" She breathed into me.

"Amber, I said fucking stop." I was practically shouting.

She stopped, frowning, sensing my tone.

"Okay." She raised her hands in a defensive gesture and got up, crossing her arms over her chest.

"Sorry, I just…' I looked at her standing in front of me, her mouth set in a hard line. "This was a mistake. I'm going."

I got up and pushed the other side door open, making it to the bathroom just in time for me to puke, emptying myself of the anxiety and despair I'd been carrying around for the past few weeks.

What the fuck was I doing here?

Drew was waiting for me when I finally got up and made my way back out into the room. I looked around, the girls had gone.

"What are you doing?" I wiped my mouth with the back of my hand.

"Waiting for you."

I frowned. "You didn't have to, you can stay."

"Nah, I'm not feeling it either." He tugged on the back of his neck. "Sorry man, we thought we needed to take your mind off Freddie, but we did a shit job."

I sighed. "No, you didn't. I just don't think this place is for me right now. I need to figure this thing out with Freddie before I do anything. That's if she'll ever fucking speak to me again."

"She will, don't worry." He pulled me into a hug. "Come on, let's get the fuck out of here. Now I'm not in the mood, this place is making my skin crawl."

A'int that the truth.

27

FREDDIE

The doorbell rang for the third time.

"I'm coming, for fucks sake."

Admittedly not moving as fast as I probably could, but I also gave zero fucks about anything right now, so the delivery guy could wait until I was ready to open the door.

I already knew what would be on the other side.

"Good morning, Miss Danvers. Still not forgiven him then?" Fred, the delivery guy, passed me a bouquet of red roses.

There had to be at least fifty in here, it was almost too big to hold.

"Still not minding your own business?" I peered around the bouquet. "Thanks."

He took off towards his van, chuckling. "See you tomorrow, no doubt."

I kicked the door shut and walked down the hall into the kitchen, where another five hundred roses waited in various states of bloom. They'd been arriving for two weeks now and I'd run out of surfaces.

Thank fuck they'd come with vases.

I put it on the floor with a deep sigh, picking out the note attached, opening it.

I know I hurt you, Baby, and I'm so sorry.
If I could take it all back, I would.
I miss you so much.
Please call me.
Coop xxxx

I put it in a drawer with the rest.

The ache in my chest started to get heavy again. Over the past two weeks it had ebbed and flowed, but never fully disappeared. When he'd left, he'd taken a piece of me with him and my heart was struggling to beat without it.

I missed him.

I missed him so much it hurt.

I missed the way he'd made me feel.

The way he'd opened my eyes to new experiences.

But what I missed most was his friendship and how much he'd made me laugh. That I got to see a different side to him than everyone else did.

I heard my front door open and close, footsteps heading towards the kitchen.

"Franks?" Murray called out as he walked in, Jack beside him.

They took in the sight.

"Fucking hell, you could open a florist." Jack walked over and picked me up in a hug. "How are you doing?"

I shrugged. Unsure.

It had been two weeks. What felt like the longest two weeks of my life.

I'd been existing in a fog, an alternate reality where heartbreak didn't exist. Pretending everything was normal until I realised it wasn't.

After the wedding I'd driven back home and crawled into

bed, not emerging until Murray had dragged me out two days later. I cried until the tears had run dry and my throat was hoarse. Until the intense pain of him leaving had subsided into a dull ache.

I hadn't been able to decide what was worse. Him unable to tell me he loved me or him leaving without saying goodbye.

Or deep down knowing it was my fault that he had.

I'd screamed at him to fuck off, and he'd followed my instruction to the letter.

I only had myself to blame.

As I'd laid in bed, pictures of the wedding had begun appearing on social media. His beautiful face staring out at me from every picture, bringing my humiliation and shame back into sharp focus.

I didn't want to see him or know what he was doing.

Ravaged by anger I'd blocked him from every form of communication I could think of. If he didn't want the whole of me then I certainly wasn't going to allow him to have parts of me.

But I'd never predicted the daily onslaught of floral arrangements. Even the random cookie. Each one saying he missed me but none of them telling me what I wanted to hear.

You can miss someone and not want them completely.

And I knew no matter how much it hurt now, that I was better than that.

Murray walked over to the kettle and switched it on. Taking some mugs from the cupboard he proceeded to make tea for the three of us.

"Thank you." I took a steaming mug from him and sat down at the table.

"Fred, have you got any biscuits?" Jack asked, wandering aimlessly around the kitchen.

"Yes, in the pantry."

He walked into it and I could hear him rummaging, before he came and sat down with three different packets. I opened the chocolate digestives and dunked one in my tea then stuffed it in my mouth, whole.

My sugar intake had taken a sharp increase since Cooper had left.

They were sitting opposite me, staring, as though I was on an interview. Both wearing an identical expression of revulsion.

I wiped crumbs off my face and dunked another one. "Anyway, what are you two doing here?".

Murray leaned back in his chair. "We came to see how you're doing. And also to tell you we're going out later and you're coming."

I groaned. "I dunno. I don't really feel like it."

"I don't care. You're coming. You can't stay here forever waiting around for another delivery. I bet the only people you've seen the past two weeks are us and the delivery guy." He gestured between him and Jack.

He wasn't wrong. And the fact that I was now on first name terms with the delivery guy was kind of depressing.

I looked at the two of them. "Where do you want to go?"

"Anywhere, we don't care. The pub? It doesn't matter, just anywhere but here. Between your mood and these flowers, we may as well be in a funeral home."

I scowled. "It's not that bad."

It was.

"Franks, it is. And you know it." He glared as he sipped his tea.

"And I'm not waiting for deliveries. They just keep arriving. It's not like I'm ordering them." I huffed.

Jack looked at me. "How long do you think it's going to take until he gets the message?"

"What message?"

"That you don't want anything to do with him."

The pain in my chest dialled up a notch.

Is that what I was doing? Sending him a message that I didn't want anything to do with him?

Would he stop?

I never even thought about that. Once they'd started arriving every day, it hadn't occurred to me they ever wouldn't.

Is that what I wanted?

My eyes started to get hot and watery.

Murray reached over and rubbed the back of my hair. "Is that what you want?"

"I don't know."

"Look." Said Jack. "As much of a wanker I still ascertain he is, all this," He gestured around the kitchen. "Is a little extreme if you only want to apologise."

I lifted my head from where I'd dropped it on my arm. "You think?"

"You could sell tickets for the amount of flowers in here. He must have wiped out all florists in West London. I'd say that was extreme. Not that I'd know for certain of course, I'm too perfect to ever have to apologise for anything." He smirked.

His joke raised a weak smile.

"I dunno. He says he misses me. And wants me to call him. But that's it. Maybe this is a normal reaction in his world."

"Franks, I'm pretty sure he's never sent flowers to a woman before. He's never been in a relationship."

"Apart from his marriage." I grumbled, standing up. I was done with tea. If we were going to talk about Cooper then I needed something stronger. I took some wine from the fridge and three glasses, putting them down on the table.

Jack took the corkscrew from me and opened the bottle, pouring it out, sliding the glasses across the table. "But that was over a decade ago. What do you want him to say?"

I shrugged.

Murray sipped on his wine, pondering. "I'm not defending him, but I do think you're being a little bit stubborn." He raised his hand before I could interrupt in protest. "He told me his marriage was a mistake, so I'm sure this was just him freaking out, that's all. You love him and he's trying to get in touch with you, and because you blocked him he's apologising in the only way he can get hold of you. But I'm certain he loves you back."

I stared at him as I drank.

"No Murray, he doesn't. I told him I loved him and his reaction was to leave the country. To me, that's extreme. He said he didn't know how he felt about me and that fucking hurt. So excuse me for being a bit sore and not quite ready to open the channels of communication again." I opened another packet of biscuits, this time chocolate chip, before Murray moved the rest of them out of my grasp.

He raised an eyebrow at me as I frowned at him.

"I know you're hurting, Franks and I want to hurt him for that. But, maybe he just didn't realise at the time."

"Have you heard from him again?" A little flutter of hope escaped from my heart.

He shook his head. "No, not since I told him he needed to figure it out."

I turned to Jack. "What do you think?"

"I told you, I think he's a wanker. But, I also think Murray has a point. And you are definitely stubborn." He replied, pouring out more wine.

"My stubbornness didn't get me into this." I snapped.

"No, but it's not helping you get out is it?" He shot back.

Maybe he was right.

But I was nursing a broken heart and my brain was only trying to protect me. I pulled on my necklace running it between my fingers, thinking.

"Have you spoken to Wolf about this?" Asked Murray.

I shook my head again. "No, she's not back until next week and I didn't want to burst their honeymoon bubble."

Next week she'd be back in New York.

Where Cooper was.

Where she'd see him.

My head started pounding at the thought.

I sighed. "I don't know what to do. I don't know what I want to do. I fucking miss him. I really miss him. But I keep seeing his face when I told him I loved him and after that he ran away. And it hurts."

"I know, Franks. Talk to Wolfie, she'll know what to do." He reached out and stroked my shoulder. "You remember I'm flying there in two days to look at offices?"

I rubbed at the pressure building in my temples. "No, I'd forgotten."

"Do you want me to see him?"

I shook my head. "Just do what you would have done anyway. Don't change anything on my account."

He placed his hand over mine. "People make mistakes, Franks. Don't let your stubbornness get in the way of your happiness."

"Yeah." I stood up. "I'm going to get changed, then let's go to the pub."

"Fuck yes, we're getting drunk." Jack picked up his phone and started tapping away. "Uber will be here in five."

Thirty minutes later we walked into our favourite pub which, given that it was a sunny Saturday afternoon, was unsurprisingly heaving.

"I'll go to the bar, you find somewhere to sit. Maybe outside."

"Okay." Jack turned around as Murray went through to the back. "You want me to help you?"

"No, I'm good." I leant across the packed bar, trying to get the barman's attention. Being shorter than average definitely had its disadvantages, although it took less time than expected.

The barman nodded to me for my order.

"Two pints of IPA and a gin and tonic please."

He started pouring them out.

"Freddie?" A voice next to me asked, I turned to see Stuart standing there.

Fuck.

The last time I'd seen him was when I'd been collecting the suits, when I was kissing Cooper. The kiss that started everything.

The pain in my chest flared up again.

"Hey Stuart. How are you?"

He glanced down at his feet. "I'm okay."

"Great, glad to hear it." I leant back across the bar again, where were these drinks?

Stuart picked my hand up off the bar. "I really miss you, Freddie."

What the fuck? How could he possibly?

I looked at him, easing my hand out of his grip.

"Stuart, we don't even know each other. We went on two dates, we barely kissed. There's no way you could possibly miss me."

"But we can get to know each other. Let's try again, whatever you want to do." He pleaded, his face hopeful.

Before I could stop it, I laughed in his face.

There's no way Cooper would have given me the option, he'd have just done it.

Suddenly, I missed him more than I ever had. I had to speak to him.

I took a deep breath. "No, Stuart. I'm sorry, but it's never going to happen. I'm in love with someone else. You'll find the right person and she'll be very lucky, but I'm not her." I smiled kindly then faced the bar again, ending the conversation, hoping he'd move away.

I saw him slink off from the corner of my eye.

The barman finally put the drinks on the bar and I paid. Picking them up, I walked through to the garden where I found Murray and Jack.

"I'll speak to Cooper and listen to what he has to say." I put the glasses down on the table and slid into the bench.

Murray raised his eyebrow as he sipped his pint. "Why the sudden change of mind?"

"I just bumped into Stuart."

"Who's Stuart?" Asked Jack.

Murray rolled his eyes. "Some douche that Franks went on a few dates with."

I waited for their conversation to finish.

"Because I'm not going to stop missing Cooper. So I'll listen to what he has to say."

"I think that's a good idea." Jack stood up.

"Where are you going?

"To get shots." He headed into the pub.

I started to dread the hangover I'd have in the morning.

28

FREDDIE

"It's so good to see you. I thought you were back tomorrow."

Wolfie's tanned face peered out at me through my computer screen. The last few weeks had felt so much harder without her there to counsel me. And I just plain missed her.

"We decided to come back a couple of days early and not tell anyone. Just have private time in the house before the season starts, so it didn't feel like Jas just got back then left for practice." She smiled at me, looking so happy.

On Cloud Nine.

That must be what love is like.

I hadn't yet spoken to Cooper, even though more flowers had arrived. I hadn't yet built up the courage to hear what he had to say, in case it wasn't quite what I wanted to hear.

"Anyway," Wolfie continued. "Enough about me. What about you? We saw Murray yesterday, he told us about Coop. Are you okay? I can't believe he left. Why didn't you call me?"

I picked up the computer and carried it through to the kitchen, placing it on the countertop.

"Because I didn't want to disturb your bubble of love and

I knew if I told you, you'd be calling every day. And that wouldn't have been fair on you or Jas."

I walked to the freezer and pulled out a tub of Ben & Jerry's Phish Food. Sitting on the stool in front of her, I took a spoon from the drawer and dug in.

"Freddie…" Her face filled with sadness.

And that's why I didn't tell her.

"Wolf, stop. Don't feel bad, Murray was here and I really didn't have much to say."

"So have you heard from him?"

"We haven't spoken but he's been sending me flowers every day and telling me that he wants to talk." I turned the screen so she could see everything.

"Woah."

"I know." I ran my spoon around the edge of the tub, scooping more ice cream.

"And you don't want to talk?"

I shrugged. "I do, I really miss him, I'm just nervous."

"Hang on. You're making me want ice cream." Wolfie started walking through her house, until she reached her kitchen. "Anyway, what about?"

She walked to the freezer before returning with her own tub.

"I don't know. He told me he didn't know how he felt about me. I don't know how that will have changed and I'm not sure I want to hear it again."

I watched as Wolfie started digging in, holding a spoonful up to the camera.

"Like old times." She put it in her mouth. "Jas saw him this morning, they went to the gym together."

"And?"

"He said he'd never seen Coop so miserable. Or bad tempered."

My heart skipped a beat. The eager bitch.

"Did he say what he'd been doing?"

"No, but I didn't get the impression he'd been doing much. Jas just said he seemed really withdrawn and cut up. Francesco, you need to speak to him, just message him while I'm here. Rip off the band aid."

She was right.

"Okay." I looked around for my phone. Seeing it on the windowsill I jumped off the stool and grabbed it.

I'd found his number and unblocked it.

"Hey, do messages come through from a number when you unblock it, if they've been sent while it was blocked?"

She frowned while trying to make sense of what I'd said. "No, I don't think so. You won't have any messages come through from Cooper if he sent them while he was blocked."

"Oh." While I was thinking about what to type out I went into his Instagram and unblocked him there too.

He hadn't added anything new since the week of the wedding, a picture taken of our group. I was looking up at him as he grinned at me.

I brushed my fingers across his face.

Like always, I was taken aback by how beautiful he was. Even more so as I'd been avoiding all pictures recently.

I flicked to see if he'd been tagged in any more from the wedding, with the most recent images coming up. There were dozens of them. And they weren't from the wedding.

I scrolled through.

What was I looking at? They seemed to be long lens shots. I zoomed in.

It was dark and grainy but that was definitely Cooper. And that was definitely a pair of tits in his face. There was a naked woman sitting on his lap, his hands were on her back, her long blonde hair hanging down as she arched into him. His mouth was open, his eyes closed, enjoying the ride she was giving him.

In the next one her hands were on his chest. He was

kissing her. I was no expert, but I was fairly certain lap dancers didn't kiss.

I stopped scrolling, my body shaking with a cold sweat.

And as I noticed the time stamp, I swear I heard the sound of my heart cracking in half.

It was two days ago.

"Fred. What are you looking at? Just message him."

I snapped out of my trance.

"No, I don't think so."

"What?"

I held the picture up to the camera. "Doesn't really look like he's that withdrawn. Or cut up about me."

She squinted at the screen. "What am I looking at?"

"It's on his Instagram. Looks like he was tagged in a picture." My voice was shaking, fighting off the tears.

I felt sick.

Jealousy was battling it out with hurt, trying to win the title of my strongest emotion.

I watched as she flicked through her phone and found what I'd been showing her, her eyes opening wide as she took it in.

Her mouth dropped in horror.

"Oh, he's a fucking dead man." She snarled.

29

COOPER

I ran my hands through my hair, amazed there was any left after the last twenty four hours of tearing it out.

"Mary…" I tried to interrupt my manager while she was ripping me a new one.

"I'm speaking right now, Cooper." Semantics but actually she was shouting. Although to be fair, she was always shouting. "How could you be so fucking stupid? What do I always drill into you? For fuck's sake."

I stayed silent, pacing through the kitchen as she screamed at me over speakerphone.

"Well?"

"You said you were speaking."

"This is not the time to be a wise ass." She was still shouting.

"You think I don't know." I shouted back, leaning across the table directly over the phone. I wanted her to feel my rage. Rage at myself, at the club, at Drew and Felix. Even rage at Freddie for giving me the silent treatment.

I would never have been there if she'd simply replied.

"How the fuck did these photos get out? How the fuck

was there even a camera in there? I DIDN'T EVEN WANT TO FUCKING BE THERE."

In my entire life I don't think I'd ever had a worse few weeks.

I'd fucked up so badly with Freddie, not a single one of my attempts to reach her had gone through.

Everything met by silence.

And I'd been perfectly happy with my bottle of whiskey and pity party for one, until those two fucking clowns got involved.

I wish I'd never gone to the fucking Black Door.

A shudder ran though me as I thought about the pictures again. Whoever had edited them made it look like I was shooting a fucking porno.

And not even a good one.

They were all over Page Six.

The worst of it was that I had no way of knowing if she'd seen them. And for the first time ever I was grateful she wasn't in this country.

I started pacing again.

"I've spoken to them. Apparently, the son of the man running to be the new governor was there and the photographer was supposed to get him. But he saw you and a couple of other people too, so took advantage."

Fucking politicians.

"But how did they even get in? It's members only, you can't take guests. Everyone's searched on entry."

She sighed, sounding frustrated. "I'm not clear, they said they're dealing with it."

I didn't want to ask what that meant, Mary could out-inquisition the Spaniards. So, if she hadn't managed to get any more information it must have been serious. And I would not want to be on the business end of being dealt with.

"Fine, then how the fuck did they miss Drew and Felix?"

It wasn't even about the pictures. It was the fact that Freddie could see them and jump to the same conclusions that any normal person would.

That I was a sleaze.

That I didn't care about her.

That I'd cheated.

That I wasn't thinking about her every second of every day.

"I don't know." She replied.

I didn't dare ask her what she did fucking know.

"So, what does this mean?"

"Nothing, not much anyway, just lay low. Having a lap dance isn't illegal. But it's a good fucking job that place is so well protected. I've spoken to the PR team at the club and they've said there'll be no repercussions, especially given everyone else who'd been caught. An injunction has been placed on Page Six and any other press sniffing around, so nothing else will come out about this for the foreseeable. But the Black Door is under investigation."

"Nothing will happen, I've seen the Attorney General in there."

Not that I gave a single fuck about anything other than if Freddie had seen them.

"We'll see. Just keep your nose clean and, I mean it Cooper, do not fucking go anywhere for the next few weeks without my say so. In fact, don't even fucking breathe. You have the charity game coming up and then the season will start."

But I'd stopped listening because at that moment Jasper stalked into my kitchen, followed very closely by Murray who walked straight up to me and punched me hard in the face. I reeled backwards, hitting the stool on the counter before falling back on the floor, smacking my head on the polished concrete.

"Cooper? Are you listening?" She barked.

"Mary, it's Jas. He's going to need to call you back." He hung up the phone and I almost laughed. She would definitely not be happy about that. You didn't hang up on Mary.

I lay on the floor, my head and nose throbbing. My face felt warm and wet, pulling my hand back after touching it, it was covered in blood.

I felt my nose. Yep. Broken.

Well, this was just fan-fucking-tastic.

The cherry on top of my shitty, shitty life right now.

Fuck.

Did I deserve a broken nose? Probably.

Was I pissed about it? Definitely.

"You broke my fucking nose, you dick." At least that's what I hoped had come out, but couldn't be sure. I now sounded like I had the worst cold in history.

Murray leaned over me, peering down. "I told you if you fucked her about my fist would be in your face. Don't say I didn't fucking warn you."

Jasper shoved him out of the way and held his hand out to me. "Get up, Coop."

I took it and he pulled me to standing.

My nose started pouring blood.

I tilted my head back to stem the bleeding, pinching the bridge, but the throbbing was making it hard to focus. I made an attempt to walk to the freezer for an ice pack but couldn't see where I was going and banged into the wall, which jarred my elbow, knocking my nose.

I grunted out in pain.

"Cooper, sit the fuck down." Jasper guided me to a chair. "Where's the first aid kit?"

"In the laundry room."

He returned a few minutes later, along with an ice pack.

"Let me see." He pulled down my t-shirt which I'd been holding to my face to stop the bleeding. "Shit. This is a good knock, it needs realigning. Do you want me to call the doctor? Or Molly?"

"No, you do it."

He grimaced. "Are you sure? It's going to sting."

"Just do it, Jas." I gritted my teeth. It's not like I'd never had a knock before, but this felt so much worse than anything I'd ever experienced.

And I deserved it.

Absolute retribution.

"Okay, take a deep breath and count to five." He took hold of my nose.

I didn't even get to three before I heard the crunch of cartilage and bone as he moved it back into place. Pain lanced through me, spearing my brain. I yelled out as fresh bleeding started up and tipped my head back again.

"Are you okay?" He asked.

"No, I'm fucking not." My eyes were watering from the pain, I tried to wipe them with the t-shirt but it was sticking to me from the blood. "Can you help me get this shirt off?"

"Yes hang on, let me fix this first." He padded my nose up with gauze, then placed an ice pack on it, taking my hand to hold it in position. "What did you do to your hand?"

I'd forgotten about that.

My hand was also a mess, bruised and swollen. Yesterday, when Mary had called to tell me about Page Six and the images I'd punched a hole in my wall. Or punched a dent. It was a hard wall.

Luckily I didn't break my hand too, or I'd be seriously fucked for the season.

"I punched the wall yesterday."

"Jesus, Coop." So as not to knock me further, he took a pair of scissors and cut my shirt off. I didn't care, it was ruined anyway.

"Thanks. Can I get up? I want to clean my face."

"Yeah, but go slowly."

He helped me stand and I walked into the bathroom off the laundry room, stopping in front of the mirror.

I wasn't a pretty sight.

I looked like I'd been on the losing end of an MMA fight.

Dried blood was caked around my face, as well as the fresh blood still damp on my nose. But Jasper had done a good job of packing it up and it had stopped running, so that was something at least. I held a wash cloth under warm water and wiped away as much as I could without causing any more damage.

The swelling had been immediate, both my eyes starting to turn black from the punch. I had to give it to Murray, he landed a good one. I was almost impressed.

Almost.

Searching the cupboard I found some painkillers, swallowing them without water before picking up a clean shirt from the laundry basket easing it gently over my face.

When I walked back into the kitchen Murray was leaning against the table, where Jasper had taken a seat. Taking three beers from the fridge I handed them out before moving out of arms reach against the island, in case he got any more crazy ideas about attacking me.

I twisted the cap off and took a sip, before holding the ice pack on my face again. "How bad is it?"

Jasper pinned me with a stern glare. "It's bad."

I rolled my lips together. "So, Freddie's seen them?"

He nodded. "You have to fucking fix this."

Fuck. Bile started to rise up my throat.

Any hope I'd had of salvaging this mess and getting to her before she found out had been completely ripped to shreds. A long sigh escaped, tension building in my temples and I tried to rub it away. I'd wanted to be able to explain it to her.

Now I wouldn't get a chance.

A crushing emptiness took over.

I pulled out one of the stools and sat down. Ignoring

Murray's death stare I directed my question to Jasper. "What's Wolfie said?"

"Wolfie is pissed at me, that's how much she's pissed at you. And I don't get any sex when Wolf is pissed. So I'm telling you, fucking fix it now. And I don't care how you do it."

Wolfie and I had always had a good relationship and the thought of her being mad at me filled me with nothing but shame. The pressure of the last few weeks was starting to hit boiling point.

"I'VE BEEN FUCKING TRYING. SHE WON'T FUCKING SPEAK TO ME."

I dropped my face in my hands, the yelling hurting my head. I held the ice pack back on it.

"And what? You're just going to give up?"

I shrugged. "I don't know what else to do. Nothing has worked. This will have put the final nail in the coffin."

Murray picked up his beer, swigging from the bottle. "You're such a fucking pussy. You don't deserve to be with her if you're going to behave like this."

I narrowed my eyes at him.

"Coop?"

I turned my attention back to Jasper.

He titled his head, contemplating. "That's Amber in those pictures. Did you fuck her?"

If he was asking, then Freddie definitely would.

"No, of course I fucking didn't. I barely allowed her to touch me before I pushed her off. Jas, I was wasted and even in that state I knew I didn't want her."

Murray's death stare returned. "Odd. Doesn't really look like you're putting up that much of fight."

I turned to him, my lip curled up in a snarl. "You know what, if you're not going to say anything helpful then get the fuck out."

"I'm not trying to be helpful, you wanker." He spat back.

At that moment two more uninvited guests marched into the kitchen.

"What the fuck are you doing here?"

"Jesus." Felix pulled the ice pack off and examined my face before putting it back. "Who did that?"

"Anthony Joshua over there." I nodded towards Murray.

He glanced at him in silent disbelief and a flash of reverence, before taking two beers from the fridge as Drew hugged me gently.

"Dude, we're so sorry."

He turned to Jasper and Murray. "This is completely our fault." He motioned between him and Felix. "He didn't want to go and we made him. He was already drunk when we picked him up. He's been so miserable about Freddie the last few weeks that we wanted to cheer him up a bit. Honestly, he wasn't interested and Amber hardly touched him before he puked in the bathroom. That photographer got fucking lucky. Coop and I were probably only in there twenty minutes tops, then we left."

I sat in silence, drinking.

Jasper frowned taking in his words, then looked at Felix. "And where were you then?"

He had the good sense to appear sheepish. "I'd already gone upstairs."

"What's upstairs?" Asked Murray.

"Beds."

I swore I saw a sly smile cross Murray's face for a split second before the death glare returned, pinning me with it.

"Cooper?"

I glanced over to him.

He rubbed the stubble on his cheek. "Do you love her?"

I sighed. "More than anything."

He crossed his arms over his chest. "Then why haven't you told her?"

"Because I didn't realise I did until I got on the plane and then only when I arrived back home it hit me how much."

"But you still haven't told her."

I took a deep breath. "What part of 'she won't speak to me' do you not understand? And I'm not telling her via a fucking florist."

His eyebrow raised, unimpressed.

"I know I've fucked up. But I've sent her flowers every day, I even sent her a cookie. I've emailed her. I don't know what more I can do." My shoulders slumped. "She's probably better off without me anyway so what's the fucking point? She's ignored me for weeks, I don't even know if she does actually love me."

I prayed that wasn't true.

"God, spare us the self-pitying diatribe." Murray rolled his eyes at me. "You're both as stubborn as each other."

"What does that mean?" I grumbled.

"It means it took her two weeks to decide whether she wanted to talk to you again, because in all your notes you didn't tell her you loved her and she couldn't admit you might have just freaked out. Then when she decided she was going to, she saw those pictures. And now you're saying you're going to give up and she's better off without you. Which, right this second, I'm not disagreeing with." He looked me up and down, disgust written all over his face.

I gritted my teeth. "What exactly do you want me to do?"

"Oh fuck off. I've helped you enough."

"Murray, please." I begged.

He sat there, silently looking at me, his eyes narrowing as he rubbed his beard. I held his gaze, waiting for him to break.

"Fine. You need to use your brain. You want to get your apology heard? Think about what's important to her."

"What the fuck does that mean? Can you stop with all this cryptic shit? I've apologised every day."

And my head was fucking hurting from it.

"Freddie doesn't give a shit about flowers. That's Wolf territory."

I drummed my fingers on the countertop. What was important to Freddie? What did she love?

"Should I buy her a house to renovate?"

"Oh Jesus." Snorted Felix as he pushed off the counter and walked to the pantry. I watched him come back out with a packet of chips, head to the fridge, take out some dip and walk back to where he'd been standing. He looked up as he stuffed chips in his mouth. We were all staring. "What?"

"Got any better ideas, dipshit?"

"Better than buying her a house? Yeah." He scooped out some dip and dropped it into his mouth.

I waited until he looked up.

"Then by all means, do share." I sarcastically swept my hands in front of me.

He sighed like I was some kind of annoyance. "Coop, you can buy whatever you want, do something that isn't so easy. Something money can't buy. You've been in love with her since you met her, so you need to show her that and make her really believe it."

Why couldn't anyone just say what they meant. This wasn't a fucking treasure map.

"HOW? HOW DO I DO THAT?"

He stared at me like it should have been obvious. "Girls like effort, so put some in. Freddie likes music. I dunno, make her an apology playlist or something."

Oh my god.

If I wasn't worried about bleeding everywhere again I'd be smashing my head against the counter.

"I'm not a fucking fourteen year old with a crush."

"Really? Because that's how you've been behaving."

I glared at him.

"Look, Coop, I love you and I'm honestly really sorry for fucking things up more for you. But you have been behaving like a teenager with a crush. I get it, this is the first time you've ever liked a girl, but you're terrible at romance."

My head was throbbing and instead of smashing it against the counter like I wanted to, I placed it gently on the cool marble straight into a puddle of condensation from the melted ice pack.

This was a disaster.

Jasper walked over and squeezed my shoulder. "Coop, this isn't the worst idea, you know. Freddie loves music."

"Yeah, but a playlist? It's as lame as a cookie." I groaned.

"Hey!" Protested Drew as he walked past me to the fridge, taking out more beers and snacks, placing them on the table.

It didn't seem like they were planning on leaving any time soon.

"No it's not, she's always making them."

I sat up again. That *was* true.

I ran my hands through my hair, tugging on the ends. Thinking.

I wasn't convinced.

As much as I hated to admit it somehow Felix, the biggest manwhore in the continental United States, was right. And I was about to take romance advice from him.

But I was at rock bottom with nothing left to lose.

I needed to make more effort.

If I did this, I would it make the best fucking playlist she'd ever heard.

It would be a love letter.

I slid off the stool and walked over to where Murray was making his way through a bowl of popcorn.

"Muz?"

He looked up at me.

"I'm really sorry about this mess, I need you to know I never intentionally meant to hurt her. I love her more than I've ever loved anyone. I'll fix this."

He sighed. "You'd better. She loves you, Coop. I've never

seen her as miserable as she's been the last few weeks. You just both need to pull your heads out of your asses."

I nodded. "Yeah."

"I'm sorry about your face."

"It's okay, I deserved it."

"Yes, you did." He smirked but held his beer up to mine in a symbol of peace.

I tapped his bottle, then took a long sip. My brain started to fire up with a plan.

I rocked back on my heels. "When are you headed back to London?"

"At the end of the week."

I looked around at the boys in my kitchen, all waiting expectantly for me to say something. The plan was building in my head.

"Okay, I'll have everything ready for then. We have a charity game next Wednesday, can you bring her back for that?"

A smiled curled from the corner of his mouth. "Yes."

Fuck, I hope this works.

30

FREDDIE

"I'll pick you up at eight, make sure you're ready."

I groaned. In the four days he'd been back from the States Murray had been nagging me like an old lady to get up and get out of the house, get some fresh air. Something I really did not have the inclination to do. I also hadn't yet plucked up the courage to ask if he'd seen Cooper and as he'd not offered up the information I assumed he either hadn't or it wasn't good news.

It had made my heart break all over again.

Since I'd seen those pictures my heart had barely beaten, surviving with a desperate ache deep in my chest. The ache the only thing showing me I was still alive. The only thing I could feel.

Everything else numb.

I was existing in a world of beige.

I wasn't even angry. The fire, extinguished.

I tried so hard not to miss him or want him, but I knew deep down from the way my heart fluttered every time the doorbell rang I was still hopelessly in love with him. But Cooper had stopped with the daily delivery of flowers and apologies. There'd been nothing for a week. Nothing since the day of the photos.

I took it as a sign that he'd also given up.

That I'd been so easy to move on from.

I needed to move on too, but it was proving harder than I thought. Murray was right, I needed to get out.

"Yeah okay. Where are we going?"

"It's a surprise. But I'm taking you away and I'm going to cheer you up. Also do me a favour, shower and wash your hair or I'm going to need to bring some smelling salts. You were pretty ripe yesterday."

I gritted my teeth, another point he was correct about but it was something else I couldn't be bothered to do.

"How do you know I didn't today?"

"Did you?"

No.

What I did was move from my bed to the sofa, cried, watched depressing rom coms which made me cry more, ate a pint of ice cream and cried again.

I stayed silent.

"Thought as much." His voice dropped, softening. "Come on Franks, you need to get out. This isn't like you, I know you're hurting but I hate seeing you like this. You're stronger than this."

My eyes started getting hot, the tears not far away. "I thought I was but maybe I'm not."

"You are." He shot out, his tone filled with frustration. "Now get off the sofa. Put the ice cream down and get in the bath before a good night's sleep."

I didn't have the strength to argue, turns out surviving a diet of ice cream and sugar doesn't actually make you feel that great.

"Okay. Are you going to tell me what to pack?"

"Just casual is good. Whatever you want as long as you're out of those bloody pyjamas."

"Alright, point taken." I grumbled.

"Good, took you long enough to get it." He fired back. "Eight am, Franks. I'll see you in eleven hours. Now go to bed, okay."

"Yeah, yeah. See you in the morning, I'll be ready."

I hung up and walked upstairs.

True to his word he was waiting outside at eight am, the car horn shattering the silence as he leaned on it for long beeps. My neighbours were going to love me.

I threw my bag in the back of the car and got in, closing the door.

Murray gave me a once over. "You look better." He sniffed me, smirking. "And smell better."

I narrowed my eyes at him. I would have retaliated with a pithy retort if there was even a semblance of inaccuracy in his statement, but there wasn't. Last night I'd walked upstairs dead set on crawling straight into bed and then I'd caught sight of my reflection in the mirror. My hair, greasy and stuck to my head, my skin as grey as the cloud I'd been living under. I suspected there were corpses looking more alive than I did. I turned the shower up at hot as I could manage and got in. But as the water washed away the grime I'd accumulated, so the grip around my heart began to ease.

I'd fallen asleep within seconds, descending into a heavy, dreamless sleep.

"Yeah, well. You said I had to get out of my pyjamas."

"Damn right." He pulled me in and kissed my head. "Come on."

"Are you going to tell me where we're going?"

His jaw twitched as he held my gaze for a beat too long before looking away. "Not yet."

Okay, that was weird.

He started the engine and drove off. I closed my eyes, my lids still heavy from the sleep I'd recently emerged from.

When I opened them again we were pulling into the airport. Into the private terminal.

Something wasn't right about this.

"Murray, where are we?"

He stopped in front of the entrance, switching off the engine.

"At the airport." He replied without looking at me. "Come on, get out."

The doors were opened by the concierge and Murray threw him the keys as he rounded the car collecting our bags from the back. I could barely keep up as he stalked through the doors, his long legs carrying him further than mine did with each stride. It was almost like he wanted me to run alongside him, like he was trying to get away from me.

"Murray, where are we going?"

"I told you, it's a surprise. And we're running late, so chop chop Franks. We can't miss this slot."

He handed our passports over to the customs guys.

When did he get my passport?

My head was fuzzy from my recent lack of sleep and proper nutrition. I'm sure if I'd been up to par I could have worked it out sooner.

Another concierge greeted us, Murray shaking his hand while I stared on mutely, following them both across the tarmac and up the steps into the cabin, stopping short at the huge bouquet of roses sitting on the table.

My stomach bottomed out, butterflies filling the hole it left, blood pounding through my ears.

A thousand and one thoughts flew through my brain.

"Why are we flying private? Who organised this plane?" But I already knew the answer and I didn't want to believe it.

I gripped onto the doorframe, Murray pulling me into the cabin before my legs gave way, gently guiding me to a chair.

I didn't understand what was happening.

Murray put our bags on the seat before giving a nod to

someone behind me. I heard the cabin doors shut and the engine start. He leaned over to me, pulling the seatbelt across my lap and tightening it.

I frowned, trying to find an answer in his eyes but he was already looking out of the window. We started taxiing and I felt the front wheel lift, my anger and panic simultaneously rising up like a missile from its silo.

"MURRAY WHERE THE FUCK ARE WE GOING AND WHO THE FUCK ORGANISED THIS PLANE?"

He turned to face me, holding my glare, challenging and not backing down. "New York. And Cooper."

I stood up without thinking and toppled forward. The plane was still climbing.

"Jesus Franks, sit down will you." He pushed me back in my seat refastening my seatbelt like I was an errant child, glaring until we levelled out.

My blood reached boiling point. "TURN THIS PLANE AROUND RIGHT NOW. YOU'VE FUCKING KIDNAPPED ME."

The dick rolled his eyes at me, then stood up and moved to another part of the plane.

"MURRAY."

"We'll speak when you've stopped shouting and stopped being so dramatic." He put his headphones on, ending our conversation.

My fists clenched in rage.

A steward walked down the cabin, handing me a menu. "Ma'am, can I get you anything to eat or drink?"

"Just a coffee and some water please." I felt too sick to eat. The butterflies were having a rave in my stomach.

Why had Cooper organised this plane and made Murray kidnap me? The last time I'd heard from him had been six days ago, the day of the photos.

Why not just apologise? Kidnapping was extreme even for him.

Because you blocked him. And hadn't replied to any of his previous apologies. A tiny voice said.

Shut up, I was going to before I saw a naked woman writhing on his lap.

Jealously rose up, the knife twisting in my heart again. I couldn't unsee those images.

"Thank you." I looked up at the steward as he placed a coffee in front of me.

He smiled with kindness in his eyes before walking off. There's no way he hadn't heard my yelling, so he must definitely be wondering what the fuck was going on. Although he didn't seem too concerned about my blatant kidnapping. Cooper had probably paid him off.

Fucker.

I sipped my coffee and glanced over at Murray his headphones still on, flipping through a magazine. I still didn't have any idea what I was doing here and knew I wouldn't get any answers unless I kept my anger at bay.

I took a deep breath and plonked myself on the chair in front of him. "Speak then."

He pulled his headphones off, his eyebrow raised.

"Murray."

"Yes?"

I gritted my teeth, willing my anger to subside. "Could you please explain why we're on this plane?"

"It was the only way Cooper could get you to speak to him."

"BY KIDNAPPING ME?'

He ignored me, so I attempted a normal decibel again. "And you're helping him? Have you not seen those pictures?"

He took a deep breath, putting the magazine down. "Yes, I have. And believe me, I was angry. So fucking angry. But he explained it to me and it's not what you think. He deserves to be heard out."

What?

285

"Wait, you saw him?"

My heart began hammering against my rib cage and a wave of nausea crashed through me.

"I did. He's really torn up over this, and he looked like shit. As bad as you."

"I don't look like shit."

Lies.

His eyebrow raised again. "You don't look great."

"I can't believe you didn't tell me you saw him. You're supposed to be on my side."

"I am on your side. I am. But I also know how much you've been hurting. If I told you I'd seen him then all hell would have broken loose and you wouldn't have come, mostly because I also know how stubborn you are."

I crossed my arms over my chest, defeated. I was being forced into a situation I wasn't ready to face. Deep down I knew I didn't want to hear his explanation because then what if I forgave him and he hurt me all over again.

I knew I wouldn't survive.

Murray leant over and scooped his bag off the other seat. Unzipping it, he reached in and pulled out a square box placing it in front of me. It was tied in a navy ribbon, which was securely holding an envelope in place. An envelope with my name on it.

I glared at it suspiciously. "What's that?"

"It's from Coop."

My eyes started to get hot and my throat thickened until I could barely swallow.

"Look, just listen to what he has to say. If you don't like it then we'll fly back tomorrow. But at least you get to see Wolfie."

I took a deep breath, the thought of seeing her the only thing mollifying me. I watched Murray get comfortable on the sofa, plumping up the pillow behind his head and lying back. He closed his eyes, putting his headphones back on.

"Open that or don't open that, but I know you want to and you'll regret it if you don't."

I sat and stared at the box as tentatively as I would a live grenade. Knowing what was inside contained a blast just as powerful. A blast whose only victim would be me.

Would be my heart.

I stared until my eyes blurred over and it turned into a blob. Then I pulled out the envelope and stared at that too. It was thick and weighty. It started shaking and I could barely hold it from the force, until I realised the shaking was coming from me. I was shaking, the adrenalin rolling through me like thunder, my nerves frayed.

If I was going to do this, I needed something to steady myself.

I looked around and caught the eye of the steward as he peered out of the galley door at the end. "Please could you bring me two large brandies?"

He disappeared, popping out a minute later with two glasses on a tray. Amber liquid, the colour of Cooper's eyes, stayed steady as he placed one in front of me, the other nearer to Murray.

"Can I get you anything else, Ma'am?"

"No, not right now, thank you." I downed one glass, reaching over and pulling the other nearer.

The steward picked up the empty one. "Just let me know when you need anything."

I smiled, gazing back down at the envelope as he walked off.

It was now or never.

I curled my legs up underneath my body, shrinking as small as I could get and stuck my thumb into the edge of the thick cream paper and ripped, sliding out several pages covered with his handwriting. I unfolded them until the top page stared up at me, my eyes filling up with tears which spilled over as I read the first sentence. Before I could wipe them away fat drops fell onto the paper, smudging the ink.

My darling Francesca,
I can call you that because you are, mine. Even though you might not feel it right now, you are. And I am yours. I belong to you heart and soul. I'm so sorry for the pain and hurt I caused you. I'm sorry it took me so long to realise what I should have known all along, but know that I will spend the rest of my life making it up to you if you'll let me.
I wish I could say these words to your face, but I can't because we haven't spoken and I know I deserve the silent treatment you've been giving me. These last few weeks have been the most painful and miserable of my life. Even the broken nose from Murray was nothing compared to this desperate emptiness dragging in my chest because you're not here.

What? I re-read that last sentence. Broken nose? My eyes shot to Murray, softly snoring, oblivious.

And the week we spent together was undoubtedly my happiest. Being with you made me feel more alive than I've ever been. More than every time I lace up my skates and get on the ice, more than every puck drop, or goal scored. You've given me life beyond hockey.
I've been trying to find the words to explain to you how I feel. It sounds too simple to say I miss you. But I do, so so much it's almost unbearable. I miss your laughter and your fire. I miss the way your hand fits into mine. I miss your sharp tongue when you're angry and your soft tongue when your mouth is pressed against mine as I kiss you. I miss the way you hide into me because the sun has woken up earlier than you wanted to. I miss the way you look at me like I'm the only man on earth. I miss the greedy noises you make and your demands for more when our bodies are fused perfectly together. Your body that was made for mine.

In French we say 'Tu me manques', but this means more than I miss you, its connotation is 'You are missing from me', but I actually think it's more accurate.

My perfect Francesca, you are missing from me, like a limb would be missing, or like my heart is missing. You are missing from me. And you are. I'm not whole without you.

I know you might think it's easy for me to say sorry and that my words might not mean so much to you, so I'm going to prove to you I'm telling the truth. Prove to you you've always been with me.

I have some instructions for you.

Open the box.

I sniffed loudly and wiped my eyes as I put down the letter, struggling to read any more in my current state. I pulled on the ribbon to untie the bow, lifting the lid off I peered inside finding a brand new pair of rose gold noise cancelling headphones.

My heart caught in my throat.

I took them out of the case, turning them over in my hands, running my fingers against the smooth metal and leather. They were so pretty, they were the pair I told Cooper I was going to buy, but since everything happened I hadn't got around to it. I went back to the letter, using my sleeve to mop up the fresh tears which had started flowing again before the steward silently placed a box of tissues in front of me.

Now tell Murray to send you my email.

I frowned. Murray was still fast asleep, but I wasn't about to wait for him to wake up. I shook his foot. He grunted.

"Murray. Cooper says you have to send me an email."

His left eye opened a fraction. "I already did."

I picked up my phone, checking my email. Sure enough there was one from Murray, looking at the time stamp he'd sent it as we boarded. I clicked into it, finding a link, taking me straight to Spotify. To a playlist called A Love Letter for Francesca.

I loud gasp rolled up my throat as I tried to catch my breath.

He'd made me a playlist. An actual playlist.

You're always making playlists and I wanted to make one for you. This is my love letter to you, this is our love story.

Put your headphones on and press play.

I did as instructed, a melodic disco beat starting up before I turned it off. I flicked through the rest of the playlist, looking at what he'd put on it. It was so random and eclectic, I wondered where he'd come up with half of them. This was so un-Coop, I couldn't even imagine him sitting down to do this. Hope flickered like a candle and warmth began flooding through me as the first smile I'd had in a week broke through my misery.

I knocked back the second brandy and went back to the letter.

The very first time I saw you was at Jasper's house. Do you remember? You came with Wolfie and spent the night. You were wearing a white dress and I could see the outline of your heavenly body as the sun backlit you when you walked down the garden. Fantasy by Earth, Wind and Fire was playing on the speakers in the pool house and I remember because that song was stuck in my head for days. Last week I was driving home and it came on the radio. It took me right back to that day and I realised that every time I hear it I think of you. I always have.

Last Halloween you were dressed as Wednesday Addams (I'd like to revisit that school uniform by the way...) We were all on the dance floor, you and Wolfie were jumping around to Bust a Move by Young MC. You were screaming the words so loudly for such a tiny person – although I'm well aware your size is deceptive - I thought you were the most entertaining and hilarious woman I'd ever met. You loved life and didn't care who was around to see it, you were so refreshing and such a breath of fresh air to me. I've never met anyone like you. You are one of a kind.

I know you've been recently reminded that on New Year's Eve I lost my shit at that douche trying to dance with you. But I bet you don't know why. Earlier that evening we'd been at Jasper and Wolfie's and you'd been dancing on the table to Fleetwood Mac's Everywhere. I'd hugged you when I walked in and you'd smelt like cinnamon from all the cookies you'd been baking that day. Cinnamon and love. And that dickhead didn't deserve to breathe in any of it. He didn't deserve to share the same air as you. I didn't know it at the time, but I was jealous of anyone who breathed the same air as you. I still am.

January 27th was the day you sent me my first ever playlist, it was made up of your favourite British bands. The first song on there was Wonderwall by Oasis. We had a big game that night against Philly and I listened to it all day. I scored four goals. I'm not saying it was because of the playlist, because I know it wasn't. It was because of you. You're my Wonderwall, Tiny.

One day, Jas and I were running along Riverside Park. During our run, we passed a busker singing Bleachers Don't Take The Money. It was the first warm day of the year and the sky was the colour of your eyes. I drove home from Jasper's still thinking about them. They see right through me. They did then and they do now. I go to sleep praying I'll see them again.

It was the night of the cup finals in Chicago and the teams were skating around during warm up before the game. Sam Smith

*Promises was playing over the speakers and the crowds were chant-
ing. I remember seeing you sitting next to Wolfie, you were
laughing at something she'd said, your face creased up and your
head thrown back. You were wearing my jersey and it made my
heart beat faster. You looked so beautiful and I knew even then that
I wanted to see you in it always.*

*When we flew in from Vegas I didn't know then that my life was
about to change, that I'd finally wake up. We'd been playing Jamie
XX in the car and you were driving like a madman, scaring the
crap out of me. I was looking at you while you were mouthing
along to Loud Places, watching your nose scrunch up and your
perfect, soft lips – lips I can still feel on mine if I think about it
hard enough – curl up with every word. When you kissed me you
jump started my heart again, my heart I kept blocked from
accepting I was already madly in love with you. It was the best kiss
of my life.*

*The Doors Light My Fire. Do you remember because I do? Have
you noticed you're still missing your panties?*

*I'd like to say I remember what was playing the first time we had
sex, the first time we made love. But I can't. My focus was one
hundred percent on you. I have never experienced anything more
perfect. More perfect than you. More perfect than the way our
bodies fit together and I know I never will. So instead I'll tell you
that I remember you playing Prince when we drove to your parents'
house the next day.*

*When I left you, Maggie Rogers Light On was playing in the car.
I'd never heard it before but I made the driver tell me what it was
and put it on repeat. I was still listening as I walked up the steps to
the plane. I finally recognised the pain in my chest was from my
heart breaking and the more I listened the more I realised what I
was feeling and how much I loved you. And how badly I'd fucked*

up. I'm so sorry. Baby, please know, I will always leave the light on for you.

Lamb, Goreki. This last one is our song. You don't know it yet, but it is. I've listened to the lyrics over and over. They sum up how I feel more perfectly than I ever could.

So you see you've always been with me, my love.
Always.
I never realised how much I loved you until I left. It took me a little bit of time to get there, but I'm here now and I've never leaving again.
Please forgive me. Please come back to me and make me whole again.
I love you with all my heart and soul, forever.
Coop xxxx

Tears rolled down my cheeks, dripping off the end of my nose and chin as I reread the last paragraph.

He loved me.

Cooper loved me.

And the relief suddenly became too much to bear.

Covering my face in my hands, pain finally ripped through me. Like a dam bursting its banks every shred of self-doubt, every ounce of tension that had festered inside me, every fragment of despair I'd built up over the last few weeks flowed out of me in great rasping sobs until my chest heaved and I was gasping for air.

They echoed through the cabin, waking Murray. He sat up and pulled me into his body, stroking my hair, letting me cry into him and absorb his calmness.

"Shhhhh." He whispered over and over. "It'll be okay, it's okay. Don't worry, Franks. It's all good, you'll see."

I let my sobs subside before lifting my head up to look at him.

His eyes widened, taking on a teasing glint. "Woah. Your face is in serious need of a cold wash cloth."

I had no doubt, even without looking I knew it was red and puffy.

He smiled and pushed my hair away from my face. "What did his letter say?"

"That he loved me and he was sorry. Oh and that you broke his nose." I frowned.

He laughed loudly. "Did he really?"

I nodded. "Is that true?"

"Yes. I didn't mean to break his nose, but I did tell him if he fucked you over my fist would be in his face. And I stay true to my word. To give him credit, he took it well."

I leaned up and kissed him on the cheek. "Thank you. You better not have ruined his face, but I do really appreciate it. Let's hope he learnt his lesson."

"I'd say he did." He peered down at me. "So does that mean you've forgiven him?"

"Almost, but I'd like to hear him say it himself." It then dawned on me I had no concept of what was happening when we got to New York, I was merely a pawn in their game. I sighed. "And seeing as you masterminded this kidnapping, I assume you know when I'll see him?"

He smirked. "We're heading to Wolf's when we land, then tonight Jas and Coop are playing in some star-studded charity match with a few of the guys. We're going to watch."

My chest deflated like a shrivelled balloon. "I won't see him until after?"

Now I'd decided I was going to speak to him I wanted to do it as soon as possible.

"No, and you should count it as a blessing. You need all the time you can get to make your eyes go back to normal." He pointed his finger at me. "No more crying."

My mouth curved up in one corner. "I'm good, I don't think I have any tears left."

"Good. Right I'm starving. Let's get you some water and both of us some food. I fancy a burger." He patted his six-pack.

My stomach rumbled, deciding it too was ready for some proper food after being made to survive on ice cream alone.

And for the first time in nearly a month I felt like things might be okay.

The elevator doors opened to Jasper and Wolfie's apartment. We heard a screech before we saw her, hurtling down the hall and skidding on the polished floor wrapping her arms around both of us.

"You made it." She squeezed us tightly before stepping back and giving me a full once over. "Are you okay?"

"Yes, I'm good. I'm better anyway. Or I will be once I've seen him." I linked arms with her as she dragged us into the kitchen. "Have you seen him?"

"Only today when he came to pick up Jas. He's not dared show his face around here. Although I have to say, he looks terrible. He's really been suffering."

A pang of guilt shot through me before I could push it away. I didn't like the thought of him suffering, even if it was a situation of his own doing.

Mostly his own anyway.

Alright, fifty fifty.

"Did Murray tell you the plan?"

"I did." He piped up, his head deep within the refrigerator. That boy was always hungry.

"And you're going to come tonight?"

I nodded.

"Good, Cooper left something here for you." She walked over to the coffee table and picked up a package, handing it to me.

I took the card from the top, opening it.

I meant it when I said I wanted to see you in it always.
I love you.
Cooper xxxx

I reached in and pulled out a soft parcel wrapped in tissue paper. Ripping into it, I uncovered a hockey jersey. The logo and the date for tonight's game stitched on the left breast, turning it over I found his name on the back. He loved me and he wanted me to wear his name. The butterflies started fluttering around my heart, causing a flush to run over me.

"Oh amazing, now we'll be matching." Wolfie retrieved a bottle of wine from the fridge placing it in front of me alongside three glasses.

Murray took the bottle from her, twisting the corkscrew in and popping the cork out.

She glanced up at the clock while Murray poured the wine out. "Right we have three hours to drink this and make ourselves look presentable before we have to leave."

Having seen myself in elevator mirrors on the way up, I prayed that would be enough time.

Klaxons were blaring around the stadium as we made our way to our seats in the family section of the stands, right by the ice. The nerves that had calmed down when I'd arrived at Wolfie's were now through the plexiglass roof, nerves that even a few glasses of wine couldn't tamper.

Wolfie squeezed my knee as we sat down. "It'll be okay, don't worry. You'll feel better once you've had a chat."

I managed a weak smile. Even though he'd finally said he loved me, he'd made me a playlist and sent me his jersey – which I was wearing – my insecurities were still fuelling a small part of me to wonder if he really meant it. We hadn't seen each other in a month. What if he changed his mind once he saw me?

Murray put his hand on my leg. "Franks can you stop fidgeting please. Your bouncing is giving me motion sickness."

I looked at my watch, they should be on the ice by now.

I turned to Wolfie. "Where are they?"

Just then, the lights dropped and spotlights zoomed around the stadium. The announcer introduced the game and started calling names as one by one the players came out, shooting across the ice before heading to their team bench.

"AND NUMBER 17, CENTRE FROM THE NEW YORK RANGERS, COOPER MARKS."

I watched as he skated out.

My heart was rapidly beating through my chest, the air caught in my throat. He looked so much bigger than I remembered, more imposing, more powerful. He skated around, removing his helmet as he arrived at the benches.

And then he looked up, stopping dead still.

Our eyes locked and every unspoken word, every unac-knowledged emotion tangled together in a ball of fiery heat and lust passing between us. I watched his eyes fill with tears before a grin split his face so wide you could have seen it from space. My heart pounded and pounded against the walls of my ribcage, like a prisoner begging to be set free.

The moment was broken as Felix exited the ice and knocked straight into him, sending them both flying.

I laughed so hard, tears were soon clouding my vision. It was exactly the light relief we needed to break the tension and I knew without a doubt that everything was going to be okay. As they straightened themselves he turned back around winking at me before taking to the benches.

Cooper's team won in a 5-0 shut out, three of the goals scored by him. I'd been screaming so loudly my throat was burning and my voice hoarse. Wolfie grabbed my hand and pulled me out towards the locker rooms, Murray following quickly behind.

I was finally going to see him again.

Eleven minutes and forty two seconds later, he walked out. His imposing presence drew everyone to him, but he didn't notice, his eyes scanning round with one singular goal - finding mine.

He stalked towards me, invading all my space and sucking the air out of my lungs but stopping a fraction too far away. Holding my gaze, he dropped his bag on the floor and I soaked him in, studying him. His hair still wet from the shower, he was dressed in his team trackpants and hoodie, not the usual post-match suit, and he looked so fucking edible my mouth dried up.

As imposing as he still was, he looked thinner and the dark circles under his eyes were from lack of sleep and worry, rather than Murray's broken nose. I knew because I carried the same scars.

"Hi Tiny." His voice deep, gruff and drowning in emotion.

He still hadn't touched me. My body was almost twitching with desire and desperation to wrap myself around him and never let go.

"Hi." My fingers lost the battle and I reached out, running my thumb along his cheek, under his eye. "I'm sorry about Murray."

He leant into my palm, his eyes closing for a second as he held his hand against mine, trapping it. "I deserved it."

Tears began swimming in my eyes again. We needed to talk and I desperately wanted to be alone with him.

His gaze turned apprehensive. "Look, there are post-match drinks. But unless you want to go, please can we leave?" It was as if he read my mind. "I'll do whatever you want though. Just being next to you is enough right now."

He looked so nervous, it served to settle mine still swimming around at Olympic speeds. "No, we can go."

His eyes lit up, taking my hand from his face he kissed my palm. "Thank you."

Curling my hand in his, holding it tight, he bent down to pick up his bag from the floor. He turned to Jasper and Murray who were chatting to Wolfie. "Hey, we're going to take off."

They all looked at me, silently asking my permission to be okay with it. I gave Wolfie a one-armed hug. "I'll call you later."

We walked to the stadium's underground parking, towards his car. He didn't let go of my hand until he had to close the passenger door and get in the driver's side. Reminiscent of the morning we'd left mine and he'd stopped Simon harassing me, he gripped the steering wheel breathing deeply, steadying himself.

I sat, silent, waiting for him to speak before he turned to me, tension thickening the air. He scanned across my face, as though committing me to memory again, and cupped my cheek.

His touch sent shockwaves down my spine.

"I was going to drive back to mine, is that okay?"

I nodded.

His expression morphed into pain. "I know we have a lot to talk about, but before we go anywhere I want you to know that those pictures, that woman..." His voice drifted off, his eyes dropping. "I'm so sorry... it was stupid... Drew and Felix took me to a strip club, to cheer me up. I'd been so miserable and I was drunk off my ass, but I should have known better. She was there for less than a minute before I pushed her off, but I know how it seemed." He looked back up at me. "I swear nothing happened. Baby, I love you so much and I'm so so sorry I hurt you. I'm sorry I didn't tell you sooner."

They were the words I needed to hear and seeing the anguish on his face released the anger I'd been holding onto. The anger that had slowly been eating away at me, fuelling my refusal to acknowledge him and his pain.

We both had to concede defeat.

"I'm sorry too. I'm sorry it took me so long to speak to you. I should have done it sooner, I should have done it when the first bouquet of flowers arrived." A smile tipped my lips. "I was so hurt and I know my silence didn't help either of us but I never stopped loving you."

He tucked my hair behind my ear before his gaze dropped to my lips. Running the pad of his thumb across it, pulling on it, a heavy throb started up between my legs igniting the fire that had died when he left.

He snatched his hand away like he'd been burned. "We need to get out of here. I'm not going to be able to stop at a kiss."

He started the engine and exited the car park.

With one hand firmly on the top of my thigh he sped through every crossing and every light whether it was green or amber. It was a wonder we hadn't been pulled over.

And he called me the crazy driver.

With every mile the air grew thicker, his grip on my thigh tighter.

Twenty minutes later he pulled off the interstate onto a dirt track, surrounded by trees, the clearing dark in the twilight of the evening. He cut the engine.

I looked around. "Coop? Where are we? Why've we stopped?"

"I can't wait until we get home." He turned to me, grabbing the back of my head, pulling me into him.

His lips crashed onto mine with no finesse, his tongue sweeping across my mouth, pushing inside with a level of desperation I matched. We collided together in a frenzy, sucking on each other, taking what we needed, rediscovering each other from the month we'd spent apart.

It wasn't enough.

I tried to move and found myself trapped in the seatbelt. Undoing it he pulled me into his lap so I straddled him. His magnificent cock already rock hard underneath me.

How had I managed a month without it? Without him.

He dragged his hands through my hair, tilting my head back, licking along the column of my neck and biting at my jaw, growling against me. The sensation sent a flood of wetness to my knickers, soaking them.

I rocked against him, rewarded with a groan in my ear while he sucked on the lobe. Pressure was building up inside me and I craved the release more than I needed to breathe.

"Coop, I need you." My plea primal and dripping in desire so feral it was unrecognisable.

He grabbed a handful of hair and jerked my head back, locking my eyes into his, incandescent with hot, hungry lust.

He nipped at my lips, making me whimper. "This won't be gentle, Francesca. I can't do that."

"Good. Give it to me. I need it."

My words ignited a frenzy to get inside me, lifting me to my knees he unbuttoned my jeans, yanking them down as far as they would go. But taking one look at my knickers, he simply ripped them in half and I nearly came there and then.

His dick sprung free from his sweatpants as he pulled them down, barely giving me a second to catch my breath before lifting me back up and impaling me in one long thrust, making me take him right to the hilt.

"FUCK." My head flew back as we both screamed.

I was fluttering around him, my clit throbbing and my chest heaving as it acclimated to the sensation of him inside me, the delicious feeling of being stretched out by him again, until it wasn't enough.

He pulled my mouth to his, running his tongue against mine, allowing me to settle to his size. "Baby, you okay?" His voice had dropped an octave.

I scrapped my fingers through his hair, bringing his gaze to mine. "I need more, I need you to move."

As if he'd been waiting for the green light, he gripped onto my hips. "Hold on tight." He started pistoning me onto his cock and curling one big hand around the back of my neck he began ramming me down so hard I was seeing stars.

An almost overwhelming pressure began building and I knew I was about to be ripped in half by an orgasm with the force of freight train.

"Fuck, baby you're so perfect. So tight. I can feel you throbbing around me. I'm so close, wait for me." He hissed, sucking air through his teeth.

His words were enough to tip me over the edge.

"Now, fuck." I screamed as the freight train I predicted barrelled through me, taking Cooper along for the ride, exploding inside me with an identical strength. I collapsed against him, spent and sweaty, while his cock continued to jerk making my pussy throb.

He began tracing patterns across my back, soothing me while he waited for our heavy breathing to subside, keeping the silence intact. I lay against his chest, my heart banging at full throttle, at a pace it hadn't since before he'd left.

And I knew it had finally healed.

I sat up and he held my gaze, his eyes brimming with heavy emotion. He was right, we were two halves of a whole. I had been missing a piece of him just as much as he'd been missing a piece of me.

And now we were one.

He cupped my face. "I love you Francesca Danvers. I'm so sorry it took me so long to realise, but I will spend the rest of my life making it up to you."

It was all I needed.

He was mine as I was his.

A sly grin curled up on my lips. "You'd better. Now take me home."

He shook his head. "So fucking bossy."

"But you love it."

He smacked his lips to mine. "Yes, yes I do."

EPILOGUE

COOPER

Nine months later

I stopped pacing and looked down at my phone as it buzzed.

Drew: *She left two hours ago, she shouldn't be too long*

For fucks sake, always fucking late. Where the fuck was she? Probably stopped for a coffee on the way home.

I checked the trunk of the car for the umpteenth time. Reaching into the pockets of my bag curling my fingers around the little box, the tension in my chest eased slightly.

I was about to call when I heard her car tearing up the driveway screeching to a halt in front of the house. In nine months, her driving hadn't improved.

I'd almost go as far to say it was worse.

She jumped out and ran into the house. "Sorry, sorry." She called.

I don't think she'd even noticed me standing outside, in too much of a hurry to even switch the engine off.

Good job we had security gates.

I rolled my eyes as I rounded her car and reached in to shut the engine. I checked my watch again.

"Francesca, can you hurry the fuck up." I yelled.

"Coop? Where are you?" I heard her call again.

"I'm out here, where I was when you ran into the house."

She appeared at the door, looking sheepish.

"Are you ready? Can you get in the fucking car please?"

Deviousness flashed across her face before she launched into a full sprint, hurling herself at me. I caught her mid air and she wrapped her legs around my waist, kissing me, her tongue sweeping round my mouth, stroking against mine.

My cock started to stir, him and I both powerless to her charm. I pulled away before I made us even later, carrying her over to the car and depositing her in the passenger seat.

"Do not move." I ordered, brushing my lips to hers, never missing an opportunity to touch them.

"Jesus Christ, you're so bossy today. Don't boss me on my birthday." She grumbled.

"It's not your birthday until Saturday." I smirked. "And I'm the boss, we both know that."

"No you fucking aren't."

And I wasn't actually. Not totally.

In the nine months since we'd got back together we'd fallen deeper in love every day. She'd given me a level of happiness I couldn't have predicted.

We were so similar that while our stubbornness could have been a recipe for disaster, instead we learned what pushed each other's buttons and knew instinctively when one of us needed space or company. And in the same way she called me out on my shit, I called her out on hers and we'd quickly synced into a pattern of living and working with an ease we'd never experienced before.

Because her job was easily transportable she rented out her house and moved over immediately into mine, or ours as it is now. The fact that we built it together, making it all the sweeter.

Wolfie and Jasper were expecting a baby and with Murray spending more time in the city, our friends had merged into one big happy group. Soon after, Drew had managed to persuade her to help with his renovations, finally giving him his beloved disco ball. It was almost finished and I was so proud of how hard she worked, even on the days I had to curb my jealously when he monopolised her time.

I'd also discovered a level of passion in her ten fold to the one I'd found in London. We were rarely parted, even during my long away spells, craving each other's bodies with an intensity I didn't know could possibly exist.

I never not wanted her.

We were perfect together.

She'd become my best friend, the face I wanted to see at the beginning and end of every day. The ghosts of my past had been well and truly exorcised and I couldn't imagine ever being without her.

Which is why I was so desperate to get the fuck out of here.

I walked back to the house and locked the door, checked her car was locked, then got into my car, before getting out again and checking the trunk one more time.

I slid back into the seat. "I have your bags in here. Have you got everything you need? There's nothing else you want to take?"

She looked at me like I'd lost it. "No, Coop, everything is in there. I told you I'd packed before I left for Drew's."

"Yeah, okay." I took a deep breath, trying to calm my racing heart and leaned over to her. "Kiss me please."

She obliged pulling back before I could deepen it and get carried away, a quizzical look on her face. "Are you okay? You're being weird."

I sat up. "No I'm not, you're just going to make us late. We can't miss our slot."

She rolled her eyes as I started the car and drove out of the gates before my hand gravitated to where it always sat, firmly on her thighs.

The concierge at Teterboro lifted the bags from the trunk before I could stop him.

I reached for the smallest, most precious one, snatching it from his grip. "I'll take that. Thank you." I pressed a wad of cash in his hand before he could also decide I'd lost it.

I held my hand out to Freddie and she took it, walking through the airport together, towards our plane.

She made herself comfortable as I stored the bags, the steward fussing around her.

"Can I get you both a glass of champagne?" He asked.

"No thank you. Just some fresh mint tea would be good."

Weird. She never turned down a glass of champagne and she normally hated mint tea.

I stroked her head. "Baby, are you okay?

She smiled up at me, always momentarily rendering me speechless. "Yes, just didn't feel like it right now."

I sat down next to her as the cabin doors closed, leaning over to fasten her seatbelt and kissing her again briefly, never getting quite enough. She put her hand in mine as the plane taxied and lifted off.

Before it had a chance to level out, she unbuckled and moved into my lap, curling into me. I wrapped my arms around her pulling her closer, kissing her head, inhaling her intoxicating citrussy scent.

She snuggled into me. "Mmmm, this is nice."

My dick twitched, filling me with regret I hadn't hired a larger plane with a bed.

"I can't wait to get to Palm Springs and have some time alone before everyone else arrives."

A pang of guilt and panic flashed through me. We weren't exactly going to Palm Springs.

I kissed her head. "I know, Baby. Me too."

I looked up as the steward approached. "Can I offer you anything else to drink? Champagne or more peppermint tea?"

"Just a beer if you've got it? Thanks man."

"And I'll have more tea please." Freddie added.

Okay, something wasn't right. I unbuckled us, carrying her over to the long sofa. Shifting her so I could see her face while she sat in my lap.

"Francesca what's going on? What's with all the tea?"

Cupping my cheek, she tilted her head as a soft smile crept across her face. "I'm sorry I was late today."

"Baby, I don't care that you were late. You're always late. I've learned to build it in to departure times." I grinned. "Wait, what's that got to do with you drinking tea?"

She rolled her eyes. "Nothing. I was late because I was at the doctor."

I spun her around so she straddled me, my eyes searching for something wrong. "Francesca, tell me now. What's the matter? Are you okay?"

She pursed her lips at me, before running her fingers through my hair. "Calm down. I'm fine."

A deep sigh of relief escaped.

"But I am pregnant." She searched my face.

Come again?

It's possible my heart stopped.

I stared, unblinking. "What?"

Her hands snaked round my neck. "Coop, I'm pregnant. We're having a baby."

I stared down at her flat stomach, gently placing my hand over it. "For real?"

She nodded.

"I'm going to be a father? We're having a baby?" My voice broke, my heart fit to bursting. My eyes became hot and overspilled with unshed tears, which she wiped away.

She nodded again.

Oh my fucking god.

She smiled down at me. "Really? You're really happy? You don't feel like I've trapped you?"

My eyes widened. "Are you insane? Baby, trap away. I love you so much, this is the best thing I've ever heard."

And that was the god's honest truth.

I pulled her mouth to mine, desperate to close the already narrow gap between us, needing to taste her, feel her inside of me. I moaned into her mouth, running my tongue softly along hers, savouring every stroke.

She tasted like her tea.

I released her lips from mine before we passed the point of no return, placing my hand back on her stomach. "How did you know?"

She smirked. "I didn't, but I was at Wolfie's yesterday and she'd left some pregnancy tests lying around so I tried one for a joke, and it came up positive. So, joke's on us really."

I shook my head, laughing as I imagined her reaction, so typical Freddie. My excitement died slightly as I briefly wondered if Wolfie had known before me.

"I haven't told anyone but you. I wouldn't do that." Reading my mind she ran her thumbs over my frown, smoothing the creases out. "I thought it must have been broken, but I couldn't stop thinking about it so I left and bought some more and they were all positive. And the doctor confirmed it this morning, but we can go back next week for a proper scan. I didn't want to do it without you."

Fuck, I loved this woman more than seemed logical.

"How many weeks?"

"Four."

"And we can still have sex without hurting the baby?"

A mischievous glint immediately twinkled in her beautiful blue eyes. "We can. And I'm feeling really horny, so how long until we get to Palm Springs?"

Shit.

"What?" She must have noticed my panic, because she narrowed her eyes.

Okay, I couldn't not tell her.

I ran my hands over her back, pulling her into me, kissing her nose. "Baby, we're not going to Palm Springs."

Her frown deepened, her faced dropping in disappointment. "Oh, okay. Where are we going then?"

I'd planned everything out to the nth degree to make sure this weekend was perfect. Planned for everything except a baby, so maybe I needed to change things up and wing it.

I stood up with her still in my lap, placing her back on the sofa. Grabbing my bag I pulled out the red box I'd been guarding with my life, sinking to my knees in front of her.

Her brows knitted together as she wondered what I was doing.

"We're going to Italy."

Her eyes opened wide. "Seriously?"

I nodded.

She flung herself forward, hugging me. "That's amazing. Oh god, Coop. Thank you, thank you. What a brilliant surprise."

Relief flooded through me, until I remembered why I was on my knees.

I stroked her cheek as she looked down at me. "You're welcome, Baby. But there's more. I'd planned a whole weekend of birthday surprises, but as you've given me the biggest and best surprise, I'm bringing some events forward."

I reached for the box and tipped out the velvet case inside, holding it out in my palm.

"I don't want to go on for another second without you being officially tied to me and us trapped together."

Her eyes brimmed. "Cooper, what's that?"

"Open it." I pushed it forward for her to take and she did, tentatively.

She flipped it open, her hand flying to cover her mouth as she gasped.

I knew she wouldn't want a ring like anyone else's, and I'd worked with our architects to design the perfect one for her based on the symmetry she'd created in our house. A chunky gold band with art deco diamond inlay, holding a four-carat pale blue sapphire, the colour of her eyes, in place.

It was her.

"Francesca Rose Elizabeth Danvers, you're everything I never realised I wanted or needed. You're my best friend, my favourite person in the world and soon to be mother of my child. I love you more than I can put into words and I'm so grateful to you every day for choosing me. I want to spend the rest of my life with you and I promise to spend the rest of my life working to make you as happy you make me. Baby, please say you'll marry me."

I wiped away the tears pouring down her cheeks, her smile breaking through them like sunshine on a cloudy day.

She leant down, touching her lips to mine. "Yes. I will. Of course I will. I love you so much."

Taking the ring from its box, I slipped it onto her finger then stood, scooping her back onto my lap, covering her mouth with mine. Our cheeks both wet with each other's tears.

She pulled back, looking at her hand. "This ring, Coop. It's so beautiful."

I gave myself a secret high five. "Just like you."

She stared at it, sitting perfectly on her finger, turning it to catch the light.

"So if we're going to Italy does that mean we get a whole weekend of alone time?"

"Not exactly, but I promise you alone time soon." A thought suddenly dawned on me, my hand on her stomach again. "How are you feeling though, Baby? Are you tired? Do you feel sick? I can stop everyone from coming?"

She gave me that look again, the one she used when she thought I was going crazy.

"Because I had plans but we can change them. Just promise to tell me if you're not feeling good."

She raised her eyebrow. "Are you going to tell me these plans?"

I had a feeling she was going to get very annoyed with me in the subsequent eight months, but tough shit.

That was my baby growing in there.

"Yes, but remember we don't have to do any of them."

She waited for me to continue. I took a deep breath, this could go horribly wrong.

"So, remember last summer when we went down to your parents and were looking around the barn?"

She nodded.

"You said you didn't want a big fancy wedding, just a three day party with all your closest friends and family, where everyone was eating, drinking and dancing their asses off."

She nodded again.

My chest tightened as I waited for the penny to drop.

Her eyes flashed in realisation. "Cooper Marks. Have you planned a wedding?"

"No, I planned a three-day birthday party where everyone will be eating, drinking and dancing their asses off. But," I held my finger over her lips, poised to interrupt. "At the end of it, if you want him, a priest will bless us."

She sucked her cheek in as she thought, a move which always made my dick stir. "What about our parents?"

"They'll be there. Everyone important is coming." I reassured her.

"Okay."

I leaned forward, making sure I'd heard correctly. "Say again."

She placed her hands on my face, kissing me. "Okay, yes I'll attend your three day party where I can eat, drink and dance my ass off before I marry your ass at the end of it."

She kissed me again, long and hard, full of love and passion and life.

"Tiny, you've just made me the happiest man in the world, for the third time today. But just one thing." I mumbled against her lips. "You won't be drinking."

She pulled back. "Oh god, this is going to be a long nine months isn't it?"

"Have I told you how fucking beautiful you are?" We were standing in the bedroom of our suite in the huge villa I'd rented for everyone.

Outside I could hear the chattering of our friends as they made their way to the private cliff top over-looking the harbour in Portofino. True to my word we'd spent the weekend partying and dancing our asses off, all throughout Freddie glowed with happiness and I'd fallen in love with her all over again.

This afternoon we told our families that we were getting married today.

At twilight.

In fifteen minutes.

And I couldn't fucking wait a second longer.

She was standing before me in a long, white silk dress that clung to every delicious curve on her body. I ran my hands over her stomach, desperately wishing it was bigger already but we'd agreed to keep the baby our secret a little longer, as something special between us.

"You don't look so bad yourself." She tipped her face up to mine, silently asking for a kiss.

I leant down, obliging, gently brushing her lips without mussing up her make up. "Ready to become Mrs Marks?"

"So ready."

"Then I'll be the one waiting for you at the end of the aisle. Don't be late."

She smiled her smile.

I don't know how I'd got so lucky.

She was perfect.

She was mine.

I walked towards the door, turning back to her before I opened it allowing her to once again take my breath away.

"I love you."

THE END

ACKNOWLEDGMENTS

To my fellow residents of Romance Land, each and every single one of you - you make my days with your funny tweets, posts and pics. Your kindness and love brings colour to what's otherwise grey and gloomy. It's an honour to be part of this world.

ABOUT THE AUTHOR

Lulu has been in love with ice hockey since she first saw Eric Lindros take to the ice with Philadelphia in the mid nineties.

She's currently working on the next New York Player's Novel. Drew and Emerson's story will be released in June.

instagram.com/lulumoorebooks

ALSO BY LULU MOORE

Jasper

You will meet Drew in June

Printed in Great Britain
by Amazon